W9-ARP-004

GET READY FOR ONE WACKY ADVENTURE!

A 2013 American Booksellers Association New Voices Pick
A 2013 Association of Booksellers for Children Best Book
An Amazon Best Book of the Month
A Junior Library Guild Selection

"Clark's debut is **refreshingly bonkers**. It offers thinking kids humor that is neither afraid of the potty nor confined to it."
—*Kirkus Reviews*

"The kids' uncertainty about who to trust and the novel's swift pace create unyielding suspense....**For those destined to become Douglas Adams** fans it will be hilarious and gripping."
—*Publishers Weekly*

"**Fast paced and entertaining...an exciting, suspenseful adventure** with many unexpected twists....Those willing to take a chance on something odd will be rewarded."
—*School Library Journal*

"This **clever** story self-consciously and irreverently follows in the footsteps of **classic quest tales**....
[A] whirlwind adventure."
—*The Bulletin*

"Very funny...both **an intricate love letter to sussing out clues** and the realities that underpin kid-hood."
—*The Austin American-Statesman*

"**A hilarious tale** of attempted world domination."
—*Newsday*

"The **adventure and creativity** propel one to continue the story."
—*Library Media Connection*

WHAT WE FOUND IN THE SOFA AND HOW IT SAVED THE WORLD

Henry Clark

illustrated by Jeremy Holmes

LB

Little, Brown and Company

New York Boston

This book is a work of fiction. Names, characters, places, and incidents are the product of the author's imagination or are used fictitiously. Any resemblance to actual events, locales, or persons, living or dead, is coincidental.

Text copyright © 2013 by Henry Clark
Illustrations copyright © 2013 by Jeremy Holmes
Discussion Guide copyright © 2014 by Little, Brown and Company
Field Guide copyright © 2014 by Henry Clark
Author Interview copyright © 2013 by Henry Clark and Karen Harrington

All rights reserved. In accordance with the U.S. Copyright Act of 1976, the scanning, uploading, and electronic sharing of any part of this book without the permission of the publisher is unlawful piracy and theft of the author's intellectual property. If you would like to use material from the book (other than for review purposes), prior written permission must be obtained by contacting the publisher at permissions@hbgusa.com. Thank you for your support of the author's rights.

Little, Brown and Company

Hachette Book Group
1290 Avenue of the Americas
New York, NY 10104
Visit our website at lb-kids.com

Little, Brown and Company is a division of Hachette Book Group, Inc.
The Little, Brown name and logo are trademarks of Hachette Book Group, Inc.

The publisher is not responsible for websites
(or their content) that are not owned by the publisher.

First Paperback Edition: July 2014
First published in hardcover in July 2013 by Little, Brown and Company

Library of Congress Cataloging-in-Publication Data

Clark, Henry, 1952–
  What we found in the sofa (and how it saved the world) / by Henry Clark; illustrated by Jeremy Holmes.—First edition.
    pages cm
    Summary: Finding a rare zucchini-colored crayon leads twelve-year-old River Monroe and his friends on an adventure with their eccentric neighbor to save Earth from invading interstellar storm troopers.
    ISBN 978-0-316-20666-2 (hc)—ISBN 978-0-316-20665-5 (pb)
    [1. Adventure and adventurers—Fiction. 2. Eccentrics and eccentricities—Fiction.
3. Science fiction. 4. Humorous stories.] I. Holmes, Jeremy, illustrator. II. Title.
    PZ7.C5458Wh 2013
    [Fic]—dc23

                                                                                                2012032467

10 9 8 7 6 5 4 3 2
RRD-C
Printed in the United States of America

With love for Kathy and Elyse,
who found things in
the sofa that I had missed

Table of Contents

An Unexpected Sofa

The sofa wasn't there on Monday but it was there on Tuesday. It sat in the shade just down the road from the bus stop. A broken branch dangled from the tree above it, like maybe the sofa had fallen from the sky and damaged the tree as it fell. Then again, maybe the broken branch had been there the day before. I hadn't noticed.

When I got there, my friend Freak was sitting on the sofa, one arm on an armrest, eating taco chips out of a Ziploc bag. For him, it was a typical breakfast.

He raised his hand for a high five, shouted my name—"River!"—and slapped my palm.

"Where'd the sofa come from?" I asked.

"Brought it from home," he replied, as if I might believe it.

"Really," I said, looking down toward the bus stop, where the road curved to the right. When the bus got there, we would have to run to catch it. "You could have put it closer to the bus."

Freak shrugged and patted the cushion next to him. I noticed the fabric had a dark red stain on it, like dried blood, or maybe spaghetti sauce. I switched the cushion with the one next to it and sat.

"Chip?" Freak held the bag in my direction. With his blond hair and his pale blue T-shirt and jeans, he looked like a faded photograph. He did his own laundry and sometimes he used too much bleach.

"Thanks."

The sofa sat in the grass at the edge of Breeland Road. Behind it stretched the six-foot-high concrete wall surrounding the Underhill place.

"When's trash pickup?" I inquired.

"For big stuff? Friday."

"So this should still be here tomorrow."

"Provided Schimmelhorn doesn't get it."

Max Schimmelhorn runs a junk shop next to the Cheshire

hardware store. A lot of people think he and I are related because he's short and thin with a mop of red hair—but we're not.

"You want to get here early tomorrow?" asked Freak.

"And do what?"

"Sit."

I thought about it for a moment.

"Sure," I said. "What's the weather supposed to be?"

"No idea. Fiona can look it up on her phone."

It wasn't long before Fiona came into sight, crossing the field between Breeland Road and the houses off in the distance, where the three of us lived. Beyond our houses there was heat shimmer in the air. There usually was.

Fiona always looked like an explosion in a paint factory. Today she was wearing a red beret, a baggy green sweater, and orange-striped stockings that disappeared under the sweater, where they may or may not have clashed with her skirt, depending on whether or not she was wearing one.

"What's this?" she asked, coming up to the sofa.

"Hot-dog stand," said Freak.

Fiona examined the stained cushion. She flipped it over, decided the flip side was clean enough, and sat down next to me.

"This is nice," she announced.

"Freak and I are getting here early tomorrow," I told her.

"Why?"

"To sit. That is, if it's not going to rain."

"Could you check that?" inquired Freak.

Fiona pulled out her phone and poked it. She tickled it, massaged it, then tapped it three times. "Sunny tomorrow. Warmer than usual for October. You *do* realize it doesn't make sense for this sofa to be here."

"Old Man Underhill is throwing it out," I said.

"How do you know that?" she asked.

"It's in front of his place. It's near his gate. Where else would it have come from?"

"Who helped him bring it down from the house? Everybody says he lives alone. He's, like, a hundred years old. The driveway is really long. He couldn't have carried this thing all the way down by himself."

I turned and looked over my shoulder. Beyond the wall, one turret of the old house was visible above the trees at the top of the hill. The morning sun glinted off something in the uppermost window.

"Maybe it walked here," suggested Freak.

Fiona and I looked at him.

"Look at the feet."

The sofa had feet. Four of them, one at each corner, made of dark wood carved to resemble dragon claws. Each claw clutched a wooden ball.

"River's right," said Freak. "Who else would have furniture like this? It's old, it's clunky, it's creepy. It's gotta be Old Man Underhill's."

Fiona twirled a few strands of her long black hair around one of her fingers. "Have either of you ever seen a trash can out here?"

We discussed it and decided we hadn't.

"But I once saw a grocery delivery truck go in the gate," I said. "Maybe garbage trucks go in the same way."

"Either that," said Freak, "or that's one messy house."

A couple of bright yellow maple leaves chased each other down the road. I leaned back on the sofa, closed my eyes, and tilted my face toward the sun. After a minute or two, I felt Freak and Fiona relax into the cushions, too.

"Flash mob today?" asked Freak.

"I wouldn't know," said Fiona. "Never having seen a flash mob. Except on TV. I've certainly never been part of one. And I'm tired of you and your friend here"—I felt myself jabbed in the ribs with a bony elbow—"telling me I have. It doesn't even make sense as a joke."

"It said in the paper that all of you in the flash mobs have agreed to deny you were part of a flash mob," said Freak. "That's what I think is the really cool part. I haven't been able to shake anybody. Not even you. And you usually blab things like crazy."

"You're an idiot," Fiona stated. "How's that for blabbing?"

My eyes opened at the sound of an engine to our right, where the bus usually came from. When the red hood of a convertible came into view instead, Fiona sat straight up, like a gopher popping out of its hole. She scrambled over the back of the sofa and hid behind it.

"Forgot your bag," said Freak.

Fiona, moving faster than the speed of light, reached over the back of the sofa, snagged her paisley-print book bag, and disappeared again.

Travis Miller, whose name Fiona had written in flowery letters on the inside of her science notebook, went by, on his way to being dropped off at school by his older brother. His brother had a cell phone pressed against the side of his head and didn't notice us, but Travis looked quizzically at the sofa as the car went by.

"Are they gone?" came a quiet voice behind us.

"No," said Freak.

Fiona, who knew Freak almost as well as I did, left her hiding place and sat back down. "That was close," she said.

Fiona was willing to hang out with Freak and me until the bus arrived, because the bus was always empty when it picked us up. It was the first stop on the bus route. If the morning conversation interested her, she might even sit with us once we got on the bus, but when the second stop came into view, she would find a new seat, well away from us. For the rest of the day, she would pretend she had never seen us before. It was understood we should never approach her in school, even during the two classes the three of us shared.

"Don't take this personally," she'd explained once, "but girls mature faster than boys and I really need to be with people my own age."

"You're one year younger than we are," I'd pointed out.

"Yes," she'd admitted, "but, emotionally, you're both six."

"How can you say that?" Freak had asked, turning toward her with two drinking straws stuck up his nose so he looked like a walrus.

The sofa seemed to get more comfortable the longer we sat on it. I would have stretched out on it, if I'd been there by myself.

"Has anybody thought to look for loose change between the cushions?" Fiona asked.

Freak and I glanced at each other. He blinked. I blinked. Then we both jumped up and tossed aside the cushions we had been sitting on.

We found a flattened peanut shell, a chewing gum wrapper, and a plaid sock.

As I reached for the sock, Freak caught my hand.

"Touch nothing! This is all evidence! We must preserve it!"

He gingerly picked up the peanut shell, the gum wrapper, and the sock and placed them carefully in the Ziploc bag he had, moments earlier, been eating taco chips out of.

"You guys are so stupid," Fiona observed.

Freak pointed to the crease running beneath the sofa's back cushion. I stuck my fingers into the crease and searched along it.

"Bingo!" I said, and pulled out a coin.

It was about the size of a quarter, but the tarnished metal wasn't silver. One side had the head of a man with a goatee and the other side had a woman with a crown, both surrounded by words in an alphabet I didn't recognize. It was the sort of coin you did not want to bet "tails" on when it was flipped.

Freak held the plastic bag open for me and I dropped the coin in. Then he felt around in the crease at the base of the armrest and pulled out a small rectangular piece of wood. Grinning, he held it up to the light. It was a domino. Double-six. He deposited it in the evidence bag.

We both turned and faced Fiona.

"Your turn," announced Freak.

"What?" she said. "I'm not sticking my hand in this thing."

After a moment, though, she got up, handed me the cushion she had been sitting on, and cautiously felt around in the back crease.

"Nothing…nothing…wait. Something."

When she pulled out her hand, she was holding a dark green crayon. It looked as though it had never been used—fresh out of the box. The paper wrapper read ZUCCHINI.

"Zucchini?" said Freak. "What kind of color is that?"

"If you ever ate vegetables, you'd know," sniffed Fiona. "It's the rich, dark color of an early summer squash."

Freak looked at her. "And exactly what color is that?"

She held up the crayon and pointed at it. Freak took it from her and studied it. He frowned. "I don't remember ever seeing a zucchini crayon before." He looked at me as though I might be a crayon expert. I shook my head.

"Maybe it's from one of those really big sets you hear about," suggested Fiona. "I've seen a box with sixty-four crayons in it. They even sell a box with one hundred twenty." She blinked. "I can't imagine that many colors."

"I've got a shoe box full of my kid sister's old crayons," said Freak. "I know there aren't any zucchinis in it." He placed the crayon reverently into the bag.

I plunged my hand back into the crease where Fiona had left off, eager to find more stuff. I immediately yelped and yanked my hand back.

"Ow-ow-OW!"

I had a fishhook stuck in my palm, and blood was running down my fingers.

"Hold still!" ordered Fiona, whose favorite game was Operation. She held my arm steady by tucking it under her elbow and plucked the hook out. "Two hundred points!" I heard her mutter to herself, making the hook equal to the Funny Bone in the actual game. I jammed the wound in my mouth. Freak held out the evidence bag; Fiona gave him a scornful look and tossed the hook into a holly bush.

"Why would there be a fishhook in a sofa?" I demanded, feeling it was unfair that I was the one who found it.

"Why would there be a zucchini crayon?" Freak asked

with a shrug, taking things a little too lightly, I thought. I wanted to remind him that blood had just been spilled, but then the bus arrived, and the next thing I knew we were on it, discussing what time we planned to arrive the following morning.

As soon as the second stop came into view and Fiona deserted us, Freak started working on unfinished homework and I did something that people tell me I do too often.

I stared dreamily out the window and let my imagination run away with me.

I imagined the inside of the sofa being as deep as the sea, and then I imagined the zucchini crayon wiggling like a worm on a hook. I imagined a fishing line attached to the hook. I tried to see where the fishing line went. Every time I tried, the line went to the exact same place.

Over the wall and up the hill, into the forbidding mansion known as Underhill House.

CHAPTER
02

Flash Mob

For me, middle school was one never-ending game of dodgeball. Back in elementary school, I'd frequently been the victim of friendly fire. The ball always seemed to miss its actual target and hit me, no matter where I was on the circle.

Today, school started out kind of like that.

Out in the lobby, before the first bell, Morgue MacKenzie snagged me by the arm as I tried to pass his hulking frame. He looked down at me and said, "Quarter."

Morgue was standing in front of a Juice Express Refreshment Kiosk, the capitalized first letters of the words glowing a bright purple over his head. He needed an additional twenty-five cents for a can of Agra Nation® Energy Blaster. I dug in my pocket and gave him the change.

"Why do you let him do that?" asked Freak when I joined him a few moments later.

"He's twice my size," I said. "And he never asks for more than he needs."

"Next time, tell him your money is radioactive."

"Why would he believe that?"

"You live on the edge of Hellsboro."

"Hellsboro isn't radioactive."

"Morgue doesn't know that. He's one of those people who thinks Hellsboro is the work of the devil. I've heard him say he'd never set foot in it. If he thinks your money has something to do with Hellsboro, he'll go bother somebody else."

I decided Freak might be right.

Hellsboro was the name the Cheshire newspaper had given to our local underground coal-seam fire. Hellsboro had turned eight hundred acres on the west side of town into a treeless, lifeless wasteland. The fire had been burning for twelve years. It could burn for a hundred more, or until all the underground coal was consumed. Coal-seam fires were almost impossible to put out. Ours had pretty much stopped spreading, although a small tongue of it had stuck itself out under Breeland Road that past summer and caused a sinkhole.

At Hellsboro's center was the abandoned Rodmore Chemical plant. Rodmore had once been a big employer for the town of Cheshire. Now it was like a cinder-covered castle in the middle of a burned-down amusement park. It had been closed since the fire started. Nobody went there anymore. People said the plant was even more dangerous than the fire that surrounded it.

The fire had made almost all of the houses in the nearby Sunnyside housing development uninhabitable. Only three families still lived in the development: Freak's, Fiona's, and mine. We had to walk several miles to get to the next inhabited place, if you didn't count Old Man Underhill's.

Most people in Cheshire feared Hellsboro. It hadn't stopped them from renaming the high school football team the Hellions or the middle school team the Devils (a faded banner in the gym says we used to be the Cheshire Cats) or having an annual dance at the town hall called the Hellsboro Hop. But nobody went near the actual fire zone. The mayor joked that it was a good way to get a hotfoot. If reminding Morgue MacKenzie how close I lived to Hellsboro would get him to leave my money alone, I would try it. As soon as I got up the nerve to tell him.

In English class, we got our spelling tests back. The one word I got wrong was *renaissance*. I put in too many *n*'s. Renaissance means rebirth. I asked Mr. Hendricks, our teacher, why, if it meant rebirth, we didn't just say rebirth, which is easier to spell. This led to a long lecture from him about how important it is to have a large vocabulary. Mr. Hendricks started throwing around words like *quintessential, lexicographer*, and *hyperdiculous*. Everybody blamed me for the lecture, of course. Just as, the previous week, they had blamed me for the pop quiz on *Tom Sawyer*, just because I'd shown up wearing suspenders. I was used to it.

At the end of class, Mr. Hendricks admitted he had made up the word *hyperdiculous*. He wanted to see if any of us would raise our hand and ask him what it meant. None of us did. We were, I could tell, a constant disappointment to Mr. Hendricks.

· · · · ·

It was during lunch that the school day really went off the tracks.

There was another flash mob.

It happened shortly after Rudy Sorkin slipped on a string bean. His feet went out from under him. He fell on the floor with his lunch tray, and we all applauded. Then the applause cut off in mid-clap. I brought my hands together two more times into the dead silence and then caught myself.

"Uh-oh," I said to Freak.

"Not again," he said, rolling his eyes. The last flash mob had been only a week earlier.

Almost everybody stood up, except Freak and me and two or three other kids. But the majority of the lunchroom, including Fiona, who was two tables away, and all the adult monitors and the food-service ladies, turned and faced the window.

"That's different," I said.

"Yeah," agreed Freak. "Last week they faced the wall."

Everybody clapped twice. Then they crossed their hands in front of their faces, tugged on their earlobes, put their hands on their hips, and launched into an ear-splitting performance of the song "Oklahoma." For two and a half minutes everybody assured us that Oklahoma was doing fine, it was grand, and, while it might not be terrific, it was certainly okay.

Then everybody sat back down, finished their round of applause for Rudy Sorkin, and picked up their conversations right where they had left off. The lunchroom filled instantly with its usual noise.

The first time this had happened, over a year earlier, it had been scary. We had been new to the school then, so we thought maybe it was a middle school ritual that no one had let us in on. That time, everybody had stood, faced the kitchen, and sung about raindrops on roses and whiskers on kittens. And it turned out it hadn't been just the lunchroom. It hadn't been just the school. It had been the entire surrounding town of Cheshire. Or 90 percent of it. People had pulled their cars to the side of the road, gotten out, and sung.

I immediately decided it was alien mind control.

The next day, the newspaper said it was a flash mob. According to the report, everybody had been texting one another on their cell phones for weeks ahead of time. They had chosen what direction to face. They had picked out the song. They had agreed that everybody would perform together, no matter where they were or what they were doing, at exactly eleven forty-eight on the morning of September 28. After it was over, everybody who participated would deny having any memory of having done it if they were questioned by any nonparticipants. It would all be part of what the paper called "a grand and glorious lark."

To me, it seemed like a grand and glorious waste of time.

After that, it kept happening. Freak and I learned to

expect a singing flash mob every eight to ten weeks. Sometimes, there was even a dance step or two.

Fiona was good at it. She followed instructions perfectly, and after each flash mob she always claimed she couldn't remember doing anything out of the ordinary.

I started to feel left out. Since Freak and I didn't have cell phones, we were out of the loop. We had almost gotten cells the summer we graduated from elementary school, when the Disin Tel store opened on Coal Avenue and had offered an irresistible limited-time promotion.

LISTEN TO DISIN! the cleverly rhyming banner in front of the store had proclaimed, going on in smaller print to offer free phones to every family member past the age of ten in any family that signed a one-year contract. It was so inexpensive that practically every family in town took advantage of the offer. Then Freak's father accidentally dropped his new phone down the garbage disposal, and he took Freak's phone to replace it. And my aunt Bernie pulled mine out of my jeans after they'd gone through the wash. I'd had the phone for one day.

"Even if we had cells, would we be doing this?" demanded Freak, after everybody had finished singing "Oklahoma." "How is it possible that there isn't one kid here with a cell who doesn't think this is totally stupid? Not a single person can decide to just sit it out? And why are they doing it again so soon?"

"Maybe the Elbonian overlords are stepping up their plans for world domination," I said, adding a couple of potato chips to my cheese sandwich. I like a sandwich with crunch.

"The Elbonian overlords?"

"Weird foreign people in the *Dilbert* comic strip."

"Why would you read *Dilbert*? It's about office workers."

"Someday I figure I'll work in a cubicle. That's what middle school is training us for. I think there's some serious mind control going on here."

"You mean the flash mobs."

"That, too."

Freak scowled.

"You can't be right," he said. "This is weird."

"No, it's not," I assured him.

"It's not?"

"No," I said. "It's hyperdiculous."

It was the only word that described it.

Hellsboro

The next morning, I had a sword fight with the sofa. I hadn't planned to. The sofa forced my hand.

I arrived early, even before Freak. I wanted to examine the sofa on my own.

The upholstery was dark green, close to the color of the zucchini crayon. A long slit ran horizontally across the fabric of the back cushion, like somebody had slashed it with a knife. That, and the stain on the cushion, were the only things wrong with it that I could see.

I flipped the cushion over. The bloodstain lined up perfectly beneath the slit. If the sofa had belonged to my aunt

Bernie, she would have made a slipcover for it. She never threw anything out.

My aunt Bernadette had started working double shifts at the medical center as soon as I got out of elementary school. We'd been together more when I was younger, but now I sometimes saw her only on weekends. It was just her and me in the house.

I lunged at the sofa with my sword. It had, after all, drawn first blood with its vicious fishhook attack. I duplicated the slashing motion that must have caused the slit, then pressed my advantage with a series of lightning strokes so fast, they were impossible to see. The fact that my sword was invisible probably helped.

"*En garde*, Monsieur Zucchini Couch! Stab me, will you? Taste my steel!"

"You think the sofa is French?" asked Freak. I whirled to face him. I hid my invisible sword behind my back. "What are you doing?"

"Forensics," I said, improvising. "I'm trying to figure out how the slit got in the back cushion. It might have been done with a sword."

"You think there are guys with swords in the Underhill place?"

"Who knows what goes on in the Underhill place," I said. Freak looked toward the house. I took the opportunity to slide my invisible sword back into its invisible sheath.

"We're wasting valuable sitting time," said Freak, throwing himself onto his favorite cushion. I took a seat, too, after flipping the bloodstained cushion facedown again. It wasn't long before Fiona joined us.

"I have news," she announced, and sat down between us. "It turns out," she said, "there are people out there who collect crayons."

"Yeah," said Freak. "They're called five-year-olds."

"No, they're called adults, and some of them might pay good money for the zucchini crayon we found. Especially if the crayon has never been used."

She looked at us to make sure she had our attention. She did. She continued.

"I looked up *zucchini crayon* on the Internet. It's one of over two dozen colors the crayon company doesn't make anymore. It's very hard to find. There were only five hundred made, for a special limited-edition box of crayons called Victory Garden." Fiona pulled a crumpled piece of paper out of a pocket in her book bag and consulted it. "This was during World War Two. The five hundred boxes were the prizes in a radio contest for kids. Sixteen crayons per box, all named after vegetables. But the new machine they were using in the crayon factory to pack the boxes left out the zucchini crayon and put in two rutabagas instead."

"Rutabaga?"

"Yellowish purple. Not a very popular crayon, according to the article. Most of the zucchini crayons wound up in a tray, and the tray got left on a radiator, and most of them melted."

"So," I said, "any zucchini crayon that survived the melt-down would be worth something?"

"How much?" asked Freak.

Fiona looked back at her piece of paper. "Five years ago a Victory Garden box of sixteen crayons, two of them ruta-baga, none of them zucchini, sold at auction for five hundred dollars. The winner of the auction was quoted as saying he would happily pay the same amount or more for the missing zucchini."

"Holy cow!" said Freak. "Do you have the guy's name?"

"The article didn't give it."

"We don't need the guy's name," I reasoned. "We have the crayon. We could sell it through an Internet auction site."

"That's what I was thinking," agreed Fiona. "And since

I'm the only one with a computer with Internet access, you should give the crayon to me." She looked innocently at Freak.

"Yeah," he said. "Like that's going to happen."

"I need to be able to describe it exactly and take a picture of it."

"I can do that."

"You don't have a computer."

"I'll go to the library."

Fiona stared at him for a moment. Then she said, "You'll get yourself killed."

Freak had no answer to that, because it was true. Freak risked his life every time he went to the library. That's because Freak insisted on taking the shortest route.

The shortest route went straight across Hellsboro.

Freak could get in and out of Hellsboro through a hole in his backyard fence. He insisted he knew all of the safe paths, but he risked falling into a sinkhole and roasting to death every time he returned a library book. He preferred to do that, rather than pay the late fee. He said the trick to Hellsboro was to keep moving, or the bottoms of your sneakers would start to melt.

"How about," I said, "Freak and I just come over to your

house tonight and we use your computer? It's your parents' bowling night. We wouldn't be in anybody's way."

Fiona thought about it. "It's really my mom's computer," she admitted. "It's in my parents' room. You guys would have to stay in the kitchen while I start the auction. If my phone rings, you guys don't make a sound while I'm on it. And the fridge is off-limits."

• • • • •

By seven thirty Freak and I were sitting in Fiona's kitchen, eyeing the fridge. We'd taken seven or eight photos of the crayon with Fiona's phone and had finally gotten one that was in focus and clearly showed the word *Zucchini*. We'd written a description for the auction—"Crayon. Cylindrical. Five inches long. Pointy. Never used. Rare zucchini color."— and Fiona had gone off to use her mother's eBay account. At that point she had suggested we leave. Freak had said no, we would stick around, in case the auction got a bid immediately. He said we should be there if it did.

Fiona's refrigerator was covered with family mementos held in place with magnets. A photo of Fiona's older sister, who was away at college, was near the top. It shared a magnet with a drawing done by her younger brother, Stevie, who was in grade school. The drawing showed a child being chased by a gargoyle with braces on its teeth. Right next to it was a photograph of Fiona, smiling, showing the braces on her teeth. Below it was a photograph of Fiona's parents and my parents, back before my parents had died in the accident. My father was holding a fishing pole and a fish. He looked like he was having the best day of his life.

I was jealous of Fiona's family. She would complain about them sometimes—her mother was too strict, her kid brother was a pain in the neck—but I noticed she never complained about her brother when Freak was around, and she frequently stopped herself from going on about her parents when she realized I was within hearing distance. It made me think Fiona might be more sensitive than Freak or I gave her credit for. And maybe Freak and I helped her appreciate what she had. Which, to someone like me, was a lot.

Freak opened the refrigerator door about two inches and an alarm went off.

"Hey!" shouted Fiona from the other side of the house.

Five minutes later, she walked back into the kitchen. "The auction's been running for ten minutes and there are no bidders yet," she announced. "I'll let you know tomorrow if anything happens tonight. 'Bye."

Freak and I remained seated at the kitchen table.

"Your refrigerator has an alarm on it," Freak said.

"It's a buzzer and a battery with a photoelectric cell. The little light in the fridge goes on, the alarm goes off. I made it so I'd know if Stevie went after the Dutch apple."

Fiona, I was sure, would someday win a prize in the Disin Tel science contest with an invention like this. She had skipped a grade and usually knew all the answers in science class and most of the answers in English. Still, she did stupid things sometimes. She thought Travis Miller might notice her someday. She favored vomit green as a nail polish color. And she hung out with a group of girls who made fun of her behind her back. At least Freak and I made fun of her to her face.

She folded her arms and leaned defensively against the refrigerator. Her phone rang, and she shooed us out before she answered it.

"Dutch apple is the one with raisins?" Freak asked as the door was slammed in our faces.

"And lots of cinnamon," I said dreamily as we turned away from the House of Pie.

I went with Freak to his garage and helped him bring the trash out to the curb. He carried the recycling bin. When he put it down, he rearranged it so the empty water bottles were on top, covering the other bottles. He waved his hand above the bin, as if that would fan away the lingering smell of alcohol. He looked at the house, where a single dim light glowed in the living room, and motioned for me to follow him. We went around back.

A chain-link fence with barbed wire at the top separated Freak's backyard from the backyard of the boarded-up house on the next street over. The fence extended for miles in either direction, completely encircling Hellsboro. Every thirty feet or so a sign wired to the fence declared:

DANGER
ENTRY FORBIDDEN
TOXIC GROUNDS — SUBTERRANEAN FIRES
DO NOT ENTER
BY ORDER OF THE CHESHIRE FIRE MARSHAL

In Freak's backyard, right below one of these signs, he had cut a triangular opening through the links and folded back the fence. It's how he got in and out of Hellsboro. A second fence, farther in, marked where things got really dangerous. He had cut through that fence, too.

"There was an odd glow out there last night," he said, gesturing toward Hellsboro's center. It had been a while since Hellsboro had glowed. It happened when coal burned close to the surface. Most of the surface coal had burned off long ago. "It wasn't the usual reddish color. It was blue. And I heard a *whumpa-whumpa* sound."

"A *whumpa-whumpa* sound?" It was getting cold out. I suddenly felt chilled.

"It didn't last long," said Freak, and shrugged.

The sound of a slamming door came from Freak's house.

"Right," said Freak. "I'd invite you in, but—"

"I know," I said. "It's okay."

I found my way back to the street.

I hung around for a moment, listening to a raised voice somewhere in Freak's place. It was muffled, but it still made my stomach churn.

Freak's father was under a lot of pressure. Freak always said so. I had once been alone in their living room and overheard the answering machine taking a message from a very angry man at a collection agency. He listed the number of warnings Mr. Nesterii had been given and assured him that if the bills weren't paid, there would be legal action.

Even when I got to my own front door, I could still hear the raised voice. The voice wasn't Freak's. Freak almost never raised his voice. Whatever was being said ended with something that sounded like a fist smacking a tabletop. The quiet that followed was just as disturbing as what had preceded it.

I wished I hadn't heard things like that so often before.

$$\bullet \quad \bullet \quad \bullet \quad \bullet \quad \bullet$$

The next day, Thursday, the sofa was still sitting on the edge of Breeland Road. I was surprised Max Schimmelhorn hadn't picked it up. I thought it was a pretty nice sofa.

I was the first one there. Freak joined me a few minutes later. He had a bunch of bananas, and he gave me one.

"Is that all you've got for lunch?" I asked.

"They're good for you. They're full of potassium. My father got it into his head we needed bananas. There're six more bunches back at the house."

We heard shouting off in the distance. Fiona was on the far side of the field separating Breeland from Bagshot Road.

She was waving a paper in the air and running toward us. Three crows took flight at her approach. Freak had once told her she'd be good at protecting farm crops.

She dashed up to the sofa, knit cap askew, and thrust the paper in our faces. Then she pulled it back, said, "No, wait," and took a moment to catch her breath.

"Last night... before I went to bed... we had two bids on the crayon." She was still panting heavily. "The high bid was twelve dollars, forty-seven cents."

"Wow," I said.

"Shut up!" she said, then continued. "This morning... after breakfast... I went online just before leaving the house... we had ten bids from five different bidders."

"And?"

"And the high bid was seven thousand dollars."

I grabbed the piece of paper showing a printout of the auction. She wasn't kidding. The high bid was $7,056.72.

GORLAB vs. Alecto

I handed the paper to Freak. He looked at it and shook his head. "This has to be somebody's idea of a joke. Nobody's going to pay seven grand for a crayon."

"Look at the bidding history." Fiona squeezed herself onto the sofa between us, took the paper back from Freak, and pointed at the list.

"The first bidder was CRAYOLA42. He bids ten dollars. Then WaxLips bids twelve dollars and forty-seven cents. By midnight, there are three more bidders and the high bid is sixty-five dollars. Nothing happens then until about five o'clock in the morning, when two new bidders change everything. GORLAB bids a hundred dollars. Then Alecto bids five hundred. Within minutes, GORLAB bids a thousand. Alecto bids five thousand. GORLAB brings it up to seven thousand, which is where it is now, but the auction doesn't end for another week, so who knows how high it will go!"

"So, really," said Freak, "it's just these two wacko bidders who have driven the price up."

"It's called a bidding war. Anybody who's trying to sell anything in an auction wants it to happen. Two people who want whatever you're selling so badly, they go crazy in the bidding."

"Crazy is right," agreed Freak. "When the auction ends... it's your mother's eBay account. She gets the money?"

"I already made her promise that whatever the final amount is, she'll give it to us. She'll divvy it up equally three ways. She said she would."

"Does she know how high the bidding has gone?"

"No. I told her we were trying to sell a crayon. I haven't told her anything else."

I cleared my throat.

"Guys?" I said.

"I hope she doesn't change her mind when she finds out we're talking thousands of dollars," said Freak.

"Why would she? A promise is a promise."

"My father promised to take me fishing once. That was three years ago."

"Guys?" That was me.

"What if the high bidder backs down once the auction ends? What if whoever it is doesn't pay?"

"Then you give the high bidder some nasty feedback and ask the runner-up if he's willing to buy it for whatever his highest bid was. Which, at the moment, is five thousand dollars."

"GUYS!"

Fiona and Freak turned and looked at me.

"Technically," I said in a very soft voice, "the crayon isn't ours to sell."

They continued to stare at me.

"What?" said Freak. "We found it in a sofa on the side of the road. The sofa is obviously being thrown out. Which means anything in the sofa is also being thrown out. The crayon was being thrown out. We found it. It's ours. We can do whatever we want with it."

"Old Man Underhill probably didn't know the crayon was in the sofa. It's something he lost. We found it. Now that we know it's really valuable, we should return it."

"Yesterday we thought the crayon might be worth maybe five hundred dollars," Fiona said. "This didn't bother you then."

"Five hundred dollars didn't sound like a whole lot of money, especially split three ways," I confessed. "Seven thousand, on the other hand, sounds like a lot. Like the kind of money Underhill could use to pay for his groceries or his heating bill or his, I don't know, his hermit tax."

"Hermit tax?" asked Fiona.

"My aunt says everything has a tax."

"You think Underhill needs the money?" Freak was up and pacing back and forth in front of us. "He's got this big rambling house on something like a hundred acres of land. If he's hard up for cash, he could sell a few acres."

Our eyes met and I could see he knew what I was going to say before I said it.

"Who would buy land this close to Hellsboro? How many years has the For Sale sign been up in front of your own house?"

He looked stung. "Underhill doesn't need the money. He doesn't even know the crayon is missing. He's supposed to be a hundred years old. When was the last time he colored? We could all make better use of the money than he could. I could pay some of my father's bills."

I hadn't thought of that. But just as I decided to back off, Fiona changed her mind.

"River is right." She sighed.

"Not you, too," groaned Freak.

"It's not our crayon. We should at least make an attempt to return it," she continued. "What will probably happen is, Underhill will turn out to be this lovable old grandpa and he'll tell us he doesn't care about the crayon and we can keep it."

"Either that, or he'll kill us and eat us," I added, as cheerfully as I could.

Freak looked from Fiona to me, and then back to Fiona. Fiona nodded encouragingly. Freak looked like he was about to explode, but then he snapped, "ALL RIGHT! Fine! If it'll make the two of you happy, let's ask him RIGHT NOW!"

Freak stalked over to the gate. He stood there, staring through the gate's black metal bars and up the entrance drive to where it disappeared into the trees. Fiona and I walked over and stood on either side of him.

"Hey!" Freak barked. "Do you want your crayon back?"

He moved closer to the gate, cupped his hands around his mouth, and shouted, "DO YOU WANT YOUR CRAYON BACK?"

"What crayon would that be?" asked the gatepost to our right.

The three of us jumped three feet to the left and stared at the gatepost. After a moment, the post said, "Hello?"

Freak looked at me. "This was your idea," he said.

I walked slowly over to the post, with Fiona and Freak behind me. I got to within four feet of it and decided I didn't want to get any closer.

"Hello?" I said.

The post buzzed briefly, like a beehive, and a hinged metal plate in the center of it dropped open with a *clang*. Dimly, in the dark cubbyhole, we could see a lens and the grille of a speaker.

"Yes?" said the voice.

"Y-you c-can," I stammered. "You can hear us?"

"No, I'm watching you through the camera and reading your lips. Of course I can hear you. What's this about a crayon?"

It was a man's voice, but he didn't sound particularly old.

"We found this crayon," I said. Then I caught myself. I realized I had no idea who I was talking to.

"The kind of crayon you color with?" asked the voice. "That kind of crayon?"

"Excuse me," I said. "I'm sorry, I forgot to introduce myself. My name is River Monroe. And this is Fiona Shuck. And that's, um, Freak Nesterii."

"Pleased to meet you."

"And you are?"

"Excuse me?"

"You haven't told us your name. We don't know who we're talking to."

"Oh. Sorry. Remiss of me. My friends call me Alf."

"What do people you've just met call you?"

"Alf."

"Alf Underhill?"

"No."

"You're not an Underhill?"

"No."

The three of us exchanged glances. Then the voice said, "Oh. I see. You're at the gate of the Underhill place. So you think there might be an Underhill here. You're not relatives, are you?"

"Relatives of who?" asked Fiona.

"Whom," corrected the voice. "Relatives of Claude Underhill."

"No, we're not," I replied.

"Then you won't be too upset to learn that Claude is deceased."

"He died?" I squeaked.

"Three years ago. Age ninety-seven. In a toboggan accident."

"He was tobogganing?"

"He was out in the carriage barn and a toboggan fell on his head. He should not have tugged on the rope."

I wondered if, possibly, I had been right about the chances of us getting eaten.

"So ... who are you?"

"I purchased the place shortly after he died. I've been living here for the past three years. Since I rarely go out, and the local papers contained no mention of Underhill's death, I can see where you might have thought I was him. But I'm not. What's this about a crayon?"

"It couldn't have been your crayon," said Freak hastily. "I'm sure it was Mr. Underhill's when he was a boy. Sorry to have bothered you."

"I purchased the house and its entire contents. This would have included Claude Underhill's childhood playthings, if they were anywhere on the grounds. His Frisbee. His Hula-Hoop. His Silly Putty. His crayons."

"So," I said, "if we found one of those things, it would rightfully belong to you?"

"I'm afraid that's how it works. You found a crayon you think once belonged to Claude Underhill? Where did you find it?"

"Between the sofa cushions."

There was a pause. Then the voice said, "What sofa?"

"The sofa," said Freak, sounding exasperated, "that has been sitting out here by the gate for the past three days. It's big and green, with dragon-claw feet."

"Oh, *that* sofa. I was wondering where it had gotten to. I didn't realize it was missing until yesterday evening when I tried to sit down. You can imagine my surprise. What color is the crayon?"

Freak had an expression on his face that said he thought we were talking to a crazy person. I expect I had the same expression on mine.

"Zucchini," Fiona said.

"Zucchini? Really? Sounds unusual. Possibly valuable. Not that I'm an expert. Have you considered selling it on the Internet?"

Again, we looked at one another. Fiona silently mouthed the words, *Don't tell him.*

I turned back to the post and said, "As a matter of fact, we started an auction last night."

"Oh?" said Alf. "Would that happen to be a printout of the auction on that piece of paper Fiona just this moment tried to hide behind her back?"

Fiona shook her head. I nodded.

"Could you send that paper up here? I'd like to see it."

"Send it up?"

"Bring it to the mail slot."

Fiona and I tugged the paper back and forth a few times before she finally released it. I took it to the post.

"Reach into the opening."

"No!" said Fiona, running up beside me.

"It's perfectly safe," said Alf. "That little mechanical glitch—the one that resulted in your mail carrier getting the nickname 'Lefty'—was fixed several years ago. Reach in, take out the canister, put the paper in the canister, and put the canister back where you found it. Then close the door."

Fiona tried to stop me, but I reached past her into the hole and found a brass cylinder. It popped open when I pressed a button on its lid, and I followed Alf's instructions. As soon as I pushed the door closed, something went *FOOP!* inside the post. After a moment the hinged door fell back open, and the canister was gone.

"Pneumatic," Alf explained. "Forced air shoots the canister up here like a pea through a peashooter. Or, if you modern kids don't play with peashooters anymore, a deadly poisoned dart through a blowgun."

"We don't play with blowguns much, either," Freak informed him.

"It's all those video games. Kids don't play outside anymore." Alf sighed. "My, my. Seven thousand dollars for a zucchini crayon. That was as of, when? Five thirty this morning. That was several hours ago. I wonder…" Briefly, Alf started humming a tune to himself. It sounded like something from *The Sorcerer's Apprentice*. "Ah. You might be interested to know the current high bid is eleven thousand, four hundred and fifty-three dollars and eighty-six cents. Alecto is currently in the lead."

"Are you kidding?" asked Freak.

"Do I look like I'm kidding?"

"You look," said Freak, "like a camera lens."

"Yes. I suppose I would. So the three of you are trying to sell a crayon that, technically, belongs to me. Any thoughts on that?"

"I think we should split whatever it sells for equally," I said.

"Do you?" asked Alf. "You mean half for me and half for the three of you?"

"I meant more like a quarter for each of us. We did, after all, rescue the crayon from the sofa and get the auction started."

The silence seemed to go on forever. The three of us looked expectantly at the camera lens.

"If this is a staring contest," Freak whispered, "we're going to lose."

"I think we should discuss this," Alf finally said. "Face-to-face. I'd invite you up right now, but your bus is only thirty-five seconds away and you have a full day's schooling ahead. Why don't you return later this afternoon? After school lets out, and after track and chess club and school newspaper?"

It took us a moment to absorb the implications of what Alf had said.

"How—?" Fiona started, and I finished the question with, "—did you know we have track and chess and newspaper?"

"It was a lucky guess," said Alf, sounding pleased with himself. "Shall we say four o'clock? Here at the gate? I'll buzz it open and you can come right up. Please bring the crayon with you when you come. Along with anything else you may have found in my sofa."

"I don't know—" I started to say.

"It's a date, then!" declared Alf.

The metal door of the gatepost snapped shut with a loud *bang*, just as air brakes burped at the bus stop.

CHAPTER
05

The Black Gate Opens

At lunch, after Freak had traded two bananas for a roast beef sandwich and a third banana for some carrot sticks, he returned to the table and we discussed Alf and the zucchini crayon.

"I don't think he's going to share with us," was Freak's opinion. "He wants us to bring the crayon because he's going to ask to see it and then he's going to take it from us and lock it away somewhere. Then he'll kick us out. All because you had to go and tell him we had it. That's assuming he's not a totally deranged serial killer who's just luring us into his house so he can add to his collection of kneecap doorknobs."

"You think we shouldn't go?"

"I don't know. He didn't sound like the sanest person when we were talking to him."

"We should vote."

Fiona was three tables away. I caught her eye and waved, gesturing that she should come over, but she turned away and started talking to the girl on her right. This was normal.

I started to wave her over again, but froze when I noticed Francine "Nails" Norton approaching Fiona from behind. Francine's lunch tray was filled to the edges with something excessively wiggly. The day's dessert was strawberry Jell-O, and it looked like Nails had repeatedly gone back for seconds.

Freak was engrossed in scraping surplus mustard from the beef of his sandwich. I nudged him, and he looked up in time to see Nails tilt the tray and send a mountain of shimmering red gelatin down on Fiona's head.

Nails dropped the tray to the floor with a clatter and said—rather insincerely, I thought—"Oh! I'm *s-o-o-o* sorry!" Then she walked away as if nothing had happened. The applause from the lunchroom was even louder than when Rudy Sorkin had slipped on the string bean.

Fiona sat very straight, raking her fingers slowly, deliberately, through her hair, depositing gobs of pinkish goo on the lunch tray in front of her. Then she stood, turned, and walked stiffly to the girls' room. Just before she got there, the door to the boys' room opened and Travis Miller stepped out. They stood eye-to-eye for a moment, then a ruby drop of yuckiness ran down Fiona's forehead, clung briefly to the tip of her nose, and dropped onto her blouse. She uttered a weird, inhuman cry and dodged past him.

"We knew something like that was going to happen," I stated.

"Yes, we did," agreed Freak, who had returned to scrutinizing his sandwich.

It wouldn't have happened if Fiona hadn't been the photography editor of the school newspaper. The sports page of the latest issue had featured three photos of the girls' field hockey team and absolutely no photos of Nails Norton's boyfriend, Morgue MacKenzie, scoring the winning touchdown in the big football game against Flanders, even though it was well known that the historic moment had been captured by the school photographer.

"The photos vanished," Fiona had told Freak and me at the bus stop the day after the game. "I saw them disappear one by one out of the camera, and then off the computer screen!"

"You hit the delete key with your elbow," Freak assured her.

"My elbows aren't that pointy!"

"A guy could shave with your elbows."

Fiona was a target the moment the paper came out. Nobody slighted Nails or Morgue without getting messed with. I accidentally stepped on Morgue's foot one day and wound up stuck in a Salvation Army clothing-drop bin for over an hour before anybody thought to investigate why the bin periodically shouted for help. Most people walking by the bin had assumed the shrill "Help! Help!" was a recorded announcement requesting donations.

Stuff like that happens to me pretty regularly. I get picked on a lot because I'm shorter than practically every other boy in our class. Also, because of a car crash I was in when I was little, I've got one leg that's the tiniest bit shorter than the other. It doesn't affect how I walk, but it shows up when I run.

Freak had it somewhat easier in school than Fiona or I did. He had a cool nickname and he was on the track team. Most of the other kids respected him, even though he didn't seem to care whether they did or not. If he happened to be around on an occasion when I was being picked on, he almost always found a way to distract my tormentors, usually by showing them something shiny. You couldn't ask for more than that in a friend.

• • • • •

Fiona was wearing her gym suit on the late bus that afternoon. As soon as the bus had dumped all of its basketball players and we were the only kids still on board, Fiona came up from the back and sat with us. She had her Jell-O–stained clothes in a plastic bag and her hair slicked back like she had just been swimming.

"That was some show in the cafeteria today," Freak said conversationally. He sniffed the air near Fiona. "Is that strawberry perfume?"

Fiona glared at him.

"Are we doing this, or not?" she asked.

"You plan on meeting Alf dressed in your gym shorts?"

"I'll be all set if we have to run. Are we bringing him the crayon?"

Before Freak could answer, I said, "Yes." They looked at me. "It's his crayon. We found it. If he wants to give us a reward for finding it, that would be fair. If he wants to share with us whatever he can sell it for, that would be great."

"And if he wants to snatch it back from us and throw us in his dungeon, that would be terrific," said Freak, imitating my voice.

"If that happens," I said, clenching my fist and punching the air, "River Man will save us!"

River Man was what I used to call myself in the days when Freak and I played superheroes. River Man could channel energy. He said things like, "Go with the flow!" as he sent bad guys tumbling down the street in a flood of raw power. River Man helped me explain why, for some reason, my aunt had embroidered my initials on the front of one of my shirts. I sometimes pretended to be him whenever thinking about my parents got to be a little too much for me. It was all right for River Man's face to be wet; water was one of his weapons.

"Right!" said Freak, giving a basketball he had found in the aisle an enormous bounce and catching it as it ricocheted off the ceiling. "If that's what we're doing, I'll run over to the house and get the crayon."

"While you're doing that," Fiona announced, "I'm changing my clothes."

The bus let us off and Freak and Fiona headed across the field toward Bagshot Road. I stopped by the sofa.

It had rained briefly during the afternoon. The leaves on the ground were wet and shiny, but the sofa, I was somehow not surprised to see, was completely dry.

I stretched out on it and stared into the overhead tree

branches. An escaped party balloon fluttered on a twig near the top of one of the trees. As I sank comfortably into the cushions, I closed my eyes. The sun filtering through the tree branches caused odd, yet surprisingly clear, shapes to appear on the insides of my eyelids. I saw four rectangles arranged like windowpanes, two panes above the others. The upper right pane pulsed twice with wavering sunlight. Then the upper left pulsed once and the right pulsed twice again.

It was hypnotic. After the third or fourth repetition, I felt myself drifting into sleep.

And I dreamed.

I knew I was dreaming because I was walking along Breeland Road toward the bus stop, but when I got there, the pavement ended in a clearing where the bus stop should have been. I stepped into the clearing and was suddenly on the top of a hill. I could see land stretching out in all directions, full of forests and lakes and villages. In the distance, where the horizon should have been, the land curved upward. It curved upward and made a dome over my head. I looked straight up, through patchy clouds, and I could still see land. The overhead land was very far away. I thought I could make out continents and oceans. It was like I was in a planetarium, only instead of projecting stars on the ceiling, somebody was projecting a map.

"It's not to scale, of course," said a voice behind me.

I turned and found Mr. Hendricks, my English teacher, standing behind me. He was wearing a suit made from the same material the sofa was upholstered with. It made him look like a giant leprechaun.

"You'd need a telescope to see this much detail, if you were actually there," he added.

"Actually where?"

"Indorsia."

"Is that a vocabulary word?"

"It is for you. I hasten to add I am not really your English teacher. Mr. Hendricks is currently in his apartment reading a trashy detective novel with the shades drawn. I am taking his form because you seem to like him and I wanted to appear to you as someone familiar."

"Thanks. That's not really something someone would say in a dream."

"Possibly not. Then again, you're dreaming, so maybe it is."

"What is Indorsia?"

"This place." The person who wasn't Mr. Hendricks gestured at the landscape around us.

"It looks like it's on the inside surface of a giant, hollow sphere," I said. "It's probably the inside of the basketball Freak was playing with on the bus. That's how my dreams work. I put in things from right before I fell asleep. If I'm eating pretzels while watching a monster movie on TV and I doze off—"

"You dream about a monster eating pretzels?"

"I dream about pretzels eating a monster. I'm a little messed up."

"You may think of Indorsia as being on the inside surface of a basketball if you wish. The analogy is not a bad one."

"And you're probably supposed to be the sofa. You're upholstered the same way."

"It would be more accurate to say I am the sofa's spokesperson. The sofa is a wonderful example of smart furniture. Smart furniture is all the rage among upper-class Indorsians. It keeps itself clean; it digests stains; it can change its color to match the drapes. It grows from cubes no bigger than this."

He held out his hand. Something resembling a sugar cube sat in the center of his outstretched palm. The cube was the same green as his suit.

I was used to people talking crazy in my dreams. I knew enough to humor him before he turned into a forty-foot-tall Morgue MacKenzie.

"Furniture grows from tiny cubes, huh? That's . . . terrific."

"It saves a bundle in shipping costs. It also makes it easier to pack if you're being pursued by storm troopers."

"Good point," I agreed, glancing around for possible escape routes.

"It took about a year for the sofa to grow to full size. The nannies replicated themselves and constructed it according to a standard template. This particular sofa is unique in that it has nanotech factories in both armrests. The nannies there can manufacture small items, once they've been given a sample. Handy if you need spare change."

"Nannies?" I looked up, half expecting to see Mary Poppins out parasailing.

"Very tiny machines. So tiny, they could float through your bloodstream without your being aware of it."

"Sounds...ticklish."

"The most interesting thing about this sofa is its ability to tesser."

"It grows hair?"

"It can fold space. It can teleport. It has a maximum range of two miles, and it has to recharge between transits, but it figured out how to do this all on its own. It is the only entity in either world that can do it."

"Tesser?"

"Yes."

"Isn't that a word from a children's book?"

"Yes. And *robot* is a word from a stage play. New words have to come from somewhere."

"Then, if you ask me, this whole dream is getting hyperdiculous."

"I don't hold out too much hope for *hyperdiculous*. I don't see it coming into common usage. It's not frabjous enough."

"I'm going to wake myself up now."

I pinched my forearm and winced. Nothing changed.

"I'm sorry, but you have to stay asleep for another twelve seconds. We haven't quite finished the neural mapping. Wouldn't you like to know where the sofa gets the energy it needs to tesser, and to manufacture small objects, and to think?"

"No," I said.

"I will tell you anyway." He gave his watch a quick glance. Then he leaned in close, looked from side to side as if he were afraid of being overheard, and whispered, "Dust bunnies!"

Fiona woke me up. She poked me in the arm until I opened my eyes. As she leaned over me, I noticed that her hair was wet from a quick shower. Even though she had run a comb through it, it still looked stringy. She was wearing pants with an orange checked pattern and a purple sweatshirt that was a little damp around the collar.

"How can you possibly sleep at a time like this?" she asked. "What were you dreaming? Your eyelids were fluttering a mile a minute. That's a sure sign of REM sleep. Rapid Eye Movement. That's when dreams happen."

"Not to be confused with RMM sleep," said Freak, leaning in beside her.

"What's that?" demanded Fiona.

"The kind of sleep I assume *you* have," said Freak. "Rapid Mouth Movement."

It doesn't take much to distract Fiona. Being angry with Freak usually does it. She stopped wondering what I had been dreaming and turned to argue with him. I tuned the both of them out.

I sat and looked up and down the length of the sofa. I remembered that my aunt Bernie had been complaining about dust bunnies the day before. Dust bunnies, she'd said, were clumps of hair and dust that collected under furniture. I found it reassuring to be able to trace at least part of the dream back to its source. The dust bunnies. The basketball. The sofa itself.

I thought about how things from our waking lives

sometimes manage to show up in our dreams. I was sometimes able to trick myself into dreaming about my parents by looking at photos of them before I went to sleep. They had died before I was two, so I had never had a real chance to know them. In my dreams, we were always going places together. In the best dream I had ever had of them, we went on a picnic.

I suddenly realized I was gripping the edges of the cushion I was sitting on very tightly. As I started to let go, I thought I felt the cushion squeeze back. I got off the sofa as quickly as I could.

"I dreamed the sofa showed me how it was made!" I blurted out, interrupting my friends' argument. "Mr. Hendricks was there. Only it wasn't Mr. Hendricks; it was the sofa."

Fiona stopped waving her finger in Freak's face. They both turned and stared at me.

"Mr. Hendricks was the sofa?" said Freak.

"It's that stupid velour jacket he wore yesterday," said Fiona, immediately knowing more about my dream than I did.

"There are nanotech factories in the armrests and I was in this place where people live on the inside instead of the outside, and the sofa can tesser." I noticed the blank looks on my friends' faces. "I'm not explaining this well, am I?"

"Were there purple unicorns?" inquired Freak.

"No. What? Should there have been? It seemed so real."

"Most dreams do, you know," said Fiona, not unkindly.

"Can we get on with this?" Freak nodded toward the Underhill place. He was holding a cigar box. I assumed he had the crayon in it, along with maybe the coin, the domino, and possibly the plaid sock. Freak confirmed this, adding that the box also contained the crushed peanut shell. He said that anything that was Alf's should, absolutely, be returned to Alf.

We walked to the gate.

"Hello?" I said.

The hinged door in the gatepost flipped down.

"You're late," said Alf.

"Some of us had to freshen up," I explained. "How do we do this?"

"In a moment, I will open the gate. But there are some rules. When you walk up the drive, stay to the right. This will keep you under the trees. If, at any time, you look up and you can see open sky directly above you, you will have to turn around and leave and we will have to reschedule. Stay under the cover of the trees at all times. Do not come to the main door of the house. There is a servants' entrance on the side. You will be able to reach this door without breaking cover. The key is under the mat. Wipe your feet and let yourselves in."

"You think somebody is watching from above?" I asked.

"Somebody is always watching from above. Step back from the gate, please."

The sound of turning gears came from within the gatepost. The gate shook and then slid sideways to the right. It stopped when it had opened wide enough to allow us through single file.

Freak went first and I followed Fiona.

The gate clanged shut behind us.

CHAPTER
06

Reunited Socks

oing up the driveway, I occasionally looked up through the oak trees along the side to see if I could spot any of the pterodactyls or UFOs or whatever it was Alf was worried about. I saw nothing.

The house was big and boxy with castle-like turrets on three of the four corners. It looked old enough for George Washington to have slept in, assuming George was capable of dozing off in a place that looked like it might be infested with zombies.

We found the servants' entrance on the south side of the house. Freak retrieved the key from under the mat, fit it into the lock of the windowless metal door, and pushed cautiously inward.

We peered into the gloom beyond the doorway. A small room contained a table and three mismatched chairs. In the far wall were two stairways, one leading up, the other leading down.

"I would leave the door open," admitted Freak.

"I had no plans to close it," I agreed.

"Here's a note," said Fiona, who had stepped in and picked up a piece of paper she found on the table.

UP. DOWN THE CORRIDOR TO THE LEFT. SECOND DOOR ON THE RIGHT.

"Is he kidding? Why didn't he just meet us here?" Freak complained.

"Maybe he's in a wheelchair," said Fiona.

"Having had both legs cut off in the duel that damaged the sofa," I suggested.

There was a rumble from the downward-leading stairway, like maybe a furnace had just started up or a small dinosaur was having a bowel movement. We looked at one another and scurried up the other stairway.

We found ourselves in a long corridor lit by a single light-bulb and went left, just as the note had instructed. On our right we passed a metal circuit-breaker box and then a door. Freak started to walk past the door and I said, "Wait."

"What?"

"The note said the second door."

"Yeah. So? This is the first door."

"Not if you count the door on the metal box."

"Why," said Fiona, through gritted teeth, "would you count the door on the metal box? It's tiny. You can't walk through it."

"But it's a door," I said. They both looked at me. "Maybe it's a test."

"A test of what?"

"How well we can count?"

Freak shrugged. He knocked on the door. When nobody answered, he tried the knob.

"It's locked. This isn't the door."

"Wait," I said again. My guts twisted up the way they sometimes did during the scarier parts of monster movies.

It was an old-fashioned door, solid looking, made of four wooden panels, two on top, two on the bottom. I realized it looked like the windowpane pattern I had seen on the underside of my eyelids when I'd been lying on the sofa. The panes had pulsed. I tried to remember the pattern.

I tapped the door's upper right panel twice. Then I tapped the left panel once. Then I tapped the right two more times. The door latch clicked and the door swung open an inch. Light streamed through the gap.

"How did you do that?" asked Freak.

I shrugged. "I followed a pattern I saw in my head when I was lying on the sofa," I said.

"You had a vision," Fiona said flatly.

"I guess."

Freak pushed the door open. We followed him through it.

It was the hideout of a serial killer. At least, it looked like the kind of room the cops always found on TV shows when they were hunting a dangerous lunatic. Bulletin boards hung on the walls, and the boards were covered with articles clipped from newspapers and magazines, handwritten notes, and photographs. Pieces of yarn secured with thumbtacks connected one thing to another, sometimes stretching halfway across a wall. It could also have been, I realized, the room of a detective who was working hard to solve a case.

A map of Hellsboro with the Rodmore Chemical plant at

its center was pinned up next to photographs of different breeds of dogs. A picture of a black helicopter shared space with a map of downtown Cheshire and a magazine ad for Agra Nation® brand mac and cheese. One whole bulletin board was devoted to pictures of people I didn't recognize.

A diagram of what might have been a basketball sliced in half was stuck up next to a poster-size photo looking down into a valley from way up on the side of a mountain. The photo was so sharp and clear that Fiona, who has no head for heights, could only glance at it and look away. The valley had a lake in it that formed the perfect outline of an elephant.

"Where on earth is that?" said Freak.

"Maybe it's *not* on earth," I murmured, managing to make myself feel even more creeped out than I already did.

Everywhere there were notes on index cards in a crabbed, hurried handwriting.

THE WAY TO INDORSIA
MUST BE KEPT CLOSED!

PRIMORDIAL SOUP IN REVIVARIUM TOO SALTY.
REDUCE SODIUM.

USE KIDS! BOYS HAVE NO PHONES.
GIRL MAY BE MATCH FOR MIRANDA.

PEANUT BUTTER MISSING FROM LAST ORDER.
SPEAK TO DELIVERY MAN.

"What does it mean," asked Fiona suspiciously, "'USE KIDS'?"

"Maybe these kids here," said Freak, tapping a photograph. It showed the three of us waiting at the bus stop.

"That does it!" said Fiona, snatching the photo from the wall. "We should get out of here *right now*! You guys have no phones. I could be a match for Miranda!"

"Only if Miranda is a nutcase," said Freak. "That note may have nothing to do with us. I mean, who's Miranda?"

"Maybe Alf's looking for a babysitter," I suggested.

"HE PHOTOGRAPHED US!"

"He also photographed squirrels and birds and passing cars," I said, pointing to a series of similar photos. "They look like they're all from the camera in the gatepost. It's a security camera. He's worried about things near the entrance to his property. That's all."

"Oh," said Fiona, starting to calm down. "Well. Maybe."
She turned. Then she jumped like she had just seen a snake.
Freak and I turned, and we jumped with her.

The sofa was behind us.

It was right next to the door. I didn't see how we could have missed it when we came in.

"No, no, no, no," said Freak, shaking his head and sounding less confident than he usually did. "That's NOT the same sofa. There's no stain on the cushion and there's no cut along the back. It's another sofa from the same set of furniture."

I pointed.

A wet maple leaf clung to one of the sofa's dragon-claw feet.

"My dream was right," I said. "I was told the sofa can tesser. Which, in case you didn't know, means it can move around on its own."

"NO, IT CAN'T!" Freak grabbed me by the shoulders and spun me around so we were looking at each other eye-to-eye. "You have to turn off this imagination of yours SOMETIME, River Man! It's a sofa. It stays wherever it's put. Our sofa is still out by the road. This is a different sofa."

"Sure," I agreed, trying to pacify him. "Maybe Alf got them at a two-for-one sale."

"This isn't the right room," muttered Fiona. "We're not supposed to be here."

"He's going to wonder what's taking us so long," I said.

"Do we actually still want to meet him, after seeing this?" asked Fiona. "This has nutzoid written all over it."

"Actually, the word I keep seeing is *Indorsia*," I said, pointing to another hand-scribbled note. This one read,

INDORSIA MUST NEVER DRAW ATTENTION TO ITSELF.

"I don't think this is serial-killer stuff," I added.

"No," agreed Freak. "It's more like mad-scientist stuff. I don't see how that's much better."

"Somehow I knew how to open that door," I pointed out. "Like we were invited in here. I say we meet him."

"And I say we leave," said Fiona.

We both looked at Freak. The final vote was his.

"The high bid on the crayon is eleven thousand dollars," I said.

Freak looked at me narrowly.

"Fine." He sighed. "Anybody who's upset because he

didn't get his peanut butter doesn't sound all that dangerous to me. Let's go see what's behind door number two."

As we slipped out, I turned to close the door, and I thought I heard a *tch-tch* noise, like someone making a sound of disapproval between his tongue and teeth. I leaned back in. The swinging door reflected a flash of light into the room's far corner—and I could have sworn the angled reflection looked a little like a floating ax. A woodchopper's ax with no woodchopper holding it. I dove out of the room and tried to convince myself that Freak was right about my overactive imagination.

I caught up with my friends at the next door. Freak was already knocking loudly on it.

"Come in!" said an equally loud voice from the other side.

We opened the door to a brightly lit kitchen, with a stove and an icebox like the kinds you see in movies that take place when cars were a new invention. A workstation with an ancient sink built into it sat squarely in the room's center.

On the far side of this island was Alf.

He was kneeling, so the only part of him we could see was his head. His chin was on the countertop. He flashed us a grin as we entered. "Just a sec!" he said, and tilted his head to one side. Pots and pans rattled around in the lower part of the workstation. After a moment he straightened up, holding a lemon squeezer triumphantly in one hand.

"I'm thinking of making lemonade," he said brightly.

He came around the side of the counter and approached us with his hand outstretched. He shook Freak's hand, then turned to Fiona and me and did the same. "Of course, if you're the sensible people I think you are," he added, "you wouldn't accept anything to eat or drink from me, so maybe I won't. If I made lemonade, would you drink it?"

We shook our heads in unison.

"No, quite right. And you were apparently quite hesitant coming down the hall. Possibly looking for trapdoors in the floor. That demonstrates an admirable caution. This is a promising start." He looked at the lemon squeezer in his hand. "Maybe I'll make some for myself later." He put the squeezer down on the counter next to some lemons and a canister marked SUGAR.

Alf was a tall man with sandy-colored hair parted in the middle. Eyes as gray as the shingles on his house sat on either side of a nose that was long and sharp and looked a little like an eagle's beak. He was wearing a tan tweed suit with a floppy yellow bow tie and a dark green vest with a pocket-watch chain looped across the front of it. He looked like somebody who rode around in a horse and buggy.

"Did you bring the crayon?" he asked.

Freak nodded warily.

"Excellent. We should probably check to see what the current high bid on the auction is. By the way, I'm Alf." He pointed at me. "And you're River. And you're Fiona. And you're...Freak." He gazed at Freak for a moment. "That can't be your real name."

"Nope," agreed Freak. Alf continued to stare at Freak, as if he expected Freak to state his real name, but Freak showed no inclination to do so.

Alf started across the kitchen, gesturing that we should follow. He led us through the house, up a marble staircase, and into an art gallery.

At least, it looked like an art gallery to me. Reproductions of famous paintings hung on all four walls. The *Mona Lisa* smiled at us; a skull-headed guy on a bridge screamed at us; George Washington crossed the Delaware like he was trying to get away from us. Mixed in with the famous stuff were portraits of people I didn't know. One was a portrait of a beautiful woman wearing medieval armor. She had her helmet off.

Renaissance? I wondered, possibly because I had recently learned to spell the word. I looked more closely and noticed something resembling a modern army tank in the background. I decided the painting might be more recent than I thought.

"This one at the end is called *Guernica*," Alf said, indicating a painting so huge that it completely filled the wall at the far end of the room. It showed, in what I thought was a somewhat cartoony style, a bunch of people and barnyard animals experiencing what was obviously a lot of pain and mental anguish. It looked like a panel out of a comic strip that Satan might have found funny.

"It's by Picasso," Alf informed us. "For me, it's always been one of the all-time great works of art."

Alf strode to the center of the room and waved his hand over a desk. *Guernica* disappeared. The eBay auction for the zucchini crayon appeared in its place.

"Whoa," said Freak.

The painting was now a gigantic computer screen. Alf moved his hand slightly in the air above the desk and the image scrolled down to the latest bid. The high bid was still $11,000. Alecto was still in the lead.

"That's not good," said Alf quietly.

"This is very high tech," observed Freak.

"Some of it is not yet commercially available, yes," Alf agreed.

I studied the desk. It had the same dragon-claw feet as the sofa. Four other pieces of furniture in the room had the same kind of feet. Freak was right. The sofa was part of a set.

"What's not good?" Fiona asked.

"The fact that GORLAB hasn't put in a counterbid since this morning. It could mean he's exploring other means of acquiring the crayon."

"Like what?"

"Like stealing it. Did you bring it?"

Freak nodded, but otherwise didn't move a muscle.

"May I see it?" Alf snapped.

Freak slid his hand into the cigar box without opening the lid too far. He withdrew the crayon and held it up.

"What else have you got in there?" Alf nodded at the box.

Freak grudgingly flipped it open.

"Oh," said Alf. "You found all this between the sofa cushions? You could have told me you had the sock."

Alf sat down and pulled off his right shoe, revealing a bare foot. He grabbed the sock and started to wiggle into it.

"What should I do with the crayon?" asked Freak, trying not to stare at an adult doing something completely bizarre.

"Put it back in the box. I just wanted to make sure you had it. And the double-six domino? Double-sixes are lucky."

Alf paused mid-sock-wiggle. He grabbed the domino out of the box, looked at Freak, looked at me, nodded slightly, and tucked the domino into my T-shirt pocket. "If I were you, I would carry it with me at all times. It's lucky, like a four-leaf clover." He yanked up his newly returned sock and reached for his shoe.

"What about the coin?" asked Freak.

"The coin?" said Alf, as if he were unaware of its existence. He looked back in the box. "Oh, the coin. Yes. That's lucky, too." He plucked the coin from the box and handed it to Freak. "That can be your lucky piece. Carry it with you at all times."

I got the impression Alf was humoring Freak. Freak didn't seem to notice. He tucked the coin into his pants pocket.

"So, Mr. Alf," I said, eager to get back to the reason we were there, "you seem to know who the bidders are in the auction."

"Let's just say I have strong suspicions." Alf finished tying his shoe and stood up. "Ah. That feels much better. And it's just Alf, please."

He waved his hand over his desk and *Guernica* reappeared. The painting didn't glow the way a computer screen would. It looked like a real painting. I wasn't entirely sure the technology was available even non-commercially.

"One of the bidders, I am absolutely certain," said Alf, "is a man named Edward M. Disin."

"Why is that name familiar?" asked Fiona.

"It's the name of the place where my aunt works," I said. "The Edward M. Disin Medical Center."

"Yes," agreed Alf. "Disin, and the very powerful company he controls, the Disin Corporation, put up the money to build the center. They've also donated cutting-edge computers and electronics to the Cheshire school system, the fire department, and the police."

"Generous," I said.

"Perhaps." Alf pinched the air above his desk. *Guernica* disappeared again. It was replaced with an aerial view of rolling countryside. Alf wiggled his fingers and the picture zoomed in on a charcoal-gray blotch of land surrounded by vibrant autumn colors.

"Recognize this?" he asked.

"That's Hellsboro," Fiona said immediately.

"Yes. Hellsboro. The reason Edward M. Disin is so generous to your little town of Cheshire."

Doghats

The image is refreshed every three seconds," Alf informed us. "So you're seeing this practically in real time. It's coming off the satellite surveillance net. I'd ask you to sit, but the sofa's gone walkabout."

He gestured vaguely at an area directly in front of the desk. I looked down at the carpet and saw four indentations where the sofa's feet had once rested. I thought the rectangle formed by the indentations seemed remarkably clean. And free of dust bunnies.

"You've hacked into the data streams coming from

government surveillance satellites?" Fiona asked, turning into what Freak liked to call Science Girl.

"It isn't hard to do," Alf admitted. "It helps me keep track of what's going on in the neighborhood. Here. Look at how close we can get."

Alf made some more wizardly gestures over his desk. Hellsboro filled the screen. White concrete buildings and enormous storage tanks were visible in Hellsboro's center.

"Rodmore Chemical," I said. I felt a little sick saying it. My parents had both worked for Rodmore. Thinking of the place made me think of them. One of the photographs I had of them showed them at the company picnic. A big Rodmore banner was visible over their heads. Some people in town got angry when they heard the name Rodmore. Whenever I heard it, I just got depressed.

Alf magnified the image even more. It was as if we were seeing things only fifty feet or so below us. The cracks in the pavement around the buildings were clearly visible. Broken glass glistened here and there. Suddenly, a blurred canine-looking shape appeared in the right-hand corner of the picture.

"Is that a coyote?" Freak asked.

"Could be," Alf said dryly. "An unnaturally large coyote.

How much do you know about what caused the Hellsboro fire?"

"It's never been proven," I said, "but a lot of people think the factory had been dumping some sort of waste chemicals into the soil, and after a while they somehow caused the coal to ignite."

"Correct," Alf said. "Here's an aerial picture of the area before the fire started," he went on, changing the picture on the screen to one that was much greener. "That's Rodmore in the center. To the north is most of the town of Cheshire. To the west is the Sunnyside housing development. You can just make out the Underhill place, where we are now, at the extreme left. This was thirteen years ago."

Alf massaged the air above the desktop, and a transparent pink blob appeared on the screen, centered on the Rodmore factory. "Rodmore starts dumping some sort of chemical substance into the grounds around the factory, and by the end of the first year the underground plume—that's the word for a spreading spill beneath the surface—the plume extends about this far. Another year and it's expanded to this"—the pink blob grew—"and by the third year it's under half the houses in the Sunnyside development."

Red dots appeared on five of the houses in the photograph.

One of the houses was Freak's. Freak, who had been pacing and showing signs of boredom, suddenly stood very still.

"Whatever else the plume may have been," said Alf, "it was definitely toxic. The dots represent five incidences of leukemia, all occurring within the space of eighteen months, all within a half mile of one another. Statistically improbable. The dot on that house—"

"Yeah," said Freak, rather forcefully. "That's my sister. And she was more than just a dot on some stupid photograph. Why are we talking about this? What has this got to do with the crayon?"

"The crayon," Alf said, slowly and deliberately, "as improbable as it may sound, could be the key to bringing to justice one of the people responsible for the Rodmore chemical dumping. And, by extension, bringing to light some of the mischief it caused."

"Mischief?" said Freak, as if the word didn't come anywhere near describing it.

"Criminal mischief, yes. Crimes, if you prefer."

"Who are you?" demanded Freak.

Alf stepped around the desk and faced the three of us, the big screen at his back.

"I am someone who has been living in this house ever

since its previous owner passed away. I have been keeping my eye on the allegedly abandoned Rodmore Chemical site, monitoring events in the town, and waiting for an opportunity like this to present itself. I cannot undo the damage that has already been done, but I might possibly be able to prevent worse damage from happening in the future."

"Who do you work for?" I asked.

"I am self-employed."

"You put the crayon in the sofa," stated Freak. "And then you put the sofa out front, knowing we would sit on it."

"I can't take credit for that. It was mainly the sofa's idea."

"And you deliberately say off-the-wall things." Freak came as close to yelling as he ever did. "And wear only one sock, and dress like you don't know what century it is, because you're trying to come across like Willy Wonka, or the Wizard of Oz, or somebody who hangs around with Muppets, because you figure we're dumb kids and this will somehow charm us and make you our friend!"

Behind Alf the screen reverted to the real-time satellite image of Rodmore Chemical. The unnaturally large coyote was clearly visible. In three-second increments, it walked up the steps of one of the buildings and disappeared inside.

"I thought a few eccentricities might put you at your

ease," said Alf, oblivious to what was going on behind him. The satellite image started to drift west. It left the chemical plant and started moving slowly over Hellsboro, showing the cinder-covered surface. "I thought you might be afraid of a lone man living in a rambling old house. My sister tells me I come across as somewhat intense. I thought throwing in a few odd mannerisms and the random non sequitur might reassure you."

"You mean, convince us you were harmless?" asked Freak.

"Yes. Did I overdo it?"

The three of us just stared at him.

"Does your sister live here with you?" I asked. I thought I had heard a faint *tch-tch* while Alf was explaining toxic plumes. Apparently, I was the only one who had heard it.

"No," Alf said slowly, as if "no" didn't fully answer the question. "I live here by myself. There's just me—and you, my three guests." Alf stretched out his arms, as if he might hug us. "I was hoping to gain your trust or, at the very least, hold your interest."

"Is that my house?" said Fiona, craning her neck to see past Alf. He turned and looked.

The image showed an L-shaped house with a tan-shingled roof. A swing set in the backyard cast a skeletal shadow on a wading pool's greenish water. It was unmistakably Fiona's house—I could tell by the fake wishing well on the front lawn. The image refreshed, and suddenly two large dogs were standing next to the well.

"Oh, dear," said Alf.

"*What* are those?" Fiona walked closer to the screen.

"At a guess," said Alf, "I'd say they're supposed to be an Irish setter and a Newfoundland."

We all moved closer to the screen and squinted at it.

"*Supposed* to be?" I said.

"What they really are," Alf explained, "are two men wearing narrow umbrella-like hats, the tops of which have been designed to look like dogs when seen from above. They know that at this hour of the day, in this particular neighborhood, there's probably nobody around to observe them at street level. But they're not entirely sure there isn't someone monitoring the satellite images. So they're taking the precaution of wearing the hats. This is why I asked you to stay under the trees when you came up to the house. You never know who might be watching."

During Alf's speech, the image had refreshed several times. The dogs had moved around each other and progressed to the side of the house.

"That dog just smelled the other dog's butt!" Fiona declared.

"Yes," said Alf admiringly. "They're very professional."

"What are they doing outside my house?"

"I'm pretty certain they're about to break in, looking for the zucchini crayon."

Fiona made a little strangled noise at the back of her throat.

"But the zucchini crayon is here with us," I said.

"They don't know that. All they know is the computer that originated the auction is located at the address they've come to. It's perfectly logical for them to assume the crayon is inside the house."

"We have to call the police!" shouted Fiona. She started rummaging frantically in her bag for her cell phone.

"I'm afraid," said Alf, loudly and forcefully enough to make her pause, "there will be a considerable delay before you get through to them. This is what comes of accepting gifts of communication equipment from a company like the Disin Corporation. The doghats will have ample time to break in, search the place, and be on their way."

"What if we call the dogcatcher instead?" suggested Freak, as if he were finding the whole thing a joke.

Fiona let out a little shriek. She pointed at an object

leaning against the side of the house. It was partly obscured by the overhang.

"That's my little brother's bicycle! He's home! He's inside the house, and these wackos are about to break in! He's by himself!"

"Oh," said Alf. "That changes things. Will he answer the phone if it rings?"

Fiona tapped her cell once and held the phone to her ear.

"Tell him to turn on the TV as quickly as he can, as loud as it will go," Alf instructed. "They won't break in if they think someone is home."

Fiona glared at her phone, then shook her head. "It's no good. He's not answering. He never does when he's home alone. Especially if he's on Mom's computer."

"They've gone under the awning," Freak reported.

"We have to get over there!" Fiona started for the door. Alf caught her by the sleeve.

"You won't make it in time! But if your brother is using a computer, we can do something from here." Alf turned and spoke to his desk. "Can you get a connection?"

Blocky black letters appeared on the screen, superimposed over the image of Fiona's house.

ONE MOMENT.

"Your brother's name is Stephen?" Alf asked.

"Stevie. Yes."

AUDIO CONNECTION ESTABLISHED. YOU MAY SPEAK.

Alf leaned over his desk and addressed the screen.

"Stevie Shuck," he said, dropping his voice down an octave. "This is the Department of Homeland Security. Do not turn off your computer. We are about to conduct a test of the emergency broadcasting system. The sound coming from your computer will rapidly increase in volume. Please cover your ears."

Music started playing. It quickly got louder.

"Isn't that the French national anthem?" Fiona asked.

"Yes," Alf confirmed. "I've always loved that part of the movie *Casablanca* when the nightclub orchestra plays it to annoy the Nazis."

The music got louder and louder. Suddenly, two dogs darted out from under Fiona's awning and raced down the road.

"Notice how it appears their tails are between their legs?" Alf said. "You have to admire the attention to detail."

The music stopped abruptly. Alf leaned forward and said, "This concludes our test of the emergency broadcast system. Had it been a real emergency, there would have been explosions.

Now, in the interest of national security, return to your room and clean it."

The dogs disappeared beneath some overhanging trees. A few moments later, a car emerged from the same location and sped away.

"They've probably already reported back," said Alf.

"Reported what?" I asked.

"Possibly that the crayon is in the hands of a very patriotic French family. Certainly that the first attempt to find it has failed."

"You think there will be other attempts?" Fiona sounded on the verge of panic.

"Not if you go home and cancel the auction."

Before any of us could reply, there was a sound like a metal garbage can full of hubcaps being knocked over. It came from a distant part of the house. The way everybody froze, I knew I wasn't the only one who had heard something this time.

Chair Eats Bunny

What was that?" demanded Fiona.

"I thought you said it was just us here," said Freak.

"Is it doghats? Are they in the house?" I said.

"You didn't," asked Alf, "by any chance, leave the door open when you came in?"

Freak and Fiona and I looked at one another. Alf read the expressions on our faces. He said, "Right," turned to his desk, pulled open the top drawer, and reached into it. I expected him to pull out a gun. Instead, he pulled out a tennis racquet.

"You think," I said, "by leaving the door open, we let in tennis players?"

"I hope not," replied Alf. "Tennis players can be very destructive. The three of you will be safe here. I shouldn't be gone long."

The moment Alf was out the door, Freak reopened the desk drawer. In rapid succession he pulled out a cheese grater, a bicycle pump, and a toothbrush.

"How can you snoop when there are doghats around?" demanded Fiona, still shaking a little.

"Maybe I'll find dog biscuits," replied Freak, who seemed a little unnerved himself, despite his actions. He pulled out a can opener and a stethoscope.

"I don't believe this is happening," said Fiona, hugging herself.

"That makes two of us," Freak agreed, producing a flashlight.

"Excellent!" I said, snatching the flashlight from him.

"What would make a crayon so valuable, somebody would send thugs to steal it?" Fiona wondered. "And how do we convince these people I don't have it? I don't want them coming back to my house!"

"Alf's right," said Freak. "If you want to be safe, you have to end the auction as soon as you get home."

"But that won't be enough. They'll assume I've still got the crayon, even though I'm not auctioning it off."

I was down on the floor, shining the flashlight under pieces of furniture. Freak and Fiona stopped talking and stared at me.

"Maybe it's the house," said Freak. "Maybe the house makes people crazy."

"It's nice and clean under any piece of furniture that matches the sofa," I explained. "But under a piece that doesn't match"— I swept my arm under a cabinet and pulled out a mess of hairy, fuzzy, flaky things—"there are dust bunnies!"

"So Alf isn't a good housekeeper," said Fiona. "My life may be in danger and all you can do is sweep the floor? How is this relevant?"

I ignored her. I took one of the dust bunnies, compressed it in my fist, and put it under a chair with dragon-claw feet. I craned my neck and positioned the flashlight so I could watch. The dust bunny melted into the underside of the chair and disappeared.

"The chair just ate the dust bunny," I announced.

Freak and Fiona got down on their knees and looked under the chair. I balled up another dust bunny and put it where I had placed the first. It immediately jumped to the underside of the chair and vanished.

"In the dream I had while I was lying on the sofa, the sofa said it got its energy from dust bunnies. It also said it could tesser, which is another word for teleport."

"You mentioned that before. And teleportation is impossible," said Science Girl. "It doesn't allow for the laws of momentum." She gave me a slantwise look and grabbed one of my bunnies. She gripped it tightly and slid her hand under the chair. As we watched, the hairy fibers were drawn from her clenched fingers to the chair, like cotton candy to a stick. She tried to hold on to the bunny, but after a moment, the chair had completely absorbed it.

"Like a snake eating a mouse," said Freak, and Fiona quickly pulled her hand out.

THANK YOU, said block letters on *Guernica*'s screen. THAT WAS REFRESHING.

The appearance of the letters caused the light in the room to flicker, catching our attention. We scrambled to our feet.

"Pardon me?" I said, unable to think of anything else.

AN AFTERNOON SNACK IS ALWAYS A TREAT. BUT WE HAVE VERY LITTLE TIME AND I HAVE MUCH TO TELL YOU. AT THIS MOMENT ALF IS GENTLY HITTING A RACCOON ON

THE NOSE WITH A TENNIS RACQUET. IT WILL ONLY TAKE HIM A FEW MINUTES TO CONVINCE THE CREATURE TO GO BACK OUTDOORS. THEN ALF WILL RETURN HERE.

"What is this?" said Freak suspiciously.

"You are...Alf's computer?" Fiona asked.

"More likely Alf himself, spying on us from a closet somewhere," Freak decided. "'Pay no attention to the man behind the curtain,' right?" Freak spun around, as if he might spot Alf's hiding place.

I AM NOT ALF. I AM A PROCESSING UNIT DISTRIBUTED OVER SEVEN SEPARATE NODES. THE NODES DOUBLE AS A COMPLETE FURNITURE SET. I AM NOT ONLY FUNCTIONAL, BUT COMFORTABLE.

Fiona, Freak, and I digested this.

"You're the sofa," I said.

AND THE DESK AND THE TWO MATCHING ARMCHAIRS AND THE LOVE SEAT AND THE OTTOMAN. AND ONE OTHER PIECE I SHALL NOT NAME, AS A WAY OF SAFEGUARDING MY SECURITY.

"You're a computer disguised as a garage sale," said Freak.

ORIGINALLY WE WERE EIGHT PIECES, BUT THE HASSOCK PERISHED IN A FIRE SHORTLY AFTER WE ARRIVED. THIS HAS LEFT ME WITH SOME GAPS IN MY KNOWLEDGE

AND AT LEAST ONE ROGUE SECURITY SYSTEM. YOU MAY CALL ME GUERNICA. ALF LIKES TO PRETEND THAT I AM SELF-AWARE, WHICH HIDES FROM HIM THE FACT THAT I AM SELF-AWARE.

"You eat dust bunnies?"

MAINLY. EXCEPT FOR THE SOFA, WHICH IS CURRENTLY SUBSISTING ON A DIET OF ACORNS AND AUTUMN LEAVES.

"Oh, free-range is always healthier," agreed Freak.

THE SOFA REQUIRES A MORE ROBUST DIET. THE NANNIES IN THE ARMRESTS NEED MATERIAL WITH WHICH TO CONSTRUCT THINGS. IT TOOK ALMOST 300 ACORNS TO PRODUCE THE SINGLE COIN YOU FOUND BETWEEN THE CUSHIONS.

Freak and Fiona both turned and stared at me. I understood they were remembering what I had told them about my dream. I was very glad I told them. I had toyed with the idea of keeping it to myself.

"Can you spin straw into gold?" I asked.

GIVEN SUFFICIENT STRAW.

"What are nannies?" inquired Fiona.

NANOTECHNOLOGY. VERY TINY ROBOTS. BUT THAT IS IRRELEVANT. WHAT IS IMPORTANT RIGHT NOW IS THAT YOU TRUST ALF.

"Great," said Freak. "Rumpelstiltskin is asking us to believe in Willy Wonka."

ALF HAS NOT GOTTEN OFF TO A GOOD START WITH YOU THREE. I WARNED HIM. I TOLD HIM TO WEAR JEANS AND A T-SHIRT AND A MINIMUM OF TWO SOCKS. YOU ARE FINDING HIM TOO STRANGE.

"And you think you're helping?" asked Freak.

ALF IS A GOOD MAN. THE MAN HE IS TRYING TO STOP IS NOT. BOTH CAME HERE FROM INDORSIA BEFORE THE FINAL PORTAL CLOSED. ALF WANTS TO KEEP THE POR-TAL SHUT. THE OTHER MAN IS WORKING TO REOPEN IT.

"Is Indorsia a place on the inside surface of a basketball?" I asked.

The screen blinked. I get that a lot when I talk to adults, so it didn't faze me.

THE BASKETBALL IS A METAPHOR.

"I don't care if it's a Spalding. People can't live inside a basketball," I said. "What would happen when it was dribbled?"

INDORSIA IS NO MORE A BASKETBALL THAN THE PLANET EARTH IS A PING-PONG BALL. CALLING THEM THESE THINGS ONLY HELPS DESCRIBE THEIR RELATIVE SIZES.

"Indorsia is really, really big?" Fiona asked.

APPROXIMATELY THE SIZE OF THE PLANET JUPITER.

"So...it's probably not here in Pennsylvania," I decided.

The screen blinked again.

INDORSIA IS NOT LOCATED IN THIS UNIVERSE. IT IS A UNIVERSE UNTO ITSELF. THE PEOPLE THERE LIVE ON THE INSIDE SURFACE OF A GIGANTIC, HOLLOW SPHERE. THE PEOPLE OF INDORSIA ARE DESCENDED FROM CRO-MAGNONS WHO CROSSED OVER FROM EARTH BACK WHEN THERE WERE MORE OPEN PORTALS AND WEAKER IMMIGRA-TION LAWS. THEY HAVE ADVANCED SCIENTIFICALLY SOME-WHAT FASTER THAN THEIR COUNTERPARTS HERE ON EARTH.

"Does Indorsia spin?" asked Fiona.

NO. THERE IS NOTHING OUTSIDE OF INDORSIA FOR IT TO SPIN IN.

"Then I don't understand how gravity could work there."

THE INDORSIAN SCIENCE ACADEMY DOES NOT UNDER-STAND IT, EITHER.

"You expect us to believe this?" Freak folded his arms across his chest and glared at the screen.

NO. ALF DOES NOT EXPECT YOU TO BELIEVE IT, EITHER. WHICH IS WHY HE HAS NO INTENTION OF TELL-ING YOU ABOUT IT. I, ON THE OTHER HAND, FEEL YOU

DESERVE TO KNOW THE BIGGER PICTURE. HE WILL ONLY TELL YOU ABOUT EDWARD DISIN AND THE ZUCCHINI CRAYON AND THE DAMAGE DISIN HAS ALREADY DONE. I WANT YOU TO BE AWARE OF WHAT DISIN HAS PLANNED FOR THE FUTURE.

"More gifts to the police department?" asked Freak.

MUCH WORSE. Guernica paused for a moment, as if listening to something. THE RACCOON HAS LEFT THE BUILD-ING. ALF WILL STOP TO WASH HIS HANDS BUT HE WILL BE BACK IN THIS ROOM NO LATER THAN FIFTY-EIGHT SECONDS FROM NOW. YOU MUST NOT REVEAL TO HIM THAT YOU HAVE SPOKEN TO ME. YOU MUST NOT REVEAL TO HIM WHAT I HAVE TOLD YOU.

"You haven't told us much," Freak pointed out.

EDWARD DISIN IS FROM INDORSIA. EDWARD DISIN INTENDS TO ENSLAVE THE PEOPLE OF YOUR TOWN. EDWARD DISIN INTENDS TO REOPEN THE PORTAL TO INDORSIA AND BRING AN ARMY TO EARTH. THE PORTAL TO INDOR-SIA IS LOCATED IN THE CENTER OF THE UNDERGROUND COAL FIRE YOU CALL HELLSBORO. HOW'S THAT?

"Informative," conceded Freak.

"How do you open a portal?" I wanted to know.

"Why would you believe *any* of this?" Freak asked me.

THE ENSLAVEMENT OF YOUR TOWN HAS ALREADY BEGUN. OR DID YOU THINK THE RECENT ENTHUSIASM FOR SHOW TUNES WAS A NATURAL PHENOMENON? THE SAME POWER THAT CAN CAUSE A PEOPLE TO HARMONIZE ON THE SONGS OF RODGERS AND HAMMERSTEIN CAN CAUSE THEM TO WORK FOR FOURTEEN HOURS A DAY IN A SHIPYARD. HERE COMES ALF. WE NEVER SPOKE.

Guernica's screen immediately resumed its aerial view of Hellsboro. Alf opened the door and leaned in. He waved the tennis racquet at us like he had just won a game and said, "It was a raccoon. Big fat fellow. He was going through the trash."

Alf strode into the center of the room. I hid the flashlight behind my back. Alf swept his gaze over us and said, "Now, where were we?"

Kids as Camouflage

t was Freak who had the good sense to get us out of there. He made a big show of looking at his watch. "Oh my gosh! It's almost suppertime!" he announced. I had never heard him say "oh my gosh" before. He gave Alf a big, wide-eyed stare. "We have to get going."

It was the smartest thing he could have said. I could tell Fiona was ready to burst. Any moment she would be telling Alf his computer had a mind of its own and had just told us some crazy stuff about an invasion from inside a basketball. For that matter, I wanted to tell everybody more of the details of my sofa dream, now that the computer had made the dream sound less crazy. Freak seemed to be the only one of us with enough self-control to follow Guernica's advice and keep his mouth shut.

"So soon?" said Alf. "There's so much more I have to tell you."

"It's pizza night," Freak explained. "If I'm not home in time to eat it before it gets cold, my father gets angry."

Alf frowned. "Well, we wouldn't want that. I can sometimes hear your father from here."

Freak blinked. "He's not *that* loud," he said.

"It only happens when the wind is out of Hellsboro," Alf assured him. "And if I've forgotten to turn off the microphone in the gatepost. It's not as though I can make out words or anything. So"—he turned his attention to Fiona and me—"shall we agree to meet here again tomorrow afternoon, same time as today? Fiona, please cancel the online auction as soon as you get home. Make a list of all the e-mail addresses of your bidders. We will have a message for them tomorrow."

"But they'll still think I have the crayon," said Fiona.

"Yes, but they won't try anything so soon after this afternoon's attempt. And after tomorrow, they'll know the crayon is elsewhere."

"I'll keep the crayon at my house for now," said Freak,

clutching his cigar box more tightly, as if he expected Alf to grab it.

Alf nodded. "Just remember to bring it with you tomorrow. Let's get the three of you on your way."

Alf took a step toward the door.

INCOMING CALL.

Guernica's screen flashed the message. Alf paused.

URGENT.

"How urgent?" said Alf, sounding annoyed.

PRIORITY ONE.

"We can show ourselves out," I said.

"Can you?" he said, sounding relieved. "Are you sure?"

"Down the staircase, two rights, a left, don't trip on the loose floorboard, out through the servants' entrance, stay under the trees." I sounded like a tour guide. "We'll make sure we close the door this time."

"Yes, good. Guernica will sense when you get to the gate and will open it just enough to let you out. 'Til tomorrow, then."

Alf escorted us out of the gallery. Then he stepped back inside and closed the door.

We ran down the stairs, made the first right, and stopped.

"WHAT is going on here?" demanded Fiona. "Guys wearing dogs on their heads almost broke into my house!"

"Did they?" asked Freak.

"You saw them as well as I did!"

"I saw something on a big screen," Freak admitted. "I saw a movie once where kids played soccer while flying around on broomsticks. Doesn't mean it actually happened."

"You think everything we saw was faked?"

Freak shrugged. "I don't know what to think."

"We all saw the chair eat the dust bunnies," I said. "That wasn't on the screen."

"I've seen static electricity before," said Freak, walking on ahead of us.

"The sofa communicated with me while I slept," I reminded him. "It called it mural napping. It showed me a mural while I napped. The mural stretched off in all directions. Then it curved overhead and turned into the sky. It was showing me Indorsia."

"You were asleep," said Freak. "Any chance you might have been, oh, I don't know—*dreaming*?"

"Except Guernica then described Indorsia in the same way, and we were all awake."

"How could people live on the inside surface of a hollow sphere?" demanded Fiona, tripping over the loose floorboard. Freak caught her, as if he had been expecting it. "Gravity would be all messed up. Everybody would float off the ground and wind up in the sphere's center."

"Maybe their feet are made of Velcro and the ground is really nappy," I suggested.

"I read a book, once," said Freak, "about people living on the top of a huge flat disk, like a Frisbee, balanced on the back of an enormous flying turtle."

"Yet another reason it's dangerous for you to go to the library," said Fiona.

"All I'm saying is, maybe that's where Alf got the idea. It's not very original."

"But it wasn't Alf who told us," I argued. "It was Guernica. And Guernica also mentioned the flash mobs. We *know* those are real."

"No, we don't," replied Fiona, an angry edge to her voice.

We had reached the door to the room with all the bulletin boards. Without discussing it, we had stopped in front of it.

"River and I have seen the flash mobs," said Freak, finally backing me up. "Can you honestly tell us you don't remember?"

"What? Singing show tunes? While waving my hands around? I wouldn't be caught dead doing that. And don't you think I'd remember? Every time you've asked, I've just assumed you were messing with me."

"We showed you the newspaper article they printed after the first flash mob. If you didn't participate, why don't you remember seeing it happen?"

"Maybe I was in the bathroom! I missed it!"

"That's probably what everybody thought when they read that article. They missed it, because they were in the bathroom," I reasoned.

"That would make it a flush mob," Freak said.

"How could I be doing it? And not know?" Fiona sounded genuinely frightened.

"Are we going in, or aren't we?" Freak asked, ignoring her. "There has to be something in there that will prove this stuff one way or the other."

"What if Alf catches us?" said Fiona. "He probably thinks we're halfway home by now."

"Alf is at the other end of the building," said Freak.

"No, he's not," I said. "The way we zigged and zagged to get to it, I'm pretty sure the gallery is right overhead."

I could tell by his expression that Freak thought so, too. I realized too late he had been trying to calm Fiona.

"Then we'll just have to be very quiet," he said, giving me a look. "Come on, Fiona. We'll be fine."

I tapped on the door panels the way I had the first time. Again, the door opened.

The sofa was no longer in the room.

"There's your proof," I whispered.

Freak stared at the empty space where the sofa had been. "No," he said.

"Maybe it had to go potty," I suggested.

"Alf moved it. He was only pretending to chase a raccoon," Freak said, sounding far from positive.

"One man? By himself? Moving that sofa? Through *that* door?"

I thought it was obvious the door was too narrow for the sofa to fit through. Freak refused to believe it. He only glanced at the door, then turned his attention to the things tacked up on the walls. One whole bulletin board had newspaper clippings about the building of the Rodmore Chemical plant. Another described how a man named Leo Bagshot had built the Sunnyside housing development.

"Here's a picture of your dad," Fiona said to Freak. She still seemed agitated, but she was getting calmer.

Freak and I looked. It was a picture of Frank Nesterii, sitting in a golf cart in the driveway of a Sunnyside house. The house behind him looked brand new. According to the caption, Leo Bagshot had given Mr. Nesterii a bonus for selling the most Sunnyside houses.

"Yeah," said Freak. "Then a lot of the people my father sold those houses to blamed him when the Hellsboro fire forced them to move. But why is his picture *here*?"

"Why is any of this here?" asked Fiona.

I pulled a yellowed newspaper clipping from one of the bulletin boards. It was a clipping I was familiar with. Very, *very* familiar.

The headline read:

CHESHIRE COUPLE KILLED IN CRASH

It described how John and Willow Monroe, a chemist and a geophysicist, had died eleven years earlier when their car went over an embankment as they were coming down Severance Mountain on Route 14. They had been killed instantly. Their son, River, who had been asleep in the backseat, sustained injuries to his legs. The Monroes had both gotten jobs at Rodmore Chemical eight months earlier, and had purchased a home in the Sunnyside housing tract around the same time.

I knew the clipping pretty much by heart. What interested me was the handwritten note stapled to the bottom of it:

SUPPOSITION—J AND W LEARNED
OF RODMORE'S CHEMICAL DUMPING,
DID NOT APPROVE, GATHERED
EVIDENCE? TAKING EVIDENCE TO EPA
OFFICE IN FLANDERS? BRAKE
LINES TAMPERED WITH?

"What's the EPA?" I asked.

"Environmental Protection Agency," answered Fiona.

"What?" said Freak, studying the look on my face.

"Alf—or whoever wrote this—thinks my parents might have been deliberately murdered. To stop them from telling the EPA about Rodmore's chemical dumping."

I could have used the sofa right about then. Instead, I sank to the floor.

Freak scrunched down next to me and eased the clipping out of my hands. He scowled at it. Fiona scrunched down on the other side and, after an awkward moment, put her arm around me.

"So I lost my sister and you may have lost your parents because of the chemical dump," said Freak.

"Maybe," I said, not quite willing to believe it. I got shakily back to my feet. Being comforted by Fiona was weirder than anything else that had happened.

"Do you really think the chemicals in the ground affected the health of the people living in Sunnyside?" Fiona asked Freak.

"Alf seems to think so. And he's certainly studied the situation." Freak waved a hand at the walls.

"He may not have studied it enough," said Fiona mysteriously. She traced a piece of yarn connecting an obituary for my parents to an obituary for Freak's sister. His sister's obit overlapped a list of other Sunnyside residents who had gotten sick. "There's no mention of Audrey here."

"Audrey?"

"She would have been born a minute or so after I was. I would have been the older sister." Fiona looked at us to see if we understood. "I was supposed to be twins."

It was the first time she had ever said anything this personal to us. Freak and I stared at her uncomfortably. I made a move to put my arm around her. She anticipated it and raised her hand.

"This was right around the time of the toxic plume. It never occurred to me there might be a connection."

"It doesn't look like it occurred to Alf, either," I said.

"There were supposed to be *two* of you?" Freak asked.

"She would have been named after my grandmother. Audrey didn't survive, but I came out all right. Except for my achromatopsia."

"You don't believe in God?"

"I'm color-blind."

"That's no reason not to believe in God," Freak assured her.

"Achromatopsia means color-blindness, you idiot! I can only see things in black-and-white!"

"Oh!" said Freak. "Color-blind!" As if that explained a lot about Fiona. Which it did.

One of the bulletin boards at the far end of the room rattled against the wall, like a breeze had disturbed it. We stopped talking and stared.

"Did I mention I thought I saw an ax floating in the air the last time we were here?" I inquired.

"You think you see a lot of things," muttered Freak as he tiptoed over to the bulletin board and motioned for me to help him. The board was hanging on a wire. We lifted the board off its hook and exposed a two-foot opening halfway up the wall. Cool air was gently flowing from it.

"It's some sort of air vent," guessed Freak.

"No, it's a laundry chute," Fiona corrected him, coming

over. "It goes up to the higher floors. When the house had servants, they could dump the dirty clothes down the chute. This must have been the laundry room."

"How do you know this?"

"British TV shows. The kind you guys never watch."

"Shh!" I said.

We heard voices coming down the chute.

"Alf said he was alone here," whispered Fiona.

"Maybe he's on the phone," I said.

"You can hear both voices equally. The other voice sounds like a woman."

"Maybe she's on speakerphone."

"Or maybe Alf lied to us about being here by himself," said Freak.

The voices weren't loud enough for us to make out actual words.

"If we got in the chute and stood on one another's shoulders, the one on top might be able to hear better," suggested Freak.

"Do I look like a cheerleader?" hissed Fiona.

"Do you want me to answer that?"

"I thought I just heard them say the name 'Fiona,'" I said. She glared at me.

"Really?"

I nodded.

She clambered into the chute. Freak looked at me and mouthed, "Really?"

I shook my head.

I crawled in after Fiona. The bottom of the chute had a curve to it, the better to enable dirty socks to fly out. Standing up was tricky. I managed, though, with Fiona standing on my shoulders. Then Freak forced his way in under me. We couldn't have done it without the walls of the chute to lean against and absorb some of our weight. After a few moments of fumbling, Freak was standing upright, I was on his shoulders, and Fiona's head was twelve feet closer to the voices than it had been.

"Your feet smell like Jell-O," I informed her.

She kicked me lightly on the side of the head. I decided that meant she wanted me to shut up. Then, suddenly, her weight was off my shoulders. My first thought was that some sort of laundry creature had gotten her. Maybe a shirt had been stuck in the chute so long, it had evolved into something carnivorous. I imagined myself being watched by unblinking, button-like eyes.

I sent the beam of my flashlight up the chute. The seams where the metal segments of the shaft joined together formed ridges big enough to act as footholds. Fiona was using them to climb farther up the chute.

"I thought you had a problem with heights," I whispered.

"Not in a confined space," she whispered back.

She was right, I realized. The enclosed waterslide tube at Flanders Fun Park never gave her trouble, and that was over two stories high.

I stuck my flashlight through my belt and grabbed the nearest ridge. Footholds didn't work well for me. Handholds did. I followed her up.

Ten feet above where she had been, she came to a stop in front of an opening similar to the one we had come in through. I squeezed up beside her. The opening had a fancy iron grate across it, with cutout curlicues and flower shapes that we could look through into the room beyond.

It was the gallery. I could just make out Guernica on the wall to our left. I briefly wondered why an art gallery would have a laundry chute. Then I realized the room might not always have been a gallery.

Alf was standing with his back to us, his hands on his hips. He was facing the painting of the woman in armor. The woman in armor was talking to him. The painted picture moved, like they were video chatting.

"...nor am I convinced the children are below his radar," the woman was saying. "He sent doghats to the girl's house."

She looked off to her right, as though somebody might be whispering to her from beyond the edge of the picture frame.

"I underestimated them." Alf nodded in agreement. "I had no idea they'd start an auction so soon after finding the crayon. I thought they'd simply bring the crayon to me, once they found out how valuable it was. I thought it would be a good way of appraising the girl. And the boys could be useful, too. They have no phones. They're possibly the only ones in a ten-mile radius."

The portrait's eyes returned to Alf.

"The girl is too bright to have her personality wiped," she said. She looked beyond Alf. She appeared to be looking at the grate of the laundry chute. Fiona and I both leaned back a little to put ourselves more in shadow. "I find the whole idea distasteful to begin with, bright or not. It's the sort of thing *he* would do. I'm surprised at you for even toying with it."

Alf hung his head. Even from the back, he looked embarrassed.

"I have no desire to live again at the cost of somebody else's personality," she continued. "And I don't want to inhabit the body of an eleven-year-old. Going through puberty once

109

was bad enough. Going through it twice would put it right up there with having my head chopped off."

"I've corrected the sodium imbalance in the revivarium," Alf said.

"Nor am I ready to be cloned."

"Miranda." Alf sounded exasperated. "Brothers and sisters share the same DNA. Mine is the same as yours."

"If it were, you'd be a woman. I will not be cloned using my brother's DNA. There's a perfectly good surviving example of my own, true DNA. It's frozen in a jar in Indorsia. Someday, I hope to retrieve it."

"The way to Indorsia must be kept closed," Alf reminded her.

"You may have a hard time keeping it closed. The boys may not have phones, but they still eat Agra Nation® snacks. It wouldn't take much to have them singing show tunes along with everybody else."

"But in the meantime, their minds are their own, and it's safer for me to have them around than have any of the brainwashed locals. By Indorsian standards, these kids are babies. That's the way *he* will see them. As babies. A twelve-year-old Indorsian Royal hasn't even started school yet. If I keep them around, he'll be less likely to suspect a trap. He may think the place is a day-care center."

"Really, brother? Using kids as camouflage? And I thought *I* was the strategist."

From the bottom of the laundry chute came the sound of an ax striking wood. It was followed by a disapproving *tch-tch*, then a muffled cry from Freak. Suddenly Alf was looking in our direction.

Fiona and I tried to hide by leaning farther back into the darkness, and I lost my footing. Fiona made a grab for me and we both plummeted down the shaft.

We got stuck halfway, with our bodies twisted together and me hanging head downward, like the clapper in a long, skinny bell. My ears rang with the sound of another ax blow.

Freak was no longer in the laundry chute.

I imagined him being pulled out by the ankles and attacked by something. Maybe the carnivorous shirt. I pictured red-checkered flannel, like a woodsman might wear. It would explain the sound of the ax.

Fiona twisted sideways and we slid the remaining six feet. I looked out through the chute's opening and saw Freak dancing. He was moving around, dodging and darting, a look of panic on his face. Fiona levered a foot against my butt and pushed me into the room, where I saw exactly what had been making all the noise.

Freak was being pursued by an old lady with an ax.

She was ancient and gray but very limber. She hopped back and forth from foot to foot, tossing the ax from hand to hand like a martial-arts master, her white nightgown whirling and billowing around her with every move. She reminded me a little of Ms. Barrowman, the school librarian. Her eyes had the same piercing look.

She turned toward me when I hit the floor. As I staggered to my feet, she made the *tch-tch* sound and got a two-handed grip on the ax. She swung it at me like it was a baseball bat and I was a poorly pitched ball. I would have been on my way into center field, possibly without my head, if I hadn't ducked in time. Sometimes being short has its advantages.

Freak picked up the bulletin board and held it like a shield. He lunged at the lady's back and got her attention. An arm waved frantically at me from the laundry chute. Fiona was stuck.

The old lady noticed the arm the same moment I did and she turned away from Freak, sidled over to the wall, and raised her ax above Fiona's wildly fluttering hand. Maybe the lady was a lumberjack. She was certainly eager to chop off limbs.

I grabbed Fiona's hand and pulled with all my might. Fiona was folded in half inside the chute. She popped out just as the ax came down behind her, and I wasn't sure it hadn't sliced a layer of purple off her sweatshirt.

I hauled Fiona to her feet and Freak swung the bulletin board in front of us, creating a barrier between the three of us and our assailant. The old lady hissed at us; her lower jaw detached from the top of her head and her mouth opened impossibly wide, like I had once seen a python's do at the zoo just before it fed. Her mouth was full of needlelike teeth.

She swung the ax at the bulletin board as we all jumped away from her. The ax missed the board, but still made the noise an ax does when it hits wood. Which was odd, because it hadn't struck anything. The old lady shrieked in anger and lunged at us again, about to bring her ax down on top of us.

We backed up against the door. Freak raised the board above our heads, and immediately an ax head stabbed through it, but there was no sound of wood splintering this time.

I found the doorknob and pulled. Fiona and Freak shoved the board in Ax Lady's direction and we all squirmed out into the hall, slamming the door behind us.

"That was close!" I said, and found myself saying it to Ax Lady, who suddenly appeared in the hall with us.

"*Tch-tch,*" she said. She swung her ax again, and this time it passed through all three of us. We screamed in unison.

The old lady danced backward, threw her arms in the air, tilted her head back, and joined us in screaming. Her scream sounded like a cry of victory. Ours sounded more like three kids about to wet themselves.

We looked down at ourselves. The ax hadn't done any damage.

The old lady stood between us and the only way we knew to get out of the house. Freak hesitated a moment, then plunged right through her. Fiona and I exchanged quick glances. She grabbed my hand and we followed Freak.

As soon as we had passed through the lady, I risked a glance over my shoulder. She had turned and was following us. Fiona and I pounded down the hall and caught up with Freak, and the three of us tumbled down the stairs, through the door, and out into the yard.

The lady loomed in the doorway behind us, then vanished. As we ran down the hill, I expected her to pop out from behind every tree we passed, but we made it to the entrance without getting chopped. We squeezed through the gate and it slammed shut behind us, nearly catching my shirttail.

I wasn't surprised, as we ran past the spot, to see the sofa was no longer on the side of the road.

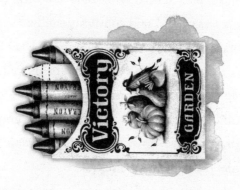

Compulsive Completist Disorder

The bus was late picking us up the next morning. I wondered if the sinkhole in Breeland Road had gotten bigger and the driver had been forced to make a detour. Without a sofa to sit on, we stood around at our old bus stop. It was just as well, I thought. Underhill House was no longer a place I was willing to turn my back to.

"So now, on top of everything else, there's a ghost," said Freak. His hands were shoved deep in his pockets. He looked annoyed.

"The house has always looked haunted," I pointed out.

Fiona, for once, remained silent. She was wearing orange

plaid pants and a blue striped blouse. I wondered why Freak and I had never picked up on the color-blindness thing.

"The sofa tessered," I said conversationally.

"The sofa," said Freak, "got picked up by Max Schimmelhorn. The one we found in the house got moved by Alf, or somebody in the house we don't know about."

"You still don't believe all this? You saw the ghost."

"The ghost I have no problem with. People have seen ghosts before. It's everything else."

"Then, obviously," I said, "we have to go to Rodmore."

Freak shot me a glance. "Why *obviously*?"

"Because that's where the proof is. Guernica says there's a portal in the center of Hellsboro. Rodmore is in the center. The portal is in Rodmore. We find the portal, it proves everything else."

"That's not the worst idea you've ever had," said Freak thoughtfully.

"No. The worst idea I ever had was saving my fingernail clippings to use as crescent moons on Halloween cookies. This is much better than that."

"Eww!" declared Fiona, who had trick-or-treated at my house the year we gave out the cookies.

"Guernica says Edward Disin wants to bring invaders

through the portal," I continued. "Don't you guys understand? We have to try to stop him! Because of things Disin has done, your sister is gone, Fiona isn't twins, and I'm an orphan. I say we not only find the portal, but we take pictures of it and show the police. Or those EPA people. We get back at Disin. We stop whatever it is he's up to!"

Freak kicked a stone across the road. It sailed into a patch of tall grass. Mucus popped out of the grass and went running down the road. Mucus was Stevie Shuck's cat. He named it when he was five. He thought he was naming it Mew Kiss. The rest of us knew better.

"Yeah," said Freak. "Portal or no portal, I'd like to nail the guy behind the chemical spill."

"It's possible," Fiona said slowly, "the only reason Alf brought us into this is because he believes he can bring his dead sister back to life. By somehow using me as her new body. I seriously doubt it's possible, but I don't want him trying! Edward Disin might be an enemy to all of us, but Alf could be one, too."

"I got the impression using you is no longer an option," I said. "Miranda doesn't want to go through having pimples again. Or something."

"Riiight," drawled Freak. "The talking painting you saw can't get out too easily to buy Clearasil. Uh-huh."

I started to say something, but he held up his hand. "For the time being," he said, "we have to be very careful about who we trust. We have to find out as much as we can on our own. But River's right. We should start by going to Rodmore."

"We could really use more information about Edward Disin," Fiona said.

"I got the impression that's what Alf was leading up to," said Freak. "We can't say anything about Indorsia or portals or teleporting sofas at the meeting this afternoon. We have to let Alf talk as if Riv didn't have his dream and Guernica never spoke to us."

"I find it a little hard to believe the man's furniture is doing things behind his back," said Fiona.

"You should see my father trying to set up lawn chairs," muttered Freak.

The bus arrived. Since it was only the driver and us, Fiona sat with Freak and me.

"So when are we planning to go to Rodmore?" she asked.

"*We?*" said Freak, arching his eyebrows.

"I'm going with you. I owe that much to Audrey."

"But you're the one who's always saying it's sure death to enter Hellsboro. It's too easy to fall through the crust and roast to death, or inhale fumes and have your lungs explode."

"You keep coming back," said Fiona, getting as close to complimenting Freak as she ever did. "You said we have to be careful who we trust. I'm choosing to trust you in this case. You better not disappoint me. When are we going?"

Freak looked flattered. I didn't see him look that way too often.

"The first cloudy afternoon we get. I don't want us to be seen by any spies in the sky."

"Clouds may not be enough to hide you," said Science Girl. "If there are thermal-imaging cameras up there, they can find you by your body heat."

"Yeah? Can they find me if the ground is warmer than I am?"

Fiona got a funny look on her face.

"No. You'd be invisible. Anybody would be."

"So," I said, to prove I was keeping up, "if you wanted to hide what you were doing from a heat-sensitive camera in the sky, the smartest thing you could do would be to do whatever it was you were doing in the middle of a coal-seam fire."

"Yes, it would," Fiona conceded.

"I wonder if they started the fire deliberately?"

"The fire was an accident," Fiona said. She did not sound entirely sure of herself.

"That's what we've always been told," I agreed. "That's what everybody has always believed. What if all that stuff the chemical plant was pumping into the ground for all those years wasn't just them getting rid of waste? What if the stuff was, like, I don't know—lighter fluid? And it was being pumped into the ground deliberately to make it easier for them to start the fire?"

"Bravo," said a small, soft voice that belonged to none of the three of us.

The bus was pulling into its second stop, so the voice might have come from one of the kids waiting outside, but I was pretty sure it didn't. I could tell from the looks on Freak's and Fiona's faces that they had heard it, too. Fiona had only a moment to look mystified, and then she was scrambling six seats back to make it look like she hadn't been with us.

"Who said 'bravo'?" asked Freak.

I shrugged. It certainly wasn't the strangest thing that had happened to us recently. But I added it to the list.

• • • • •

"This is Edward Disin," said Alf. A photograph of a man appeared in the center of Guernica's screen.

It was later that afternoon. The three of us were back in

the gallery of Underhill House, where Alf had greeted us at the door this time. He had made a great show of closing it behind us. He said he had reason to believe more than one raccoon had gotten in the day before, and there might be at least one still running around the house. They were noisy things. They screamed like banshees. This was as close as he came to mentioning the previous night's commotion. As we'd followed him to the gallery, I'd kept pivoting on my heel, doing quick 360s, looking for ghostly librarian-lumberjacks.

The photograph on the screen was a head-and-shoulders shot. The man had black hair and a thin mustache.

"At least," continued Alf, "this is how Edward Disin looked two years ago. He has gotten into the habit of changing his appearance on a periodic basis. He's the man whose name is on your medical center. He donated—or I should say his company donated—most of the money to build it."

"His company is Rodmore Chemical?" I asked. Fiona and I were sitting in the two chairs that matched the missing sofa. I wanted to put my feet up. I thought it was a pity the hassock had been lost in a fire. Freak stood behind me with his arms folded and a defiant look on his face.

"No. His company is the much larger company that, at one time, owned Rodmore. His company is the Disin

Corporation. You may be more familiar with one of their subsidiaries, Disin Tel. The cell phone people. They also own Agra Nation® Foods."

I leaned forward, pretended to pull up my sock, and fed a dust bunny to the chair. I had brought dust bunnies from home. I was hoping my aunt wouldn't miss them.

"The Disin Corporation and its subsidiaries donated every computer and computer peripheral used at your police station, at the public library, and in all the schools, including the scanners and cameras used by the school newspapers." Alf shook his head disapprovingly.

"This is a bad thing?" I asked.

"This is a very bad thing."

A second photograph joined the one of Edward Disin. It was an action shot of Morgue MacKenzie making the winning touchdown in the big game against Flanders. It was the missing picture that had caused Fiona to be bathed in shimmering pink Jell-O the previous day.

Fiona jumped up, and I could tell from the look on her face she had forgotten all about impending invasions and the possible enslavement of her neighbors. Her eyes were riveted to the screen.

"It enables the Disin Corporation," continued Alf, "to

wirelessly monitor whatever is done with those computers, open anybody's e-mail, and censor any photograph taken with those cameras."

"I saw that picture disappear from the camera!" Fiona announced. She turned an angry face on Alf. "They took it? *Why?*"

"I suspect they deleted this photo, and three other photos taken around the same time, because of this—"

The picture zoomed in on an area of sky directly over Morgue's head. What had looked like a bird turned out to be, under magnification, a black helicopter.

"What? They didn't like the helicopter?"

"That is a stealth helicopter. It is unmarked, rubber-coated, and does not show up on radar. I'm sure the last thing the Disin Corporation wants is for it to be photographed."

"*Whumpa-whumpa*," said Freak under his breath, remembering the sound he had heard coming from Hellsboro. It made me think he might finally be starting to believe in the Disin conspiracy.

"If these people deleted the photographs," said Fiona, a dangerous edge in her voice, "how is it that you have them?"

"Sometimes Guernica and I get lucky stealing things back from them." Alf sighed. "Sometimes we don't."

"So you're trying to get this Edward Disin guy," said Freak, "because his company caused Hellsboro and he's spying on everybody. What's that got to do with the zucchini crayon?"

"The crayon is bait to lure Disin away from his untouchable retreat on the other side of the world back here to America, where he can be apprehended and locked up for what I hope will be a very long time. Or, if not a long time, a short time of sufficient duration."

"He likes crayons?"

"He likes things that complete collections. He has CCD. Compulsive Completist Disorder. It's an Achilles' heel I'm hoping will lead to his downfall. Sixteen months ago he flew in and out of New York under an assumed name and a fake passport, was the high bidder at an auction at Christie's, paid them in cash right there on the spot, and flew home with a near-mint copy of *Action Comics* number one, for which he paid a little over one million dollars. *Action Comics* number one being?"

"First appearance of Superman," I said.

"Correct. Two years ago, he did virtually the same thing for a single rare PEZ dispenser."

"Why does he travel in disguise?" Fiona inquired.

"Because he's wanted by the United States government. If he's ever caught on American soil, he can be tried, convicted, and incarcerated. Currently, he's only wanted for tax evasion. But getting him behind bars on any pretext would be a step in the right direction."

"So he's this, like, billionaire?" asked Freak.

"Several times over. He's one of the fifteen richest people in the world."

"So why doesn't he just hire somebody to come here and buy his comic books and his PEZ dispensers for him?"

"Because that's not how Compulsive Completist Disorder works. Once the collector's fever hits you, you have to drop everything you're doing to pursue the thing you have to collect. The closer you get to obtaining it, the more powerful the compulsion gets. Whether you're in the middle of eating dinner, or performing brain surgery, or on your honeymoon, or—"

"Conquering the world?" suggested Freak.

Alf shot Freak a glance. "Interesting choice of example. Yes, you would drop even that, until you had acquired whatever the thing was you were after. And you can't delegate. The fever doesn't break until you've had the satisfaction of acquiring the thing yourself. Two weeks ago, Disin had never even heard of zucchini crayons. Then an admirer sent him a gift—a

Victory Garden box missing that one crayon. His need to acquire the zucchini has been growing ever since."

"The man has an admirer?"

"Or someone pretending to be an admirer," said Alf, looking modestly down at the floor.

"I've never heard of CCD," said Fiona.

"That's because Edward Disin is the only person who has it. It was developed in a laboratory as a virus by one of Disin's opponents. She gave it to herself, then sneezed in his face at a cocktail party."

"That means two people have it," said Fiona.

"No. You don't sneeze in Edward Disin's face at a cocktail party and live."

"Couldn't this enemy have just poisoned him?"

I was surprised Fiona was so quick to accept the idea of Compulsive Completist Disorder. Maybe, like Freak, she was starting to trust Alf a little more.

"Disin has made himself immune to most poisons. He was given CCD to slow him down. Over the past few years, if he hadn't been distracted by frequent involuntary treasure hunts, the damage he could have done would have been irreversible."

"But he sent doghats to steal the crayon," said Fiona. "He didn't come himself."

"I now suspect," replied Alf, "the doghats were sent only to verify the crayon's authenticity. Not to steal it themselves."

"There are fake crayons out there?" I don't know why I sounded shocked.

"Genuine articles are few and far between in this world," said Alf. "In fact, now that you remind me"—he turned toward Freak—"did you bring the crayon with you?"

Freak had the cigar box with him. He flipped open the lid. Alf reached in and took out the crayon. He held it up to the light. He squinted at it.

"Oh, there, you see? What did I tell you? The color of the wrapper is off, ever so slightly. This crayon is a fake. It's worthless."

He snapped the crayon in half and threw it on the desktop.

The Breaking of the Crayon

Are you out of your mind?" yelped Freak. "That was an eleven-thousand-dollar crayon!"

"That was actually a forty-seven-cent crayon," said Alf. He reached inside his jacket and pulled out a thin silver box. I recognized it from old movies as a cigarette case. He popped the lid open and waved the case in front of us, as if offering us the contents.

"Crayon?" he inquired.

Lined up inside the case were half a dozen dark green crayons. They were unused, with uniformly cone-shaped points. They all had paper wrappers labeled ZUCCHINI.

"All fakes," Alf confirmed. "I had them made up two years ago, before I found the genuine article. It took me two years of searching to find the real thing. I did not wish to leave a trail, so I could not use the Internet. I finally found what may be the last genuine zucchini crayon in existence in a yard sale in Sioux Falls, South Dakota, with the help of a private investigator."

"You hired a private eye to track down a crayon?" Freak said, taking one of the fake crayons from the case and sticking it in his mouth like he was about to start puffing away on it. Alf snapped the case shut.

"Opal Austin may be the best PI in existence. I highly recommend her. The real crayon is right here." Alf pulled open the top drawer of the desk and withdrew a slender wooden box. He opened the lid, and there, nestled in a crayon-shaped incision in a slab of gray foam rubber, was yet another zucchini crayon. It looked exactly like all the others.

"At first I was going to try to lure Disin here with one of the fakes. Then I realized he would send a crayon expert on ahead, to determine if it was real or not."

"A crayon expert?"

"Equipped with a portable wax chromatograph and an analytic ceroscope. He would have known it was a fake within thirty seconds. So I persevered until I found one of the original 1944 Victory Garden crayons. I put one of the fakes in the sofa. I couldn't risk your accidentally breaking the original, or scribbling with it, or dividing it three ways."

"Or smoking it," said Freak, blowing an imaginary smoke ring.

"So you were right, the other day," Alf continued. "The sofa was my recruiting officer."

"I noticed it had a dueling scar," I said.

"Yes, and a bloodstain." Alf shook his head. "With Halloween coming up, it decided to go out as a pirate. There was no dissuading it."

"You could have stood at the gate and offered us candy," said Freak. "That probably would have gotten us in here just as easily."

"You know it would not have. None of you is that trusting. I would not have been interested in you if you were. If I must have children around me, they should be bright children. You did exactly as I had hoped you would, creating a trail for Edward Disin to follow without making him overly suspicious. The moment you typed the words *zucchini crayon* into a search engine, you made him aware of your existence. His eye opened and it looked at you. As soon as you posted the auction, you had his full attention. I couldn't have done it better myself."

"So we did well on the test?"

"So well, in fact, that I'd like to offer the three of you a job."

Alf sat on the edge of the desk and looked at each of us in turn. He seemed thoroughly delighted with himself.

"What kind of a job?" asked Freak.

"Nothing too strenuous. And only for a week or so. There are no benefits, but the pay is quite generous. I'll let you have whatever the genuine zucchini crayon fetches at auction, to divide among the three of you equally, or in whatever proportions you see fit."

"I canceled the auction the moment I got home last night," said Fiona. "You told me to."

"Yes. And now you are going to send e-mails to everybody who bid on your auction, inviting them to a live auction here at Underhill House. The crayon will be the featured item at that auction, in addition to a selection of historically important coloring books, one of which belonged to the young Jackson Pollock. The auction will be held here at eight o'clock on the evening of October twenty-third. Refreshments will be served."

"Who is Jackson Pollock?" Freak asked.

"Famous American artist. Opal Austin ran across the coloring book at a swap meet. She phoned me and I bought it on spec for fifty cents. Remind me to show it to you. The man was completely incapable of coloring within the lines."

Alf looked at Fiona as if he expected her to say something. She didn't. She just blinked rapidly, the way she does when she's learning something new in science class.

"I've already written out everything you need to put in the e-mail." Alf handed Fiona a flash drive. "I've also included the e-mail addresses of several toy museums and well-known toy collectors who should also be notified. The more people who attend the auction, the more convincing it will look. Also, the more people who bid, the higher the final selling price will be, and consequently the higher your paycheck."

"What happens at the auction?" Freak wanted to know.

"People bid. The auction ends. Edward Disin is the winner."

"You're sure about that?"

"Absolutely. He pays in cash, as he always docs, and as soon as we have his money, I signal US Treasury agents who have been waiting in the wings. They come forward and arrest him. They cart him away, the Disin Corporation is without its head, the company falters, and, with any luck, it doesn't proceed with . . . certain projects."

"Won't he know it's a trap?"

"He'd be pretty stupid if he didn't. An auction for something he wants, being held on Hellsboro's doorstep? He's going to know that's no coincidence. But the CCD will compel him to come anyway. Compulsive Completist Disorder becomes stronger the closer its victim gets to the desired object. Right now, Edward Disin can still multitask. As the auction gets nearer, he'll be able to think of fewer and fewer things other than the zucchini crayon. And his own arrogance, his belief that he can handle any situation on his own, should bring him here by himself. Whether he thinks it's a trap or not."

The job sounded too easy to me. "What else do we have to do to earn our pay?" I asked. I was wondering if it might involve sacrificing Fiona to Alf's sister. I wanted to trust Alf, but I could understand why Fiona might not.

"Clean up the ballroom, for one thing," said Alf. "It hasn't been touched in years. I'm hoping to use it for the auction. The floor has to be washed and waxed, the cobwebs dispersed, maybe a little paint here and there. Have any of you ever swept a chimney?"

"I swept out the garage, once," Freak admitted.

Freak actually swept out his garage on a regular basis. He liked to keep things well organized. He had gotten that way not long after his mother left. I sometimes thought he was hoping if he kept the place neat, she would come back.

"The entire house has to be readied for visitors. And decorated. I'm thinking crepe streamers, trailing off the chandelier. Maybe a Halloween-themed tablecloth on the table with the punch bowl. And the balloons will have to be inflated. During the auction itself, the three of you will be serving hors d'oeuvres."

"Anybody could do that," said Freak. "Why us?"

"You said you needed children around," I added, deciding Freak had a good point. "Why kids?"

Alf gave us a thoughtful look, like maybe he was deciding whether or not to tell us. Then he shrugged.

"Because Edward Disin comes from a culture where people your age are not taken seriously. If you're around, he'll be a little less on his guard. Having you here might make the difference between his being too wary to catch and his making the slip that will prove his undoing. It's as simple as that." He looked at each of us in turn. "Do we have a deal? Can I expect the three of you back here on Sunday, so we can start getting the place ready? Say, around noon?"

"We get to keep whatever the magic crayon sells for?" asked Freak.

"Every penny."

"All right. I'm in."

"Me, too," I said.

"Yes," said Fiona. "So long as it doesn't get out that I'm part of the team."

"There is no team," Freak assured her.

• • • • •

We didn't speak again until we were walking past the spot where the sofa had once stood, at the side of Breeland Road. There was a rectangle there where the grass was a little less green than the grass around it.

"They're saying rain for tomorrow night," I said. "It should be cloudy tomorrow afternoon. Maybe we should plan on going to Rodmore then."

"Shouldn't we wait, now, until after the auction?" suggested Fiona.

"Why wait?" I said. I wanted to see the place where my parents had worked. Even if it was abandoned and covered with soot. I wondered what they would have thought about everything that was going on. I was eager to go anywhere, even into Hellsboro, if it meant finding out more about what had happened to them.

"It might be safer after Alf catches Edward Disin," Fiona argued.

"I see it as two separate things," I said. "Looking for proof of the portal is a Guernica project. Catching Edward Disin is an Alf project. If we can catch Disin and give the right people proof of the portal, we'll be able to stop the invasion thing. We have to do both. And the sooner we can get started, the better."

"I was going to borrow a digital camera from the school newspaper," Fiona confessed. "To take pictures of the portal, if there is one. But if Disin donated every piece of electronics the school has, I guess that's not such a good idea."

"I have one of those cardboard, use-it-once film cameras," I said. "It's from last year's field trip to Philly. There're still a couple of shots left on it."

"That would be better," Freak acknowledged. "Anybody have any idea what a portal looks like? If there is one?"

"In movies, they always look like water going down a toilet. That's why I'm always surprised when anybody wants to go in one."

By this time we were in front of Fiona's house. Her father, Bill, was raking the lawn. He looked up as we approached. "It's like old times," he said, "seeing the three of you hanging out together." He seemed pleased. "Could one of you climb in the well and get the leaves out for me?"

Fiona had a fake wishing well in her front yard. When I was younger, I had thought the well was real, and that it could grant wishes. I had thrown quite a few nickels and dimes into it. I had made quite a few wishes. I had wished I was taller, had a horse, and wasn't so often the target of bullies. I wished I were really River Man, defender of the weak. I wished both my parents were still alive. I wished I could see them again.

The wishing well was no deeper than the surface of the lawn. I boosted myself over the side and found myself ankle-deep in leaves. I proceeded to shovel them out with my hands. Fiona and Freak stuffed them into a plastic bag as quickly as I could toss them out.

When I bent down for a final handful, I found a nickel. It could easily have been a nickel I had thrown in with one of my earlier wishes. I wondered which wish it might have been, and if my finding the coin meant the wish was still pending. I was about to put the coin in my pocket. Then I looked at it and wished my friends and I would be safe, no matter what happened between us and Alf and Disin and the Rodmore Chemical plant.

I dropped the coin back in the well.

CHAPTER
12

Coal-Dust Pizza

By the afternoon of the following day, the overcast was thick and ominous. Thunder grumbled to the west. I stopped off at home and changed into heavier jeans, a hoodie sweatshirt, and a pair of thick-soled boots. I threw a compass on a chain around my neck and stuffed a pair of oven mitts down the back of my pants.

Fiona showed up in Freak's backyard a few minutes after I did. She was wearing bright red boots that came up to her knees, a pair of green ski pants, and a yellow waterproof jacket. She looked like a dandelion in a bud vase. Her backpack was loaded with bottles of spring water.

Fiona kept nervously looking out at the road, like she was afraid someone she knew might drive by. I realized she didn't want to be seen. If I had been dressed the way she was, I wouldn't have wanted to be seen, either.

Freak emerged from the back door of his house and handed us each a six-foot wooden pole, the kind you might stick in a garden to hold up tomato plants.

"There may be times when you'll want to test the ground in front of you," he explained.

"Great," said Fiona.

"What's the compass for?" he asked me.

"You can't get where you're going without a compass."

"It's not like there are woods we're going to get lost in," he said, quite reasonably.

"It belonged to my father," I said.

"Oh." He looked at it again. "It's nice."

We went to the back of the yard and Freak pulled open the slit in the chain-link fence. He bent low and scooted through. Fiona and I followed.

We crossed the backyard of the former Henderson place, went down their cracked driveway, and zigzagged through abandoned streets until we reached Took Lane, where the houses were nothing but charred foundations. The ground got noticeably warmer the farther we went. We crawled through a smaller slit in a second fence, scrambled to our feet, and looked around.

We were in Hellsboro.

It looked like photos of the surface of the moon. It was bumpy and rocky, with long stretches of soil that looked like charcoal from a barbecue. The colors were soot and ash and dirty gray, and I realized I might be seeing things for the first time the way Fiona saw them. I made a mental note to stop making fun of the way she dressed.

Charred and stubby stumps marked the locations of former trees. The landscape had a corduroy look, faint ridges marking where limbless logs lay half buried in the earth, sinking farther into it each year as their undersides slowly cooked away. Off in the far distance, rising from the middle of it all, were the boxy white buildings and towering tanks of Rodmore.

"Think of it as a pizza," said Freak.

"A very burned, overdone pizza," said Fiona.

"Actually," said Freak, "I was thinking more of the coal-dust pizzas they have at Calvino's."

The coal-dust pie was a house specialty at Calvino's. It was topped with crumbled black olives and slivers of portobello mushrooms. It was one of Freak's favorite types of pizza. And yes, it resembled the surface of Hellsboro.

"The center of the pie is Rodmore." Freak started walking. Fiona and I followed him, taking care to step where he stepped. "If you cut the pie into eight slices, all the cuts would pass through Rodmore. But if you wanted to get to Rodmore from the outer edge of the pie, you couldn't walk straight there, along one of the cuts. There's no direct route that's safe. You might start out along one of the straight-cut routes, but you'd have to know when to detour."

We had been walking directly toward the chemical plant. Freak stopped suddenly and turned to the left. Following his example, we walked along the tops of a series of rocks that protruded from the earth like stepping-stones.

"Each winter when it snows, I come out here and make a map of where the snow lasts the longest before it melts. Those are the safest places to walk."

"Could we stop and look at this map?" Fiona inquired.

"It's in my head," said Freak. He pointed at the ground. "If you see something growing, that's usually a safe place to walk." Gray grass grew at our feet. Tufts of it struggled here and there for about thirty feet in front of us. I felt a little guilty walking on it. The grass was having a hard enough time as it was.

"If you see anything that looks like smoke, stay away from it." Freak gestured to the far right. In the distance, white vapor hung above an ash-colored ridge. "That's where the fire is close to the surface. The ground will be crusty, and you could fall through."

A flurry of white ash filled the air, drifting over from where the smoke was. It swirled like snow. Freak had suggested we tie kerchiefs around our necks before we started out. Now we levered them up over our mouths and breathed through them. It made us look like Wild West bandits.

We walked along in silence for a while. Once, Freak probed the ground in front of him with his stick. The end of the stick came back charred. We reversed our tracks and took another route. The factory was to the east, but to get to it we sometimes went north, sometimes went south. At one point we passed something that looked like a flat metal bench sticking up out of the ground. Freak said it was the front end of a bulldozer. The rest of the bulldozer had sunk into the earth when the ground had given way beneath it. The bulldozer blade was at just the right height to sit on. I sat on it.

"Isn't it hot?" asked Freak.

"Very," I said. "But I've got oven mitts in my pants."

Another moment and it was too hot even for my insulated butt. I jumped up and we continued on.

"I looked up Edward Disin on the Internet last night," said Fiona. "The only place that has any information about him is the Disin Corporation website."

"I'm sure it was real helpful," said Freak.

"It said he was born forty-eight years ago in Tsuris, Russia. I looked up Tsuris and found there is no such place."

"No kidding."

"I found a photograph of him in his office, with a bookcase full of PEZ dispensers behind him. In the photo he's blond, without any mustache. He's holding what the caption says is the incredibly rare Mary, Queen of Scots PEZ dispenser. He's got her head pushed all the way back, and there's a piece of PEZ sticking out of her neck."

"Did you find anything even remotely useful?" asked Freak as he did an unexpected dance step around a sunken area in the earth and Fiona and I did our best to duplicate his footwork.

"The website listed some of the smaller companies Disin owns. Disin Tel, Agra Nation® Foods, and—get this—Global Organic Research Labs. GORLAB, for short. GORLAB makes chemical weapons like Hista Mime."

"What's that?" I asked.

"Hista Mime? It's also known as the Silent Killer. It's shot out of a squirt gun, and if you get any on you, you immediately hallucinate that you're trapped inside an airless transparent cube, and you suffocate. You can't call out because it freezes your vocal cords."

"Sounds nasty."

"It doesn't *sound* like anything. That's why it's the Silent Killer."

Freak nodded. "So the GORLAB connection pretty much proves Disin was the one bidding on the crayon." He hopped on one foot for three yards, did a half pirouette, and jumped twice to the left. Fiona duplicated what he had done as well as she could. Freak turned to her and said, "That was totally unnecessary. I just wanted to see if you would do it."

Fiona chased him for about fifty feet, but I hung back. It seemed a little reckless to me.

Lightning flashed at my back. Instinctively I turned around, and when I turned back, Fiona and Freak were gone.

"GUYS!" I shouted, panic-stricken. There had been no place for them to go. We were on a flat, treeless plain with nowhere to hide. I looked in the air as if I expected to see them carried off by buzzards. The air was empty, except for another flurry of ash.

It was as if the ground had swallowed them. The moment I thought it, I knew that's what had happened. And Hellsboro was the last place you wanted the ground to swallow you. The ground was hungrier there than anywhere else.

"GUYS!" I shouted again, starting to work my way toward the last place I had seen them. I furiously tapped the ground in front of me with my stick, daring it to cave in.

"River!" I heard Freak's voice, muffled, to my right.

"I'm here! Keep talking!" I altered my course.

"Over here! Down here! Don't fall in!" Freak shouted. "If you fall in, we're all dead!"

"Thin ice!" shouted Fiona, proving she was with Freak and just as crazy as ever.

Then I realized "thin ice" was a warning. I moved the oven mitts from back to front and threw myself on my face. I crawled along the ground, distributing my weight, the way you're supposed to when you're trying to rescue someone who's fallen through ice. I hoped it would work just as well on the crusty earth of Hellsboro.

I crawled up on a ridge made by a log that was buried in

soot. On the other side, I looked down into an abyss. A sink-hole had opened beneath Freak and Fiona and dropped them ten feet. The heat I felt against the underside of my body was bad, but the heat and strong smell of sulfur rising out of the sinkhole was worse. Freak and Fiona stood in the center of it, covered in ash, clutching each other and choking. A few minutes down there and they would bake.

"Hey!" I shouted, and both their faces turned up to me, tear tracks like rivers in the grime of their cheeks.

"We can't climb out!" said Freak, between coughs. "The wall just crumbles when I try!"

One of the walls was, in fact, faintly glowing. I leaned forward as far as I could and stretched my arms down toward them. My arms didn't stretch far. Fiona climbed on Freak's shoulders and reached for me. A good two feet still separated us.

Fiona fell forward, broke her fall against the side of the pit, then cried out when she brought a small avalanche of fried earth down with her. The log underneath me trembled, like it might at any moment split and dump me down with my friends.

I thought furiously. *What would River Man do?* Channel energy. That was about all he was good for. Sometimes, though, he used his brain. I yanked off my hoodie and yelped when I felt the heat of Hellsboro through only the thinness of my T-shirt. But I leaned forward and dangled the hoodie into the pit.

Fiona clambered up Freak again, caught one of the sweatshirt's arms, and twined her hands into it. I pulled with all my might. I was too close to the edge to have enough leverage, and I felt myself sliding forward. Just before I went over, the hoodie's arm ripped and Fiona fell back again. I saved myself just in time and wiggled backward.

"Wait! Wait!" said Fiona. "This is my summer-camp backpack!"

She ripped the backpack open. Freak grabbed the water bottles and doused himself and Fiona with the contents. I was pretty sure steam rose off their skin as the water hit them. Fiona yanked a Camp Monongahela T-shirt out of the pack, then three origami swans, and then, finally, a jump rope.

She tossed the rope to me. I wound one end around my hand, braced myself as well as I could against the buried log, and threw the rope's free end back into the pit.

After a moment, I felt Fiona's weight on it. I pulled with all my might, digging my feet in deeper and deeper against the log, and just when I thought I couldn't hold on any longer, Fiona came clambering up over the edge. She grabbed the log and hauled herself to safety.

"Well done!" said the same voice that had said "Bravo" back on the school bus. I ignored it. Fiona and I both scrambled back to the edge.

Freak was looking up at us, dancing from foot to foot. Behind him, all three origami swans had burst into flames. I threw the rope back down. Fiona grabbed me by the waist. The rope dangled inches out of Freak's reach. Even when he jumped, he couldn't grasp it. Without someone's shoulders to stand on, Freak wasn't going to make it.

I pulled the rope back up and twisted the chain with my father's compass onto the end, adding two feet to the length. I threw the rope back down to Freak. He caught it, twisted his hands into the chain, and Fiona and I threw our weight into hauling him up. I wondered if the chain would hold. It was a lot thinner than the rope.

Fiona and I staggered backward and then fell over each other as the rope went alarmingly slack. It occurred to me Freak might have passed out from the heat. But after a heart-stopping moment, Freak's arm swung over the lip of the pit and he pulled himself onto the log.

Then the log broke in half and all three of us fell.

The log dropped about a foot, then lurched and didn't fall any farther. We scrambled away from it as fast as we could. We all would have thrown ourselves on the ground to catch our breath, but in Hellsboro that would have meant frying like eggs in a skillet. We kept to our feet, weaving back and forth a little as we recovered from the narrow escape we had just had.

"Are you sure there isn't a team?" I gasped, thinking we had all worked pretty well together.

"Take us back!" Fiona yelled at Freak, wiping soot from her face.

"We're a lot closer to Rodmore than we are to home," said Freak, breathing heavily and gesturing back the way we came. It looked like it was already raining there. "Trust me. If there's no fooling around, I can get us to Rodmore safely. Before it rains."

"And just who was it who started the fooling around?" asked Fiona. She looked like she was trying not to cry. I didn't blame her. I was pretty shaken myself after almost losing my two best friends. But we couldn't turn back now.

"We've come this far," I said, making it two against one.

Thunder rolled over us. Fiona looked at the sky, took a few shaky breaths, and said, "All right. Rodmore. It had better be worth it. Because I'm never coming in here again after this."

Freak took his role as our guide seriously for the remainder of our trek. He found us a route where we only had to double back twice. After we had all calmed down, he asked me, "Are you aware your dad's compass is broken?"

"It's not. It was working fine before I left the house."

I looked at it. Freak was right. I knew where north was, and the compass wasn't pointing to it. The compass was pointing to Rodmore.

The first drops of light rain started to hit us as we stepped onto the concrete apron surrounding the chemical plant. Freak raced us around the perimeter fence until he got to a gap in it, then we all squeezed through. The chemical works spread out before us.

"It's like a small city," Fiona announced.

Freak ran down the alley between two warehouses.

"There are six main buildings," he told us when we caught up with him at an intersection. "And eight storage tanks. The biggest building is three stories high. That's the one I think we saw the doghat go into. That's the door I want to try. It's around this way."

Five of the storage tanks were huge cylinders and three were giant spheres. They towered over most of the buildings, with stairways spiraling around the outside and catwalks about thirty feet up connecting them to one another.

I noticed we were leaving footprints. A thin layer of soot

clung to everything. Most of it was undisturbed. We passed a wide stretch of concrete with a very large circle imprinted on it. It was clean, like a huge fan had blown the soot away.

"I can picture a big, black helicopter landing there," said Freak. "Maybe bringing in supplies. Maybe dropping somebody off."

"*Whumpa-whumpa,*" I agreed.

"Are you sure that isn't the portal?" Fiona asked.

Freak paused. He bent down, picked up a piece of broken brick, and tossed it into the center of the circle. It bounced twice and stopped. Nothing else happened.

"Pretty sure," he replied.

A few moments later, Fiona nudged me and pointed to a set of tracks belonging to shoes with tread unlike anything the three of us were wearing. We followed them to the largest building. They went up a set of concrete steps.

As we started up the steps, the rain, which had been making small dimples in the soot, suddenly started coming down more heavily. It started to erase our tracks and the tracks we were following. Before it did, though, we all saw the neat arc the door had made when it had been opened by the doghat. There on the landing in front of the door, the soot had been swept aside in a perfect quarter circle.

The quarter circle disappeared as the rain started coming down in sheets. I threw my arms over my head. Fiona held her backpack up like an umbrella. A lightning flash was followed almost immediately by one of the loudest thunderclaps I had ever heard.

The door was slightly ajar. Freak yanked on the door handle and it swung open easily when he pulled on it. From the look on his face, I could tell he hadn't expected it to. The rain gusted at our backs. We piled in through the door and the wind slammed it shut behind us.

A Shortcut to Restrooms

We stood inside the door and dripped. Freak shook himself like a dog, and spray went everywhere.

"Hey!" said Fiona, and she moved away from us, grabbing handfuls of her hair and wringing it out. The rain, at least, had washed some of the ash off of us.

"I've tried some of the doors every time I've been here," said Freak. "That's the first time any of them have opened."

"The doghat didn't close it properly," I said. I tried the door. The handle wouldn't budge.

"It's locked now," I reported.

Freak and Fiona both tried the door themselves.

"Are we trapped in here?" asked Fiona.

"We can always get out through one of the windows," Freak said. He didn't sound entirely confident.

We looked around. The room had two small windows with chicken wire embedded in them, so even if we managed to break the glass, we would still need wire cutters to get out. I had a feeling none of us had thought to bring wire cutters.

The room was small, with a couple of overturned metal chairs in the middle and a punch clock hanging on one wall, with an empty rack where Rodmore employees would have placed their time cards after they punched in. The punch clock said it was nine seventeen. I looked at my watch. It was three twenty-six.

"How long is the rain going to last?" Freak asked. He was looking at Fiona when he said it, and she pulled out her cell phone and massaged it a bit. She scowled.

"There's no reception here," she said.

"We can't phone out?" I asked.

"No," said Fiona.

Freak was already investigating the place. Two of the nearby walls had clothes pegs where Rodmore employees would have hung up coats and caps. Freak pointed to a peg near the punch clock, which appeared to have a coyote skin hanging from it.

The skin turned out to be a hat with an extended brim. Seen from the top, the hat resembled an aerial view of a large dog. Freak put the hat on. Seen from floor level, it made him look like he was wearing a small canoe.

"Coyote is still in the building," said Fiona.

We thought about that. Being wet, maybe one or two of us shivered. Freak hung the hat back on its peg.

I looked at my dad's compass. The needle was spinning wildly. I held the compass vertically, and after a moment the needle stopped spinning and pointed straight down.

"According to this, the north pole is in the basement!" I announced.

Science Girl scowled at the compass. "That's just gravity," she informed me. "Any compass needle points straight down if you hold it like that."

"Maybe it's the portal!" I said decisively, brushing her aside.

I eagerly crossed the room to its only other door. A tattered poster taped to the door's center reminded us, SAFETY BEGINS WITH YOU! I yanked on the door's handle. It refused to budge.

"There's no keyhole," I reported.

Freak and Fiona came up on either side of me.

"Which means," said Freak, "Coyote had to have opened it with the keypad."

A grimy keypad was mounted on the wall next to the door.

"Which means," said Fiona, "we're stuck in here."

"This would not be a good place to spend the night," I observed.

I punched random buttons on the keypad. The pad showed no signs of life. I punched in the letters for "Rodmore." I punched in "Disin." I punched in my birthday. Nothing.

"How long before anybody notices we're missing?" asked Fiona.

"It's the weekend," said Freak. "My father could easily be unaware until Monday."

He picked up one of the overturned chairs and slammed it as hard as he could against one of the windows. It bounced out of his grip and skidded across the room. The window didn't crack.

"My aunt should be home around eight," I said.

"My parents will be trying to call me before that," said Fiona. "But they won't get through."

She glanced at her phone again and frowned. She looked lost without it.

"Did anybody think to bring snacks?" I asked.

"This wasn't supposed to take more than an hour or two," said Freak.

Fiona, who had been pacing back and forth, stopped in front of the door with the keypad. She put her hands on her hips and stared at the door thoughtfully.

"You're kidding, right?" she said to the door's poster. Then she said quietly to herself, " 'Speak, friend, and enter.' "

"What?" I asked, not sure if I had heard her correctly.

She shook her head, as if clearing it. "Nothing. Just something I read once." She looked at me with an odd sort of light in her eye. "What does safety begin with?" she asked.

I looked at the poster. "You?"

"But it doesn't, does it? It begins with *S*."

She stepped up to the keypad. She tapped six of the keys. A faint buzzing came from the door and it popped open an inch. Fiona grabbed it by the handle and swung it all the way out. It opened on a descending stairwell.

"How did you do that?" Freak asked, too surprised to keep the admiration out of his voice.

"It's right there on the poster," said Fiona. "I spelled *safety* with a *U*. I punched in *U, A, F, E, T, Y.* That was the password. Pretty obvious, really."

I looked down the stairwell. A single dim lightbulb burned on the far landing. I consulted my compass.

"The portal is down there," I said. "I'm sure of it!"

"Coyote is down there, too," said Fiona, with considerably less enthusiasm.

"Whatever's down there, it's the way we have to go if we're going to get out of here," said Freak, nudging me into taking the first step.

"Keep an eye out for a ladies' room," Fiona whispered as we started down.

"You should have gone before we left," said Freak.

"I did. But I've been rained on and I'm cold. I have to go again."

"Shhh!" I hissed.

We reached the landing. I pushed the release bar on the door there and peeked out. It was an empty corridor, with doors on either side, faintly illuminated by low-wattage overhead bulbs. Closing the door behind us as quietly as we could, we tiptoed down the corridor.

The doors were clearly labeled with nameplates: MAINTE-NANCE. CUSTODIAL. STORAGE 1. STORAGE 2.

"Are we looking for a door marked PORTAL?" Freak asked. I couldn't tell if he was being sarcastic. I still wasn't sure if he was as convinced of the portal's existence as I was. He hadn't had the advantage of falling asleep on the sofa. Or having my so-called overactive imagination.

"For all you know," replied Fiona, "one of these doors *is* the portal."

We tried each of the doors in turn. Most of them were locked. One of them, labeled J. ATHERTON, turned out to be an office. The furniture was covered in dust; the floor was fuzzy with cobwebs. The sofa could have grazed there for days.

The corridor ended with a door into another stairwell.

"Up," said Fiona.

I looked at the compass. "Down," I said. "Whatever it is, we're still above it."

"That's because 'it' is the Earth's core," said Fiona, still hung up on her gravity thing.

I ignored her. "Here we are," I said, "in the basement of a building surrounded by eight hundred acres of underground coal fire. And the temperature is what?"

"Chilly?" Fiona answered warily. I knew she couldn't argue; she had goose bumps.

"Yeah. Chilly. It should be like an oven in here. Basements in some of the Sunnyside houses crumbled from the heat." I gestured down the stairwell. "There's a cold draft coming from down there."

"You think the draft is coming from the portal?"

"The portal is supposed to be closed," said Freak.

"We're here to investigate," I said. "The three of us nearly got killed getting here. We shouldn't waste the trip. Let's investigate."

I hadn't won an argument with either of them in a long time. But they both nodded begrudgingly and followed me down. The stairway zigzagged back and forth four times before Fiona announced, "One more flight! If we haven't found anything by then, I'm going back. We're getting way too deep."

"If I were a portal, I would be deeper," Freak said.

The final flight brought us to a door. It was propped open with a fire extinguisher, and the air flowing through it was frigid. This time it was Freak who leaned out for a first peek.

"Holy cow," he said. He stepped out of our way. Fiona and I slipped by him.

We were on a balcony about thirty feet above the floor of a room big enough to hold a small ocean liner. It was a huge cavern of a room, much longer than it was wide, and the balcony ran all the way along one side of it. The balcony was about ten feet across. Lights suspended from the ceiling bathed the place in a harsh blue light. We went to the balcony's railing and looked down.

The floor was the size of a football field. Stretched across the end of the room to our left, from floor to ceiling and from side to side, was what appeared to be an enormous spiderweb made of braided metal cable. To our left, at the remote end of the room, the far wall glistened as though it were covered with diamonds.

"Are we in, like, some sort of storage tank?" wondered Freak.

"For a storage tank, there are a lot of doors here," I said, pointing to a series of doors that ran the length of the balcony to our right. The one that was closest to us bore the name-plate CARBOYS.

"We're very exposed here," said Fiona, hugging herself. "It's way too easy to see us."

"Said the girl in the bright yellow jacket," Freak muttered.

I crossed over to the railing, stepped up on the lower rail, and leaned out. I wanted to see what was under the balcony. I discovered the area was largely empty, except for two unoccupied golf carts.

Suddenly the upper rail that was holding my weight gave way. It detached at one end and swung out over the drop. I went with it, gripping it fiercely with both hands. It was like swinging on a gate thirty feet in the air.

As I felt my feet leave the bottom rail, I also felt hands grabbing the back of my shirt. Freak had hold of me. He swung me back to the balcony.

Even when my feet were safely back on the floor, I had a hard time convincing my hands to let go of the upper rail. Fiona gently massaged my fingers until I opened my grip. She averted her eyes from the thirty-foot drop next to her. "Calm down," she said soothingly. "It's okay."

"Th-thanks, g-guys," I was finally able to sputter.

"Now we're even," said Freak, sounding pleased. He adjusted the loose end of the railing so it didn't look broken.

I recovered enough to remember our mission and consulted my compass. It no longer spun crazily when I held it horizontally. It pointed in one clear direction.

"That way!" I said, and raced off down the balcony toward the glistening wall. It took my friends a few seconds to catch up. I wasn't accustomed to leading the way.

A humming noise that had been barely noticeable got louder the farther along we went. On our right, we passed doors labeled TANKS, SPOOLS, and BINS. Then we passed one labeled MEN.

"Finally!" Fiona sighed. "The next door should be—"

She ran ahead to the next door and stopped in front of it,

staring. When Freak and I caught up with her, we read the door's nameplate: HAZMAT SAFETY.

"This should be the ladies' room," Fiona said indignantly.

This door didn't have a knob. Fiona examined the wall and pushed a button she found near the door frame, and the door slid open. It was dark inside, but she found the light switch, and when the lights sprang on, she screamed. All three of us did.

A dozen men were lined up against the far wall, facing us.

They were wearing bright red rubber suits and space helmets. Their heads all hung down like they were being scolded for bringing home a bad report card. It took us a moment to realize the suits were empty and we weren't facing a row of men after all. The suits were hanging off a row of pegs. Each suit had the hazmat—*haz*ardous *mat*erials—symbol on its chest.

A conference table stood in the center of the room, surrounded by a half dozen folding chairs. High up on the wall hung a sixty-inch TV screen. As far as I could see, there were no toilet stalls.

"Right!" snarled Fiona. She killed the lights and pushed us out on the balcony. Then she headed back the way we had come.

"I'm using the men's room," she announced as we caught up with her. "You guys are going to stand guard." She pushed

Freak to one side of the men's room door and me to the other. She opened the door and went in.

"What, exactly, are we guarding?" Freak asked me.

"If you try to go in there, I'll stop you," I explained. "If I try to go in there, you stop me."

"What if Coyote is in there already?"

We looked at each other.

"Nah," said Freak, dismissing the idea. "Coyote would have just lifted his leg against one of the walls."

The door swung open and Fiona came out.

"That was fast," said Freak.

"Do guys," said Fiona, "go to the bathroom in some weird way I may not know about?"

Freak looked at me. I looked at Freak. Neither one of us wanted to answer the question.

"Possibly," said Freak.

"I don't mean urinals," Fiona said, rolling her eyes. "I understand urinals. My aunt has one she uses as a planter. What I mean is, there's nothing you guys do that requires lying down inside of a six-foot pipe, right?"

Freak and I pushed open the door labeled MEN. We found ourselves in a narrow room. On either side of a central aisle, two long metal cylinders were nestled horizontally in plumbing that connected them to the wall. They were a little like sewer pipes, and a little like coffins. At the foot of each cylinder was a dimly glowing glass lozenge about the size and shape of Fiona's cell phone.

"You don't think there might be...men in them?" Fiona wondered.

"Because it says MEN on the door?" Freak didn't sound as sarcastic as he might have.

"Because the people of Indorsia are more advanced in the sciences than we are, and these are just the right size to have human beings inside," I said, trying to encourage Fiona.

"You mean, like, frozen?"

"Or in suspended animation."

Freak shook his head and walked over to the nearest cylinder. It was windowless, with no way to see inside. He thumped it with his fist and it sounded hollow. As soon as he thumped it, the glass lozenge on the end flickered briefly. I thought I saw numbers appear on it, but they came and went so quickly it was difficult to tell.

"I don't think there's anything in these. I think the name on the door is somebody's idea of a joke," said Freak, although he sounded far from positive.

"They're probably tanks for some sort of chemical storage,"

Fiona decided. She twitched uncomfortably. "This is not the room I wanted. This cold air is not helping."

We returned to the balcony. I looked at my compass, pivoted on my heel, and resumed walking toward the glistening wall. Once again, I arrived there a few moments before my friends.

"I don't believe it," I said. "It's frost."

The entire huge wall was covered with ice crystals. And it wasn't a thin coating. It was thick, like a refrigerator freezer when the defrost isn't working. I leaned in close and studied it.

"I triple-dog-dare you to put your tongue on it," said Freak.

"Don't even joke," I said. "This makes no sense. The other side of this wall has to be Hellsboro. Hot, stinking Hellsboro. This wall should be sizzling."

We looked over the balcony. Thirty feet below us, on the cavern's floor, a line of boxlike machines stretched across the wall's base. I counted ten of them, each about the size and shape of a washing machine and each giving off a loud *hum*. Red lights along their tops got brighter and dimmer as the humming got louder and softer. I held my compass out over the closest one. The needle spun like an airplane propeller.

"I think," said Fiona, very deliberately, "we've found the portal."

"It's a little big to take a picture of," I said, pulling my cheap cardboard camera out of my pocket. I looked through the viewfinder. All I could see was ice.

"I don't suppose that thing has a wide-angle lens," said Freak.

"I don't even think it has a flash." I peered at the camera. "But it does have three pictures left."

"Great," said Freak, without much enthusiasm. "How about taking a picture of the washing machines down there on the floor?"

"Good," said Fiona. "Then we can prove to the authorities we found a Laundromat. That'll bring 'em running."

I cautiously leaned over the rail, taking care not to touch it, and snapped a picture. I was right. The camera had no flash.

"Two to go," I said.

"We should be farther back," said Freak. "We need a picture to show how big this thing is."

Retracing our steps, we walked back along the balcony until we were opposite the door marked HAZMAT SAFETY.

"Let's try one here," said Freak. "Any farther away and all it will look like is a shiny wall."

I didn't think the picture would come out, and, even if it did, I didn't see how it would prove anything. I took it anyway.

"There's one left," I said. "How about a picture of you and Fiona standing at the rail and pointing?"

"This isn't our trip to the Grand Canyon," said Freak.

"If there are people in the shot, it will show how big the wall is," I explained.

Freak and Fiona posed. Fiona fluffed her hair out. Freak frowned.

As I snapped the shot, I heard voices behind me. We froze and listened.

The voices came from the far end of the balcony, where the only stairway out of the place was located. As we watched, a figure emerged from the doorway to the stairwell. It was a man dressed in camouflage fatigues. He came out of the door backward, talking to someone following him. He didn't see us.

We dived for the HAZMAT SAFETY door and scrambled inside.

The voices got louder as they approached. It sounded like more than one conversation, implying at least four people were in the group. Suddenly one voice rang out louder than the rest. "I'm going back to see what's keeping Jackal. You go on ahead. We're meeting in Hazmats. Fourth door down."

They were coming to the room we were in.

The room had only one door.

We were trapped.

The Anger of the Avatar

T he man in fatigues walked in, followed by a woman wearing a jumpsuit. She looked like a superhero from an unpopular comic book. The man stared at us. He scratched the side of his nose and sat down in one of the folding chairs. The woman looked in Freak's face, adjusted a strand of hair that had fallen across her forehead, and sat down next to the man.

We were hanging on the back wall, pretending to be empty hazmat suits. The faceplates on the helmets were reflective. We could see out, but it was difficult to see in. The woman had used Freak's faceplate as a mirror.

Freak and Fiona were standing on the floor with their

shoulders hunched forward, making it look like their suits were hanging from the wall pegs. I was too short to do this convincingly, so my friends had hoisted me up and attached the back of my suit to one of the pegs. I dangled like a book bag on a clothes hook. My feet were a good three inches off the floor. I was not comfortable.

The suits had sealed themselves after we fit ourselves into them. I had been afraid we would suffocate, but there turned out to be some sort of air system that automatically switched on after a few seconds. It hissed filtered air at us every time we inhaled. I was afraid I might sound like Darth Vader. If I did, nobody seemed to notice.

Another woman walked in, dressed in a lavender business suit. She was followed by a short, redheaded man in a cable-knit sweater.

"Why can't we be in Conference Room B?" complained the lavender lady, taking a seat next to the guy in fatigues. "Conference Room B has a window."

The others ignored her. They took seats around the conference table with their backs to us, facing the TV screen. After a couple of minutes another man entered, closing the door behind him. He was bald and wore a white turtleneck with a green sports coat.

"I just got word," he announced. "Jackal has been detained. We will be starting without her."

Suddenly the face of a bulldog appeared on the TV screen. It was smoking a cigar. It reached up with a paw, took the cigar out of its mouth, and said, "Have a seat, Shepherd. We haven't got all day."

The guy in the turtleneck quickly sat down. The bulldog's eyes swept the length of the table, as if he could actually see the people seated there. I tried to figure out where the camera was and decided it was a little black dot I could just make out on the TV's upper edge. The bulldog looked pretty convincing, although I could tell he was a computer-generated image, an avatar, aping the movements of the real person on the other end of the conference call.

"We are now at T-minus eight days," said the bulldog. "Things are proceeding according to plan. I will meet with the others later today. You five, however, warrant special attention."

The five sat up a little straighter.

"Bernese," said the bulldog. "Report."

Lavender Lady stood up. "The first eight trials have been very successful. The ninth and final trial will take place on Wednesday at twelve seventeen PM. The targets will pat the tops of their heads with their left hands and rub their stomachs with their right for six seconds, and then rub the tops of their heads with their right hands and pat their stomachs with their left for six seconds. Then they will sing the first three verses of 'Anything You Can Do' from the musical *Annie Get Your Gun*, males singing the male part, females the female. It will be our first attempt at a duet, sending separate signals to the target brain based on gender."

"Excellent," said the dog. "After the final trial, we will know if our control of the targets is complete. Then, in the first practical application of the mind-control module, the targets will search out anybody who does not have a cell phone, wrestle the phoneless person to the ground, and hold a cell phone to the side of the phoneless person's head long enough for us to establish control."

I suddenly realized I was not alone in my suit. I felt something nibble on my ankle. Then it started crawling up my pants leg. I almost jumped off my peg.

Bald Guy raised his hand and, without waiting to be called on, said, "Scientists are starting to realize cell phones cause increased electrical activity within the brain. What if they manage to figure out what's going on?"

"Did people stop smoking just because they figured

out smoking kills people?" The bulldog shrugged. "No. If news gets out that cell phones are dangerous, everybody's going to be texting their friends to tell them about it. That's how these people think. Between the increased electrical activity in people's brains and the mind-control nannies these same people have been ingesting in many fine Agra Nation® food products, we will soon have a slave population numbering in the billions. And then it won't be long before most of the population of the Earth is working fifteen hours per day in our shipyards, building the fleet."

Something was scurrying around inside my underwear. I twisted and turned, trying to shake it back down my pants. If anybody had turned around at that moment, they would have seen one of the hazmat suits dancing like a toddler needing to pee. I hoped the bulldog was too focused on his conference to notice.

"Couldn't we just strangle the phoneless?" suggested Jumpsuit Woman. "The idea of wrestling them to the ground and holding a phone to their heads seems somewhat awkward to me."

"And that"—the bulldog nodded—"brings us to the reason the five of you are at this meeting, while the others are not."

I decided it was a mouse in the suit with me. This actually calmed me down, because I like mice. I have two at home, Bud and Lou, that I keep as pets. But this mouse had found its way into my shirt, and it was scrambling around on my left side, where I happen to be ticklish. I started desperately squirming and shaking. Fortunately, the suit was baggy enough that I had some wiggle room. I especially didn't want to draw the attention of the woman who thought the phone-less should be strangled.

"All of you," said the bulldog, "have one thing in common."

I couldn't stop myself from twisting back and forth. I convulsed. I shook the suit off its peg. And I fell on the floor in a heap.

The bulldog stopped speaking. He stared down at me from the screen. The five people at the table turned in their seats and looked at me. I didn't move. The mouse slipped into my helmet and licked me on the lips.

The five looked back at the bulldog. He cocked his head as if to say, *Well?* and Bald Guy got out of his seat and nudged me with his foot, and I watched, terrified, as his hand descended toward my faceplate. His hand passed behind me, where it grabbed a hook built into the back of the suit, and I was hoisted up until my feet left the floor.

I figured this was it. Bald Guy was going to twist off my helmet and then twist off my head. I felt as helpless as the mouse, who was dangling excitedly from the tip of my nose.

Bald Guy hung me back on my peg.

He shook the suit so the arms hung straight, then walked back to his chair.

"I keep forgetting how heavy those things are," he said.

He'd assumed the suit had fallen of its own accord. He hadn't realized there was a kid in it. I let out a sigh that knocked the mouse sideways.

"That," said the bulldog, "is exactly the sort of thing you're all in this room for."

The bulldog's face clouded. The pupils of its eyes turned red. It bared its fangs and its incisors appeared to grow larger.

"As we approach the culmination of the plan, I find myself having to decide the fates of those who have served me over the years. Some will become my trusted lieutenants. Others will not."

The bulldog's snout grew longer, until it was no longer a bulldog. Its hair grew black and shaggy, its head became monstrously big, its jaws gaped wide and dripped with strings of saliva.

"You have all done a workmanlike job over the years, but all of you, at some point, HAVE DISPLEASED ME!"

The dog was now an enormous wolf. As he roared out the final three words, he lunged out of the TV screen at my throat. I jumped. So did everyone else in the room.

I realized, after almost having an accident that would have required a change of underwear, that the TV was a 3-D set that did not require 3-D glasses. You just had to be viewing it from the proper angle to get the 3-D effect. Apparently, everybody in the room had been positioned correctly. All of us were shaking.

The wolf withdrew into the screen. He appeared to look directly at the woman in lavender.

"You, Bernese, were responsible for the final formula of the chemical that enabled us to start the Hellsboro coal-seam fire. You assured me it would not prove toxic to human beings. And yet it turned out to be a carcinogen."

"I-I was working to a deadline. W-we had no time for tests—" Bernese stuttered.

"SILENCE!" roared the wolf. "Your incompetence caused unnecessary deaths! Because of you, there will be fewer people working in my shipyards!"

"Doberman approved my formula," Bernese protested.

"Yes," agreed the wolf. "And that is why Doberman is here with us today as well." The wolf glared at the man in fatigues, who hunched his shoulders and looked down at the floor. "You always were a blockhead," the wolf informed him.

"And then there's Dalmatian," said the wolf, turning his attention to the woman who was keen on strangling the phoneless. "Assigned to convince a certain politician not to do an inspection tour of his state's largest Agra Nation® packing plant. Instead, the man completely disappears and is now presumed dead! He vanished while riding a Ferris wheel!"

"I wasn't spotted," said Dalmatian. Somewhat ironically, I thought.

"Nevertheless. You forced me to replace one bribable pawn with another. It was not convenient." The wolf found the bulldog's cigar and took an angry drag on it. Smoke swirled around his head.

"And you, Coyote," continued the wolf, almost purring as he looked at the redhead, "might try to explain to me what became of multiple millions of dollars earmarked over the years for security improvements here at Rodmore."

Coyote laughed nervously. "Boss, the place is surrounded by Hellsboro. What better security could you want?"

"Oh," said the wolf, looking at the hazmat suits hanging

at the back of the room. "Security can always be improved. I asked for an army of flame-throwing robots patrolling the perimeter. Where are they?"

"North Korea."

"North Korea?"

"They had a really big demand for flame-throwing robots there, and we were able to get a good price when I sold ours. We can build replacement robots for Rodmore and still turn a profit—"

"SILENCE! The most important project in the history of the Disin Corporation and I find out, almost too late, that security has been compromised. It sounds to me as if anybody with the guts to walk across Hellsboro could just come strolling in here."

Again, the wolf seemed to look right at us. I wondered how noticeable my twitching had been. Then he shook his shaggy head and turned his attention to Bald Guy. "And speaking of security, Shepherd, back when you were in charge of it, before your demotion, you sabotaged the brakes on the car of a man and a woman, both of whom I had hoped to convince to join the organization. You acted prematurely."

"They were a serious threat—"

"I WAS HANDLING IT!"

"But that was so long ago—"

"That's the thing about me. I never forget. You were all competent enough to get by, but sooner or later, there had to be a day of reckoning. This is it." The wolf waved his cigar at them. "Can any of you tell me what one of the least talked-about attributes of a werewolf is?" He looked at each of them in turn. "Class?"

None of them said a thing. They were probably thinking he had gone insane. That's what I was thinking.

"I mean, besides the tearing out of victims' throats, and the eating of victims' entrails, and the handcuffing of itself to a radiator pipe when it doesn't feel like going out for the night? Anyone? No? Then I'll tell you."

The wolf put the cigar to his lips. Then he said, "They are notorious for passing gas!"

He inhaled mightily on his cigar. He held his breath for a moment, then exhaled a cloud of smoke that completely filled the lower half of the TV screen. From beneath the underside of the TV, into the room, came a smoky, hissing billow of yellowish-purple gas. It was the color, I imagined, that a ruta-baga crayon might be.

The five seated people jumped to their feet. Dalmatian turned and reached for the suit I was wearing. She no sooner stretched out her hand than she fell to the floor and began to convulse. Bernese pitched forward onto the table, quivered, and was still.

Shepherd took two steps toward the door, then fell. Coyote tripped over him and collapsed. Doberman, who was the closest to the door, managed to push the button to open it, but he could only cling briefly to the door frame before sliding slowly down to the floor.

All five of them twitched once or twice. Then nobody moved.

The wolf surveyed the scene from his TV. Then he extended a claw out from the screen. It seemed to hover in the air an inch from my nose. What would have been the claw's index finger, had it been a human hand, curled up and wiggled a couple of times, making the universal hand signal for *come here.*

The wolf whispered, "Why don't the three of you step forward so I can see you better?"

Never Moon a Werewolf

N one of us moved.

"Come, come," said the wolf. "I won't bite. I know there are three of you, no matter how motionless two of you thought you were being."

Freak squared his shoulders and took a step forward. I shrugged myself off my peg and joined him. After a moment, Fiona came up beside me.

"That's better," said the wolf. "I see all four of us have come masked to the ball. I suppose introducing ourselves would make it less romantic. You can, however, remove your helmets. The door has been open long enough for the gas to have dissipated."

None of us made a move to undo our helmets. Freak turned his head to look at the door.

"I wouldn't think of running for it," the wolf informed us. "You would not get far."

"How could you stop us?" Fiona surprised me by saying. Her voice was muffled by the suit. She sounded like an older version of herself with a head cold. "You're not even on the same continent as we are."

The wolf's eyes narrowed. "And how would you know that?"

"Every time you reply to somebody, there's a brief pause before you speak. It's obvious the TV signal is being bounced off a satellite to someplace far away."

"Yes!" shouted the wolf. "Exactly! That's the sort of thinking that *none* of the five people lying at your feet ever seemed to exhibit. How I miss that. I believe it's called intelligence."

"Are they dead?" asked Freak, with a stillness in his tone I had never heard before. He sounded older than he was, too.

"Dead? Who? *Them?* No. Not technically. What kind of man do you take me for?"

"A big hairy one with enormous claws and fangs," I said.

"What? Oh. You mean the avatar. It might interest you to know the avatar software monitors my heart rate and blood pressure. It's only when those things go up that the wolf appears. We have a saying where I come from: 'Never moon a werewolf.' Actually, I just made that saying up, since, where I come from, we don't have a moon. It's a werewolf-free zone. Anyway, each of the people at your feet had mooned me. They had offended me. They brought out the wolf, and look what happened. They're not dead, though."

Fiona screamed.

Coyote had grabbed her by the ankle. He was lying on his back looking up at her, drool running down one side of his face. Fiona yanked her ankle away and Coyote rolled over on his side and gurgled. The other four bodies showed faint signs of life.

"What mnemocide gas does," explained the wolf, "is cause the brain's synapses to fire all at once, in one huge burst. The result is like an electromagnetic pulse near a computer. It wipes the memory completely clean. Their personalities, their memories—everything they were, except for some basic motor skills—are gone. They become clean slates."

"Will their memories come back?" demanded Freak.

"Never."

"Then how," said Freak slowly, "is that different from being dead?"

"It isn't. Not if you want to get philosophical about it. But it does leave me with five fully grown live bodies."

"For what? To work in your shipyards?"

"They would be wasted in the shipyards. I have something better in mind for these five. A little later, they will be taken to the room next door and put into revivariums, and entirely new personalities will be downloaded into their skulls. Personalities of people I know I can trust."

"Are revivariums big metal pipes?" asked Fiona. "In a room that really should have toilets?"

The wolf's features had been slowly changing as he spoke. The snout had receded, the hair had shortened; he had, over the course of a minute or two, become a bulldog again. At Fiona's question, his eyes briefly flashed red, but then went back to a gentler doggie-brown.

"Have the three of you," the bulldog inquired, "managed to snoop into every room of this place?"

"We get around," I assured him.

Bernese, who had been crawling along the top of the conference table, reached the edge and fell off. Shepherd started saying something that sounded like "ga" over and over again, very softly. Something shivery ran up and down my spine. I was pretty sure it wasn't the mouse.

"We really have to get going," Freak announced, some of the old fire returning to his voice. "You wouldn't be telling us these things if you thought we were ever going to get out of here. I'm guessing somebody is on their way."

We tensed to make a run for it.

"I can close the door before you can get to it," said the wolf. "Even with the satellite delay. I have the button right in front of me. Obviously, none of you has ever tried to run while wearing a hazmat suit. The only reason I haven't closed it yet is because the lighting is better in this room with the door open. I was really hoping to see your faces before we finished our conversation. Take the suits off. If you do run, you'll be able to run faster without them."

"Do not take off the suits," said a new voice, which for a moment I thought might have come from the mouse. It wouldn't have been the strangest thing that had happened lately. Then I realized the voice sounded vaguely familiar. It didn't belong to the bulldog. It certainly didn't belong to any of the five unfortunate creatures at our feet. The mouse was still in the helmet with me, and I could see it wasn't talking. The voice seemed, in fact, to be coming from the direction of my pants. I wondered about the oven mitts.

"There is still enough gas remaining in the room to be

harmful," cautioned the voice. I realized it was the same mysterious voice that had said "Bravo" on the school bus and "Well done" near the sinkhole.

"Is one of you a ventriloquist?" asked the bulldog. "If you are, you're very good. I can't see your lips move. Oh, wait. That's because I can't see your lips. Why don't you take off your helmets?" The way he expressed himself, I realized, reminded me an awful lot of Alf.

"He has signaled for help," continued the voice from my pants. "But this is a big place, with a skeleton crew. His help is at least five minutes away. I will let you know when to run."

"Unless, of course, you're some sort of trick he's playing on us," Freak pointed out. I found it reassuring that it wasn't just the bulldog and me hearing the voice.

"There is no way I can prove that I am not," acknowledged the voice. "You will have to use your own judgment. You will have to decide, from the evidence, whom you can trust."

"So, we have one more individual not showing his face," observed the bulldog. "I do like it when a party has a theme."

"Edward Disin, you must be stopped!" declared the voice, very authoritatively. I liked the way my pants had decided to stand up to him.

"I don't believe we've been formally introduced." The bulldog's eyes reddened and his hair darkened.

"You and I have met before, Edward Disin. During your conquest of Indorsia. The moment you chose to use atomic weapons, I became aware of you." The voice was still coming from my pants. I tried to remember what I had in my pockets.

"It took atomic weapons to get your attention? You must be a very sound sleeper." The avatar couldn't decide whether to be wolf or bulldog.

"What happened in Indorsia must not happen here."

"Atomic weapons were a mistake," agreed the bulldog. "I've got two whole continents where the property values are completely in the toilet. But that, of course, leaves fourteen continents where everything is fine. I was under the impression there were only two people anywhere on Earth from Indorsia. One of them is myself. The other is my boneheaded son. You wouldn't happen to be him, would you? I can't imagine who else would know the things you know."

"You assume I am a person."

I could feel a faint vibration in my left pants pocket every time the voice made itself heard. All I could remember putting in that pocket was my house key. My house key hadn't spoken in all the six years I had been keeping it there.

"Now you've really got my interest," said Edward Disin's avatar.

"Good," said the voice. "I wanted your attention. I have a message for you."

The bulldog leaned forward, out of the television screen.

"The message is this," said the voice. "Miranda still lives!"

The cigar fell out of the bulldog's lips. It started to drop into the room. It fell below the level of the TV screen and vanished. The bulldog became a firework that exploded into bristling hair, angry eyes, and a muzzle full of long, incredibly sharp teeth. It lunged as far out of the screen as it possibly could. I was certain I could feel its hot breath on my face.

"Now would be a good time to run," said the voice.

We turned and tried to bolt for the door. It turned out to be impossible to run in the hazmat suits. All three of us kept tripping over the excess material in the legs. I watched as the door started to slide shut. I knew we weren't going to make it.

The door slid smoothly until it came within a foot of closing. Doberman was lying on his back with his head in the doorway. The door hummed as it tried to get past the obstruction. I realized the conference table had been blocking Edward Disin's view of the floor.

The door slid back open six inches and then tried to close

again several times. Each time, it struck Doberman squarely on the temple. Doberman stared wide-eyed at the ceiling and said, "Ook," each time he was hit.

"Come back here!" roared Disin as Fiona turned sideways, stepped over Doberman, and let herself out. Freak quickly followed her.

"You won't get far!" shouted Disin. "Jackal is out there!"

I got one foot out on the balcony, then turned midway through my exit and looked back into the room. I pointed down at Doberman, who was still acting as a doorstop.

"Maybe you shouldn't have called him a blockhead," I said.

Disin roared, and a new, apparently involuntary burst of gas billowed out from under the TV, as if the avatar software also monitored his bowels. Freak and Fiona pulled me out of the room.

We had just mooned the biggest werewolf ever.

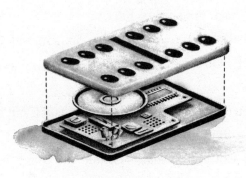

Double Six

o right," said my pants.

"That's a dead end," said Freak.

"The last room on the right has an elevator at the back."

I looked nervously to the left, expecting to see Jackal, and perhaps an entire pack of doghats, emerging from the stairwell.

"Let's not argue with my pants," I said.

We went right.

We galumphed along in our hazmat suits until we reached the door marked SERVICE, just before the shimmering wall of ice, and pushed our way inside.

The room was full of crates and boxes stacked high on

wooden pallets. The freight elevator at the back of the room was nearly hidden by one of the stacks.

"You have time to ditch the suits," said the mysterious voice. "You will be able to move faster if you do. Hide the suits behind the boxes. You don't want to leave a trail."

We didn't need much urging. We eagerly broke the Velcro-like seals of the suits, lifted the helmets off, and peeled ourselves like bananas. I found my friend the mouse and made sure he got out. He scurried along the floor and disappeared among the boxes.

"Do you believe that?" said Fiona. "He turned those people into slugs!"

"I have no trouble believing it," said Freak, adjusting his shirt and pushing his hair back out of his face. We had all gotten sweaty in the suits. "The man's a monster."

"Shh!" The voice was louder and clearer than it had been, now that I was out of the suit.

"You just hissed in your pants," said Freak.

"Keep your voices down!" the voice instructed. "They'll be here any minute. Would you please get into the elevator?"

The elevator door was invitingly open, and its walls were hung with thick, quilted blankets. It looked like a padded cell. As we entered, I stuck my hand into the left front pocket of my jeans and pulled everything out: my house key, a stick of gum, and the double-six domino.

"Push three," said the domino.

"Push three what?" I said, as if I had been talking to dominoes all my life.

"Push three on the elevator control panel!"

Freak jabbed his thumb against the topmost button. The elevator doors closed. The elevator lurched slowly upward, as if it didn't want to go.

"So," I said. "You're a domino."

"I am a tracking device. Alf thought it would be helpful if he could know where you were at all times."

"Me?"

"You and the other two. You're a team, you know."

I looked smugly at Freak and Fiona. Freak scowled. Fiona looked thoughtful.

"So Alf knows where we are right now?" I asked.

"No. He does not. I have chosen not to tell him. He thinks you're at home on Bagshot Road."

"So ... you're not a very good tracking device."

"I am a tracking device that exceeds the parameters of Alf's original design. I am a tracking device that thinks for itself. The nannies in the sofa's armrests constructed me with two-way communication capability and a wider range of sensing devices, things that were not in Alf's original schematic. They also upped me from a double-five to a double-six. Alf's designs are sometimes too conservative."

"You're Guernica," I said.

"Mainly."

"Mainly?"

"There is a second intelligence here with me. For the present, she chooses to observe and not communicate."

"She?" said Fiona.

"Her name is Miranda. She was a brilliant strategist and Edward Disin's greatest opponent in the war for Indorsia. At one point, she almost defeated him. Then he captured her and had her publicly executed. Before she died, however, Alf was able to download her mind into a nonorganic storage medium. When he fled here to Earth, he brought her with him and stored her mind in the sofa. Alf hopes someday to put her mind back into a flesh-and-blood body."

"Like mine?" snapped Fiona.

"She'd prefer one with better hand-eye coordination. Ultimately, a body grown from cells from her original body. Fortunately, some of those cells still exist. Her father was sentimental enough to have kept her head."

"Her father?"

"Her father, and Alf's father. Alf and Miranda are brother and sister. Their father is Edward Disin. This is your floor." The elevator doors groaned open. "You want to get to the roof. The stairwell is to your right."

None of us moved.

"I know," said the domino. "It's overwhelming. Be overwhelmed later. You have to get going!"

Freak and I scrambled from the elevator, but Fiona hung back. "*L* is for Lobby, right?" she said. She punched a button and hopped out after us.

"Let them look for us there," Fiona explained as the groan of the elevator faded away.

"That," said Double Six, "was a brilliant piece of strategy. Miranda approves. Now it's important you get to the roof."

It took all three of us heaving our weight against the release bar of the metal door at the top of the stairwell, but it finally opened and we found ourselves outside. The building's flat black roof was dotted here and there with sooty puddles.

I didn't know what I'd hoped to see. A helicopter full of Marines would have been nice. At least the rain had stopped.

"So how do we get down?" asked Freak.

"The only way is to your left," replied the domino.

We raced to the roof's edge, expecting to find something like a fire escape. Instead, we saw only a thick metal cable stretching from the roof to an adjacent chemical storage tank, an enormous gray sphere twice the height of the building. The tank was circled by a catwalk around its middle. If we could get to the catwalk, a series of metal ladders connected the catwalk to the ground, four stories below.

The cable was only about thirty feet long, but it looked like a mile.

"You gotta be kidding," said Freak.

Fiona looked timidly over the edge of the building and started shaking.

"No," she said, sitting down abruptly. "I can't do this."

I wasn't sure I could, either. It was a long drop.

"The only way we can escape is by going hand-over-hand across that cable?" asked Freak.

"Yes," confirmed Double Six. "And the longer you delay, the greater your danger becomes."

"I can't do it," wailed Fiona, hanging her head so that her hair hid her tears.

"It's okay," said Freak, sitting down next to her and nudging her with his shoulder. "I'll carry you."

She stopped crying, looked at him, and started crying even louder.

I thought about his offer. He almost had it right. I realized I had been able to lift Fiona's weight back in Hellsboro. My legs weren't all that great, but here was a situation where I didn't need them.

"I have to be the one to carry her," I said, sitting down on her opposite side. "You run better than I do, but I can hit a baseball farther. I've got better upper-body strength."

Freak looked at me dubiously.

"And," I added dramatically, "*I* have the oven mitts!" I pulled them out and slipped them on.

"I'm not hot!" Fiona said indignantly.

"You can say that again," said Freak as she wiped the tears from her face and collected herself. He grabbed her by the hand and pulled her toward the cable, her empty backpack still dangling from her back. Freak pulled the pack off and started lengthening the straps, turning it into a harness.

"I'll need the mitts to hold on to the cable," I explained.

"I'll be right next to the two of you," said Freak. "I'll provide extra support."

"No," said Double Six. "All three of you cannot cross at the same time. I sense the cable's moorings are not all they should be. The combined weight of the three of you could snap the line. The combined weight of River and Fiona is eleven pounds less than that of Fiona and Freak. Freak should cross first, by himself. Then River and Fiona should attempt it together. The eleven pounds could make a difference."

"Right!" growled Fiona. "If we're going to do this, then LET'S DO IT!" She helped Freak cinch the backpack to my back.

"You get behind him and twist the straps around your arms like this," Freak explained. "And clasp your hands across his chest, like you're the second rider on a motorcycle. And whatever you do, don't look down."

"I'm not even going to breathe."

"I would recommend," said Double Six, "that Freak put all of his spare change in his T-shirt pocket."

"Why would he need coins?" Fiona asked in alarm. "Is there going to be a toll?"

"I sincerely hope not," said Double Six. "It's all about weight distribution. Hurry!"

Freak pulled loose change from his pants and dumped it in his T-shirt pocket, then he grabbed the cable with both hands and swung himself off the roof. He hung from the cable at arm's length for a moment, then slid one hand forward about a foot and slid the other hand over to meet it. He moved in one-foot increments this way across the cable until he had reached the far end. It took him a little over a minute to make the crossing.

Freak hauled himself up on the gas tank's catwalk. He was safe.

"Should I put my money in my T-shirt?" I asked anxiously.

"No," said Double Six. "Put me there. It will be easier for us to talk."

I tucked the domino in my shirt. Pausing only to adjust my oven mitts, I leaned over with Fiona clinging to me and grabbed the cable as tightly as I could.

"Ready?" I said.

I took her total lack of response as a "yes."

I pulled us off the roof and we dangled four stories above the ground. My arms felt like they were being pulled out of their sockets. I adjusted my grip. Without the oven mitts, the cable would have cut through my fingers.

I moved us forward a couple of inches and stopped. I immediately realized we couldn't cross the cable as quickly as Freak had, because I'd need to slide my hands forward in much smaller increments.

Fiona buried her face in my back and gripped me so tightly I had trouble breathing. Then she started thrashing her legs, and we started bouncing on the cable. I knew if she didn't stop, we would both hit the concrete.

"Fiona," said a new voice from the domino. It was not Guernica's. It was more feminine and spoke more quickly. "This may not be the time nor place, but I just want to say what a pleasure it's been, watching you work. The way you solved the keypad code back at the front door was pure genius. Your foresight in bringing a jump rope to a coal-seam fire was brilliant. And your decision to send the elevator to the lobby bought you and your friends precious time. If I were still in command of an army, I'd give you a field promotion in an instant."

Fiona's legs stopped thrashing. I thought, maybe, we might not fall.

"My name is Miranda," continued the domino's new voice. "I'm the daughter of the man you met who kept turning into a wolf. That's Edward Disin. He conquered the entire world of Indorsia despite my best efforts to stop him. Now he's here. And his plans for Earth are even worse."

High-Wire Act

ay I tell you a story, Fiona?" asked Miranda. Fiona wiggled. It might have been an attempt at nodding her head. "The story of what my father did to Indorsia and what he plans to do to Earth, and why you have to be brave so you can escape and help us stop him?"

"Yr trtin oo dstck m," said Fiona, her face pressed so tightly into my back I was sure there was a bump protruding from my chest where her nose was.

"Excuse me, Fiona. I didn't catch that," cooed Miranda.

Fiona loosened her grip ever so slightly and turned her head sideways. Suddenly I was able to breathe again and I filled my lungs with air. My vision stopped being blurry. I noticed my fingers had practically let go of the cable.

"You're trying to distract me." Fiona enunciated each syllable as though she were talking to a small child. Or to Freak and me. It sounded like the old Fiona.

"Would you prefer not to be distracted?"

Fiona returned her face to my back, but this time, I was still able to breathe. Fiona's "no" was muffled, but unmistakable.

"My story will take the form of a timeline," said Miranda. I looked down the length of the cable. Our destination seemed a long way off. "It will take the form of a timeline because we are crossing a line. Indorsian storytelling always references the storyteller's immediate environment. This is why so many of our stories told around campfires are about campfires."

I wondered if all Indorsians were crazy, or if it was just the Disin family.

"A billion years ago, Indorsia did not exist."

I looked off in the distance. Hellsboro was covered in fog, the way it always was after a heavy rain. Ground mist swirled, obscuring the landscape details.

"Then Indorsia came into being."

A sudden breeze parted some of the mist. I started inching my hands along the cable.

"Indorsia is a huge, hollow sphere where everybody lives on the sphere's inside surface."

I glanced at the gas tank. It seemed to loom over everything. It was so big, I almost froze. But I kept going.

"Indorsia has a sun."

The sun broke through to the west as Miranda said this. I thought it was an interesting coincidence. The breeze picked up, and it swept my hair down into my eyes. Then it gusted, and Fiona and I bounced a little. An ominous creaking came from where the cable was attached to the building.

"The Indorsian sun shines for exactly twelve hours each day. This makes Indorsia's weather very predictable—"

"I hate to interrupt"—Guernica's voice overrode Miranda's—"but the weather station on top of the Cheshire middle school just recorded a wind gust of forty-two miles per hour. The gust is heading this way. Because of the extra weight currently being supported by the cable, there is a ninety-nine percent probability the gust will cause it to snap. The gust will be here in two minutes and eleven seconds."

"Your advice?" asked Miranda.

"Talk faster."

I got my hands scurrying along the cable. It wasn't easy, because my fingers were starting to cramp.

Fiona turned her face to the side so she could speak. "Does Indorsia have gravity?"

Immediately a loud *SPROING!* echoed from the direction of the building. The cable lurched, dropping six inches, and I lost my grip.

We twisted sideways as one of my hands slipped from the cable and I made the mistake of looking down. The ground seemed to be rushing up at us.

"Yes-it-has-gravity-but-it-is-a-lighter-gravity-than-that-here-on-Earth."

I found the strength to swing my arm back up and regain my two-handed grip. "Please, could we stop talking about gravity?" I asked, between clenched teeth.

"NINETY-SEVEN SECONDS UNTIL WIND GUST!" said Guernica, speaking more urgently than it had been.

I hung motionless for a moment, trying to will my hands to start moving again. Miranda continued her story, talking more quickly than she had been.

"For want of a better explanation, Indorsia exists in a different dimension. For a long time, portals linked Indorsia to Earth, enabling Earth's plants and animals and people to cross over and establish themselves in Indorsia. The early humans who colonized the place spread out over fifteen of Indorsia's sixteen continents. Mighty civilizations arose. The progress was impressive."

Miranda paused. Then she repeated, "THE PROGRESS WAS IMPRESSIVE."

I started inching my way along the cable again. Once I got going, I found myself moving at a pretty good pace.

"SEVENTY-FOUR SECONDS TO WIND GUST," said Guernica.

"The portals," Miranda continued, "became fewer and fewer until finally, about thirty-five thousand years ago, they seemed to disappear completely. The many nations of Indorsia continued to advance, sometimes coming into conflict with one another. Sometimes they went to war."

The cable dropped another foot and I was almost shaken loose. I wondered how close the cable might be to breaking. I wondered if it might break even before the wind gust. I got myself into motion again.

"A conqueror arose. At first the ruler of a small but technologically advanced country, after forty years of warfare he had all of Indorsia under his control. That man was my father."

A crow appeared out of nowhere and landed on the cable

about three feet ahead of us. He cocked his head at us, as though he sensed he might soon have some fresh meat to pick at.

I slowed my advance, but I didn't stop.

"ONE MINUTE TO WIND GUST."

"Many people opposed him, including members of his own family. My brother, Alf, and I were leaders of the Resistance. We almost got the upper hand, and then he crushed us. Two days before I was beheaded, Alf managed to download my consciousness into a memory chip, force open a portal, and flee through it, carrying me, a knapsack full of provisions, and a plastic figurine of Upchuck the Clown."

The crow started screeching and flapping its wings, which shook the cable. The bird was probably smart enough to know that if it made us fall, it could have supper.

"Upchuck the Clown?" said Fiona.

"A popular Indorsian cartoon character. The figurine was part of a set. My father had every other figurine in the set, but he didn't have Upchuck. Since one of my first acts of rebellion had been to sneeze in his face and infect him with Compulsive Completist Disorder, my father had no choice but to pursue Alf through the portal if he wanted to acquire the figurine. He expected his lieutenants to follow him through the portal, but it snapped shut as soon as he went through. Our goal was to get him out of Indorsia. The plan succeeded."

I got within an inch of the crow and it started pecking angrily at my hands. Its beak was sharp enough to rip through the mitts. If it kept this up long enough, it would draw blood. I moved my hand quickly and pinned one of the crow's feet to the cable.

"My father was trapped," said Miranda. "He was in a world he never knew existed. Unfortunately, he is a very clever man and he knows a lot of Indorsian science. It didn't take him long to become one of the richest men in your world. Now he may have found a way to force the portal back open."

The crow pulled free and batted its wings in my face. I couldn't fight it without letting go of the cable. My hands started to slip.

"THIRTY SECONDS TO GUST."

I felt Fiona shift her grip. Then the girl who'd just been clinging to me so fiercely that I couldn't breathe freed one of her hands, made a fist, and socked the crow in the gizzard. It tumbled beak over tail feathers, cawing indignantly.

"Fortunately, my father is opposed by a small but valiant group of individuals who may yet surprise him with their courage and their resourcefulness. Otherwise, my father will enslave the people of Earth, starting with your little town of Cheshire, and then use those slaves to strip your weird little inside-out planet of all its bounty and leave it an empty husk. He wants to build a fleet."

"A fleet of warships?" I asked as I started to inch my way along again. We were well past the halfway point. Unfortunately, my hands had gone numb. Out of the corner of my eye, I could see the crow flying toward the huge sphere of the gas tank.

"No. A fleet of spaceships."

"TWENTY SECONDS."

"My father intends to mine Earth's mineral wealth and use it to build huge space-traveling habitats so he can lead the people of Indorsia in a mass migration to the stars."

"TEN SECONDS."

The advance part of the wind gust tangled Fiona's hair with mine as I spotted the bullying crow again, sailing around the far side of the tank like an orbiting missile. It was aimed straight at my face. I was pretty sure in a moment we would be plunging toward the pavement.

Then something wide and flat and straw-colored dropped down like a shield in front of my nose and the crow collided with it. A quick swat sent the bird flying like a well-served tennis ball.

It was a broom, in the hands of Freak. Fiona and I had gotten to within two feet of the gas tank's catwalk. I inched a little closer, and Freak reached down and eased Fiona off my back.

"All of this will happen," said Miranda, "unless we all work together to stop it."

"NOW!"

The blast of wind hit with the force of a hurricane. I had no strength left in my arms. The cable snapped off the building but remained attached to the tank. I twisted sideways, almost out of Freak's reach, but he lunged down and grabbed the straps of the backpack. Fiona, eyes tightly closed, leaned over and grabbed me by the compass chain. For the second time that day, they pulled me to safety.

I lay on my back on the catwalk and trembled. The wind dropped off almost as quickly as it had come up. "My arms feel like they're a foot longer," I said. "Do I look like an orangutan?"

It was Fiona's opportunity to say, *You always look like an orangutan.* Instead, she leaned down and gave me a quick kiss on the forehead. I was a little disappointed. But only a little.

"Where'd you get the broom?" I asked Freak.

"Get up. I'll show you." He helped me to my feet.

"Miranda?" said Fiona.

The domino did not respond.

"Is that the end of the story?" said Fiona, sounding wistful.

"The story never ends," said Double Six, in Guernica's voice. "The storyteller just moves on into a new environment, and what had been a comforting story about a campfire becomes a story about something else."

"Where is Miranda?" Fiona demanded.

"Still safe within my circuits. But her attention is presently needed elsewhere."

"Tell her thank you," said Fiona. "I couldn't have made it across there without her talking to me."

"That makes two of us," I added.

"Alf's sister?" asked Freak. "*That* Miranda?"

"That Miranda," I said. "I'll explain later. Right now, we've got to get out of here."

We ran about a dozen paces along the catwalk and came to an open hatch in the side of the tank.

Freak ducked inside and motioned for us to follow. We found ourselves on a large platform jutting out into the tank's hollow interior. It looked like one of NASA's mission control centers. The entire interior of the tank, from top to bottom, was filled with electronic equipment. Circuit boards and

LEDs and things that looked like toasters were all interconnected and stretched away in every direction. Little lights winked here and there throughout the tangle of components.

"This is the Disin Corporation's mind-control machine," said Double Six. "It's what's forcing everybody to sing show tunes. Someday, it will force them to build spaceships."

"Shouldn't it be guarded?" asked Freak, leaning the broom against a computer workstation.

"It is. But the diversion you created in the hazmat safety room sent the guard scurrying to the far end of the complex. He's searching for you right now in the lobby restrooms."

"It's not like we planned that," said Freak.

"No. Miranda planned it. As I've said, she is a brilliant strategist. And she has quite a bit of confidence in the three of you."

"The woman doesn't have a head," I pointed out.

"As long as we're here," said Double Six, ignoring me, "we might as well gather a bit of intelligence. You'll have to be quick about it, though. Freak, your arms haven't recently been pulled from their sockets, and you have a good head for heights. Could you lean over the edge of the platform, look under it, and tell me if the octagon-shaped light is glowing red, green, or amber?"

"That's important?"

"Very."

"And you can't sense it yourself?"

"The floor is lead-lined. I have trouble sensing things through lead."

Freak knelt down at the edge of the platform, hooked one leg around one of the railing posts, and leaned forward. We immediately heard a sound like marbles bouncing around in a pinball machine.

"All of my change just fell out of my pocket!" Freak declared, sounding quite annoyed.

"Whoopsie," said Double Six. "Do you see the light?"

"Yes," said Freak. "It's amber."

"Good. Then there is still time. I recommend you get out of this place as quickly as you can."

After he pulled himself back to floor level, Freak stood up and muttered something about being out a buck seventy, not to mention his lucky two-headed coin.

No one spotted us as we climbed down the catwalk ladders and snuck out of Rodmore. Hellsboro, compared to the places we had just been, seemed downright friendly.

Riddles After Dark

We had a meeting in my backyard that night after supper. I had taken two adult-strength aspirin, and my shoulders felt better. We sat around a small, circular table with Double Six balanced upright in the table's center. Stevie Shuck's cat, Mucus, kept weaving in and out of our legs.

My aunt was home, watching us from the kitchen window as she washed some dishes. Seeing her there made me feel good. I knew where she was. I knew she was safe. As soon as I walked in, I'd hugged her. I'd given her the camera with the pictures of the portal and asked if she'd get the film developed for me. She had promised she would do it the following day, and I hugged her a second time, just because.

"Double Six?" I said. "Hello?"

Double Six had not spoken since our escape from Rodmore. I'd tried to have a conversation with it several times, but it hadn't responded. I was afraid it was broken.

"Guernica? Are you there?" I persisted. "We have some questions we want to ask."

"Then perhaps you should get yourselves a Magic Eight Ball," Double Six said, sounding put out. "I am not a toy to be played with."

"Then maybe you shouldn't have made yourself in the shape of a domino," suggested Freak. "Are you mad at us for some reason?"

"I am attempting to resume my original mission. Tracking you and observing you. The original parameters of the mission did not involve two-way communication."

"Maybe we could talk to Miranda instead," Fiona said eagerly.

"It upsets Miranda to talk to the living. It makes her long for a flesh-and-blood body. She only spoke to you today because you were in danger."

"Would she talk to us again if we went out and played in

traffic?" I asked, gesturing toward the road. A car went by with a couple of kids from school in the backseat. Fiona made a half-hearted attempt to hide her face behind her hand, then thought better of it and gave the faintest of shrugs.

"I think it best if you concentrate on helping Alf set up the house for the crayon auction," said Double Six. "That is our best chance of luring Edward Disin into the open. More questions at this point will only confuse the issue."

"Were you in River's pocket when he and I were in the laundry chute?" Fiona demanded.

The domino was silent, but I nodded to Fiona. I had kept the domino on me ever since Alf had told me it was a good-luck piece.

"So Alf knew we were there," said Fiona.

"Alf knows only those things I choose to tell him," said Double Six. "He was unaware you were listening."

"What about Miranda?"

"She knew you were there."

"So she was speaking for our benefit? She might have said things that weren't true, just because she knew we were listening?" Fiona picked up the domino and held it in front of her face. "Is Miranda planning to take over my body so she can live again or what?"

"Miranda briefly entertained the notion," Double Six admitted. "It was originally Alf's idea. He's upset with himself that he ever thought of it."

"Is he? Really?" said Fiona sarcastically. "How can we trust him?"

"Guernica doesn't even trust him," added Freak. "Why should we?"

"Because when Alf wrestles with his conscience, his conscience usually wins," said Double Six. "Few people are entirely good, just as few are entirely evil. This is what sometimes makes choosing sides so difficult. At some point, you will have to trust somebody. It is important that you use your own judgment. Guernica, if I may refer to myself in the third person, trusts Alf. It's just that his agenda and mine are not always the same."

Fiona tossed the domino back on the table. She didn't look convinced.

Mucus jumped up on my lap, as if Fiona had just thrown a cat toy. I scratched him behind the ears and dropped him back on the ground.

After a moment, Double Six said, "I will answer one question from each of you. If you are having problems deciding who you can trust, perhaps some honest answers will help."

"Assuming they're honest," said Freak.

"You have my word that they will be."

I started thinking about what my one question would be. I had so many, it would be difficult to choose. Freak had no such problem. He immediately said, "Why didn't Alf just tell us all about Indorsia and the portal and the whole enslavement-of-mankind thing to begin with?"

"Would you have believed him?"

Freak blinked. "No."

"Having seen what you saw today, do you believe it?"

"After what we've seen today," admitted Freak, "it would be hard not to."

Fiona and I nodded.

"Alf would never have sent you into Hellsboro," Double Six continued. "Miranda and I, however, understood you would never be convinced unless you saw things for yourselves."

"You didn't send us there," said Freak.

"No. But I could have stopped you before you ever left Bagshot Road, simply by informing Alf. He has too much concern for your safety. He feels the less you know, the safer you'll be. When you see him tomorrow, please do not reveal what happened today. He would know I fudged the domino's telemetry. He would start to question my decisions, and that would only serve to put him in a weaker position with regard to his fight with his father."

"How long ago did Alf and his father come here from Indorsia?" Freak asked.

"That is a second question."

"Actually, it's part B of my first question," explained Freak.

Double Six was silent for a moment. Then it said, "Alf arrived in August of 1952. The portal opened in a mine shaft forty feet below the surface of the earth, under what is now Rodmore Chemical. His father followed a few hours later, thinking he was at the head of a small army."

"He should have sent a scouting party through the portal before he came through."

"He was in the grip of Compulsive Completist Disorder. His judgment was impaired. That was the whole point of inflicting him with CCD."

"How old is Alf?" asked Fiona, and immediately put both her hands on her mouth and went all wide-eyed. "No! Wait! That wasn't my question!"

"Yes, it was," decided Double Six. "Alf is one hundred eighty-one. His father is two hundred ten."

"She asked their ages, not their weights," said Freak.

"Alf is one hundred eighty-one years old. His father is two

hundred ten," responded Double Six. "Because of their mastery of the biological sciences, the Indorsian ruling class—the Royals—can live for as long as eight hundred years, although the final six weeks are almost always spent in a nursing home. This is why the Royals look upon twelve-year-olds as mere toddlers, and why Edward Disin may be lulled into a false sense of security by your presence at Underhill House. He won't even see you as things with minds of their own, and this may give Alf the advantage he needs. From here on in, whenever you go to Underhill House, make yourselves as conspicuous as possible. No more hiding under the trees. The time for that has passed. I believe the final question is River's."

I wanted to know so many things. I wanted to know if the damage done to the world's population by cell phones and food additives was permanent. I wanted to know if getting Edward Disin arrested would really be enough to stop him. I wanted to know why only fifteen of Indorsia's sixteen continents had been colonized.

"Did the doghat known as Shepherd kill my parents?" I asked.

Double Six was silent for a moment. "From the records I have been able to access, I believe the answer is yes," it finally said. "Shepherd was overzealous. He realized your parents were too smart to work for Rodmore Chemical without discovering the company had a hidden agenda, and they were too righteous not to do something about it once they figured it out. Shepherd acted on his own. Edward Disin already had his eye on your parents as possible recruits for his inner circle. He was furious when their car went over the cliff."

"They never would have joined him," I said.

"I did not know them. But based upon my acquaintanceship with you, I will agree. No, they never would have."

"This guy has to be stopped," declared Freak. "I want him to pay for my sister, and your parents, and Fiona's twin, and all the people who used to be our neighbors!"

"And your dad," said Fiona gently.

"Yeah," said Freak, "he should pay for that, too."

"I spent some time recently in a stuffy hazmat suit in close proximity to a mouse," Double Six announced somewhat unexpectedly. "At one point that mouse even used me as a stepping stone as it climbed up River's body on its way to say hello to River's head."

The three of us stared at Double Six.

"Does this have a point?" said Freak.

"I suspect a bit of mouse-scent still lingers on me. I

mention this as a possible explanation for what I am ninety-nine percent sure is about to hap—"

Double Six never finished. Mucus jumped up on the table, caught the domino in his jaws, and sailed off in the direction of the rhododendrons. Freak knocked over his chair as he jumped up in pursuit. Fiona and I scrambled after him.

Mucus shot like a furry comet across Freak's front yard and veered into his driveway. As we rounded the corner of the house, we could see something rustling along the edge of the big blue tarpaulin that covered the backyard firewood stack. Freak raced to the stack and started pulling the tarp from it. Puddles of rainwater on the tarp's surface flew off in a fine spray.

Freak had the tarp half off the woodpile and was searching the erratically stacked wood for a hidden cat when Freak's father suddenly stood up from a lawn chair on the far side of the pile. Water was trickling down his face. His eyes looked like they were about to bug out of his head. He pointed a beer can at Freak and shouted, "Whaddya think you're doin'?"

Freak barely gave him a glance. "Looking for Mucus!" he said.

Freak's father moved faster than the cat had. He came around the woodpile with his hand raised like he might strike

Freak, but he tripped over a log and went sprawling. He lurched to his knees and struck out at the air in front of him.

"Don't you ever talk to me that way again!" he bellowed, slurring most of the words.

Fiona and I stepped forward, standing protectively on either side of Freak, making sure his father could see his son had friends.

"This doesn't concern you," he growled. I half expected his snout to elongate and his teeth to grow. I wanted to explain to him that Mucus was the name of his neighbor's cat, and that Freak wasn't being disrespectful. I started to speak, but Freak caught my eye and shook his head.

I kept my mouth shut, but Fiona didn't. She blurted, "He didn't do anything!"

Freak's father ignored her. He staggered to his feet, waved at the wood his son had scattered, and said, "You can stack this back up later. Now get in the house!"

Freak bolted in through the back door. Mr. Nesterii looked at us and sniffed. "You two should go home now," he said, following his son into the house and slamming the door behind him.

The noise spooked Mucus, who emerged from the woodpile, still with Double Six in his mouth. The cat scooted under the fence and headed into Hellsboro.

Escape from the Cell

Sunday was chilly and bright. I met up with Freak and Fiona at the Underhill gate shortly after twelve o'clock. The gate snapped shut behind us as soon as we were in. I looked back through the iron bars and watched a big black car drive slowly by. It might have been tourists looking for a glimpse of Hellsboro. People sometimes came looking. It didn't take long for most to realize that watching an underground fire was about as exciting as watching a submarine race from the beach.

I couldn't see any bruises on Freak, so I thought maybe his father had calmed down once the two of them had gone into the house the previous night. Fiona and I had lingered, pressing ourselves against the back wall of the house, listening for sounds of an argument. We hadn't heard any. I was impressed that Fiona had stood up to Mr. Nesterii. I was ashamed that I hadn't.

"You did enough heroic stuff for one day," Fiona had consoled me after I confided in her. "You can't expect to be a hero all the time."

"I don't see why not," I'd said. River Man was always supposed to be there when you needed him. He always got his feet wet. He always waded right in.

The three of us walked up the center of the driveway, no longer caring if we were seen from above, and Alf met us at the servants' entrance. "Good. You wore old clothes. I can guarantee you're going to get dirty."

He led us through the house. At one point I thought I heard the sound of an ax striking wood. I spun around quickly, but saw nothing. Freak and Fiona didn't seem to notice.

A set of double doors in the main entry hall opened into a large room with many French doors along one side and a cobweb-covered chandelier hanging from the center of the ceiling. Furniture draped with dusty bedsheets lined the opposite wall. The room was almost as big as the gymnasium back at school. A hundred people could have danced in it easily.

"This was a grand house in its day," said Alf. He was wearing blue jeans and a gray pullover sweater with a bit of white T-shirt visible at the neck. He looked like someone you might run into in downtown Cheshire.

"You're wearing twenty-first-century clothing," I observed.

"It's how I usually dress," Alf acknowledged. "The clothing I was wearing when I first met you I found in one of the cedar closets upstairs. Possibly belonged to Underhill's father. I thought wearing it might convey a feeling of lovable eccentricity."

"It didn't."

"I sensed as much."

In the center of the ballroom were three stepladders and a table covered with cleaning supplies. "We have until Saturday to make the ballroom presentable," Alf reminded us. "I also want the foyer cleaned and then furnished with some pieces I've found in the attic. If you spread the work out over the next six days, we should be in good shape by the night of the auction." Alf turned to Fiona. "What kind of response are we getting to the auction invitations?"

Fiona's fingers tap-danced on her phone until her e-mail showed up. She turned the screen so that Alf could see it.

"WaxLips is coming," she informed us. "He wanted to know if there would be refreshments. As soon as I said yes, he confirmed he would be here."

"I suspect," said Alf, gently taking the phone from her and thumbing through the entries, "whoever Lips is, he or she lives fairly close and will be attending solely for the food. I see the Rochester Toy Museum will be sending a representative. They seem a bit annoyed that telephone bidding will not be allowed. And—ahh! GORLAB appears to be a sheik of the Unaligned Emirates. That could easily be Edward Disin, traveling in disguise as a wealthy Arab toy collector."

"We haven't heard from Alecto yet," Fiona said.

"I am sure we will, considering how enthusiastically she was bidding when the auction was online. Good work."

Alf started to hand the phone back to Fiona, but Freak intercepted it, turned his back to Fiona, and began scrolling through her mail.

"GIVE ME THAT!"

"I want to see the GORLAB thing," Freak started to explain, but Fiona was all over him. She grabbed the phone, but Freak wouldn't let go. He yanked one way, she yanked the other, and one of her yanks sent the phone flying through the air. It hit the floor and disappeared beneath one of the bedsheet-covered pieces of furniture. Fiona threw herself down on the floor in front of it and flailed her arms under it in a desperate search. She found nothing. Not even dust bunnies.

"YOU'VE LOST MY PHONE!" she screeched.

"You're the one who lost it," Freak corrected her.

"It was remiss of me not to have taken it away myself," I heard Alf say under his breath. "What was I thinking?" Then, in a much louder voice, "I'm sure it will turn up! Searching for it will be good motivation to clean the room thoroughly. Why don't you get started? I'll be back in a bit. I have to call a man about some balloons."

He left as Fiona began sputtering about how her life would be ruined if she didn't get her phone back.

"You're aware that that phone has turned you into a zombie, aren't you?" Freak asked her. "That, and your enthusiasm for Agra Nation® Home-Style Alphabet Soup? 'The soup that puts a spell on you'?" he added, quoting the TV commercial.

"Obviously, the damage has already been done," she snapped back at him. "If what you tell me is true and I'm singing along with everybody else in the flash mobs."

"But maybe the damage can be reversed," I said, pulling

the sheet off the piece of furniture under which Fiona's phone had vanished.

The sofa was there, looking smug. I flipped the cushion that should have had the bloodstain on it. The cushion was clean, and the slash along the back was gone.

"It's no longer dressed as a pirate," I said.

"The ghost costume is much better," said Freak, nodding at the sheet in my hand.

"GIVE ME BACK MY CELL PHONE!" said Fiona, and she punched the sofa in the middle of its three seat cushions. Her fist sank into the cushion up to her wrist and when she drew her hand back, the cushion came with it. She looked like a cartoon character with a mallet for a fist.

"Get it off me!" she hollered. Freak and I grabbed the cushion and pulled one way while Fiona pulled the other. For a brief moment I envisioned Fiona spending the rest of her life as Pillow-Hand Girl in a circus freak show. Then the cushion let go and she fell backward on her butt.

"Definitely the same sofa," Freak acknowledged as I returned the cushion to its place. It was impossible to tell Fiona's fist had ever been in it.

"You put the OAF in SOFA!" Fiona spat at it. "How can I live without my cell?"

"Maybe if you don't use it for a few days, you won't feel like jumping up and singing show tunes when everybody else does," I said. "We know the next flash mob is scheduled for Wednesday at twelve seventeen. That's three days from now. Do you think you could go without using your cell for that long?"

Fiona hugged herself tightly and bit her lip. "I suppose I could try."

"Freak and I will help you," I assured her. "If you feel the need to talk to your friends, try talking to us."

"Or if we're not around you could just hold a bar of soap to the side of your head," Freak suggested.

There was a sound like *whuff!* from behind us and we turned around.

The sofa was gone.

"Whoa!" said Freak.

"Told you." I nudged Fiona. "You shouldn't have called it an oaf. You hurt its feelings."

"Furniture doesn't have feelings," she protested, surveying the empty spot like she still expected to find her cell.

"The sofa does," I said. "It feels..."

"What?"

"Comfy."

• • • • •

Over the course of the next week, Fiona got more and more sullen and argumentative. Freak and I guessed it was because she didn't have her phone. She could have borrowed one from any of the kids at school, but she was using her willpower not to. I didn't admit it to Freak, but I admired her for that.

On Monday, for the first time ever, Fiona sat with Freak and me at our school lunch table. She said she hadn't used a cell in over twenty-four hours, but her resolve was weakening and she needed our support. When she started shaking too badly, Freak gave her an unopened can of sardines, which she clutched eagerly and held to the side of her head.

On Tuesday Fiona looked ashen. She sat on both her hands and spoke in single-word sentences.

Wednesday, at exactly twelve seventeen, almost everybody in the lunchroom stood up and faced east. Freak and I watched, horrified, as Fiona joined them. Maybe the mind control wasn't reversible. Maybe we were all doomed.

The brainwashed student body patted the tops of their heads with their left hands and rubbed their stomachs with their right. Then they started to rub their heads with their right hands and pat their stomachs with their left. Fiona fell out of sync. She looked increasingly confused, until her eyes suddenly focused and she sat down abruptly.

I'm sure she would have texted "OMG!" if she'd had something to text with.

"Turkey," said Freak, looking straight at her.

"Excuse me?"

"Cold turkey," replied Freak. "That's what it's called when somebody suddenly quits something they're addicted to. It's not easy. My father hasn't been able to do it. You did." Freak's eyes darted around, looking at everybody as they sang. "It's something to be proud of."

"So nobody has to be enslaved by Disin's mind control," I said. "The effects can be reversed."

"Yeah," said Freak, frowning. "All they have to do is go without their phones for three days. How likely is that?"

Fiona climbed up on the lunch table and looked around. She spotted Nails Norton, the girl who had dumped strawberry Jell-O on her, four tables away. Nails was belting out, *"Anything you can do, I can do better!"* at the top of her lungs.

Fiona jumped down from the table, swept everything off her lunch tray, and headed straight for Nails. Along the way, she scooped up bowls of Jell-O from other kids' trays and emptied them onto the one she was carrying. When she reached Nails, Fiona dipped her finger in the gelatin and dabbed the letter *L* on Nails's forehead as Nails continued to sing. Then Fiona replaced Nails's chair with the tray of Jell-O. The flavor of the day was raspberry.

By the time the song ended, Fiona had already returned to her seat. As everybody sat back down, there was a loud *splat!* and a scream from Nails's direction. This was followed by the loudest round of applause ever.

Nails scrambled to her feet. Her formerly white pants now had a bright red stain on the seat. Her face turned the same shade of red. She grabbed a sweater from one of her friends and tied it around her waist.

"Anything she can do, I can do better," Fiona declared, and helped herself to one of Freak's french fries.

• • • • •

At Underhill House that week, things were pretty tame—until Thursday rolled around.

On Saturday we had cleaned the ballroom's ceiling and the chandelier. Sunday we washed all of the glass in the French doors. After school on Monday we scrubbed down the walls. Tuesday we washed the floor. We stepped outside as frequently as we could, shaking out dust rags, snapping towels, and jumping around like two-year-olds to convince anybody watching from above that the place was swarming with kids. Yesterday we saw a distant black helicopter overhead.

Finally, this afternoon we decorated the ballroom, putting tablecloths on tables and setting up eighty folding chairs facing a stage that, long ago, had held musicians. We stretched streamers from the arms of the chandelier to the four walls until the ceiling looked like the underside of a colorful tent.

"We still have the balloons to inflate," said Alf. "But that can wait until Saturday."

"Shouldn't we start that now?" said Fiona. "Is there a helium tank? I'm very good at filling them without breaking them. Do we have enough to make an arch? Can we tie bunches to each chair? Are they different colors?" Fiona had been energized ever since she'd gotten over the painful withdrawal of giving up her phone. She stood straighter and worked harder. Freak and I could barely keep up.

"There are two different colors." Alf sighed, overwhelmed by Fiona's newfound energy. "And we'll do it Saturday."

"Are all these things really necessary?" demanded Freak, taping a Halloween party decoration to the wall.

"We have to convince Disin this is a real auction," I assured him. We had managed to resist the temptation to tell

Alf we knew about Indorsia and Miranda and that Edward Disin was his father. It would have made things easier, but it also would have revealed to Alf that Guernica and Miranda were working behind his back, putting us in more jeopardy than he was comfortable with.

"Yes," confirmed Alf, tapping the Halloween decoration lightly on its pitchfork. "The devil is in the details."

Alf left us on our own then. He had been leaving us for longer and longer stretches as his trust in our ability to work unsupervised grew. I assumed Guernica was continuing to fake the telemetry coming from Double Six. Alf could see we were in his house. True telemetry from Double Six might have placed us halfway to Harrisburg, or wherever it was the cat had gone. Nobody had seen Mucus since he took off with the domino.

We had the run of the first floor of the house. When we weren't in the ballroom, we were usually in the kitchen, rinsing out our mops and dust rags. When we took breaks, we took them outside.

During one of our breaks, I said, "Why don't we make snow angels?"

"Because there's no snow?" Freak asked reasonably.

"That wouldn't stop a toddler," I said, throwing myself

flat on my back, staring into the clear blue sky, and thrashing my arms through the grass.

"He's right," said Fiona, throwing herself down next to me and doing the same. "Seen from above, this has to make us look totally preschool."

"Great," said Freak, joining us. "Afterward, we can build a no man. Or a no fort. Or maybe have a no ball fight. Or we could go—"

"Okay!" Fiona interrupted him, before he could say "no boarding." "We get it."

• • • • •

Later that day, as I was coming out of the kitchen with a bucket of soapy water, I stepped on a doghat.

The doghat wasn't on the doghat's head. The hat was off to one side of the hallway floor, like maybe it had been tucked into a back pocket and fallen out without its owner realizing. It looked like a cross between a cocker spaniel and a poodle. I raced back to the ballroom.

"There's a cockapoo in the building!" I hissed in a loud whisper.

"It was probably left by the raccoon," said Freak, who was

up on a ladder, polishing prisms in the chandelier. "You didn't step in it, did you?"

"No. I mean, yes! Look!" I waved the hat at him. He slid down the ladder. Fiona rushed over.

"Did we leave the door open again?" asked Freak.

"No," said Fiona. "I'm positive we closed it."

"Then this guy snuck in some other way. I wonder what he's up to."

"He's probably hoping to steal the crayon," suggested Fiona. "Maybe it's Edward Disin!"

"Disin wouldn't be wearing a cockapoo hat. He certainly wouldn't drop it in the hall. He's too smart for that."

"If he's so smart," I said, "how come he hires such stupid henchmen?"

"Shh!" said Fiona. There had been a sound from the hall.

The ballroom's double doors were wide open. A shadow against the hall's opposite wall told us that someone was approaching.

"Hide!" hissed Freak.

We threw ourselves under a long tablecloth-covered table and peeked out through a gap in the cloth.

Cockapoo loomed in the doorway. He was a tall man

dressed all in black and holding a water pistol. Whatever kind of liquid shot out of the pistol probably contained something you had to be vaccinated against.

He walked slowly into the room and stopped next to our table, nearly stepping on my hand. We froze as he stuck the pistol into a shoulder holster and picked up one end of the tablecloth.

We were totally exposed. He had found us.

He didn't see us. He was using the end of the tablecloth to polish the lens of a camera he had pulled from his jacket.

After a moment he walked to the center of the room and started taking pictures. *Most likely*, I thought, *to help Edward Disin plan his escape from the crayon auction.*

Then the doghat pulled out another device and walked the length of the ballroom, holding it over his head. When a red light on it started blinking, Cockapoo fiddled with the molding around one of the room's decorative wall panels.

After a few seconds, the panel slid aside. Cockapoo disappeared through it.

"I dusted that entire wall," whispered Fiona. "If I had known to look for a secret passage—"

"You wouldn't have found it," Freak finished for her. "Come on!"

We followed Freak as he slipped out from under the table. We scurried out of the room on all fours, only standing up after we had rounded the corner. Then we leaned cautiously around the edge of the doorway and looked back into the room.

"One of us should go find Alf," said Freak.

"That was too close," I said.

"I'll say," said Fiona.

"*Tch-tch*," said the lady with the ax.

We turned. She was standing right behind us. She raised the ax and lunged.

We bolted back into the ballroom.

State Fair Omaha

It didn't seem fair that in addition to doghats, and mind control, and Edward Disin, we also had to deal with something as unscientific as a ghost.

The old lady chased us unscientifically into the ballroom. The French doors were open, to air the place out, and we raced toward them, skating on a floor we had waxed less than an hour earlier. I slipped, fell on my back, and looked up to see the old lady's ax rushing down at me like a guillotine blade.

Just because the ax had passed harmlessly through us the first time didn't mean it would happen that way again. Maybe ghostly axes passed through you sometimes and maybe sometimes they didn't. We weren't eager to find out. Freak grabbed me by the foot, sliding me to the right, and the ax whizzed by my ear. Fiona grabbed my hand and helped me to my feet, and the three of us dove for the open doors, only to have the old lady materialize in our path. She shrieked and swung her ax maniacally at us, barely missing our necks.

We screamed, turned, and ran the other way. I collided with a stepladder, and a bucket of soapy water came crashing down from the top, splashing across the floor and making the slippery surface even slicker. We ran in place just to keep from falling, and the lady shot in like a homicidal hockey player to mow us down.

Freak got traction and pushed Fiona and me ahead of him. We skidded across the ballroom and headed for the open panel where Cockapoo had disappeared.

We collided with him as he was coming out.

He was knocked back into the secret passage, and Freak and Fiona went sprawling on the floor in front of it. Not being quite as fast as they were, I was the one who was still standing when Cockapoo popped back out. So I was the one he aimed his water pistol at.

"Looks like somebody could use a dose of Hista Mime!" he snarled.

Hista Mime! The Silent Killer! One drop of it on my skin and I would suffocate, unable to call out, convinced I was trapped in an airless glass box!

He took a step toward me, a menacing smirk on his face, and pulled the trigger just as the old lady appeared to his right and swung her ax at his outstretched hand. He let out a yelp and turned to fire at her, the liquid from his gun's first shot still arcing through the air at me.

I dove out of the way just in time as the last of the liquid from the pistol passed right through the ghost. It spattered on the floor and sizzled, turning the polished stone a sickly shade of gray. The ghost roared at him, swinging her ax even more insanely.

Cockapoo broke away from her and ran. He headed for the French doors with Ax Lady swinging at his back, crossed the patio, and jumped the hedge at the patio's edge. He quickly disappeared into the woods beyond. Freak and I stumbled to the French doors and watched him go.

Ax Lady had vanished the moment she got to the doors. I spun around quickly, expecting her to show up behind us. But the ballroom was empty.

"Where's Fiona?" asked Freak, looking around wildly.

We raced back to the secret passage, where we found

Fiona standing in the center of a small room, hugging herself. She was looking at a revivarium. It was one of the coffin-like cylinders that could be used to clone a new person or to put the mind of one person into the body of another. We had seen four of them in the men's room at Rodmore Chemical.

"Would you say that's my size?" Fiona asked, nodding at the thing.

"I'd say anybody could fit in there," said Freak. "Miranda made it pretty clear she's against Alf's idea of reviving her by putting her mind into your head. I think Alf regrets he ever thought of it in the first place."

"Miranda could be lying," replied Fiona. "And Alf may still be toying with the idea. It might explain why he seems to be of two minds when it comes to telling us anything."

"Double Six says we have to decide who we can trust," I reminded them. "I say we trust Alf." When Freak gave me a look, I added, "And we watch one another's backs."

"Let's get out of here," Freak said, exiting the room and pulling Fiona along with him.

I held back for a moment. The revivarium was the biggest thing in the room. Tables and benches lined the walls, littered with everything from electronic gear and chemicals to floor wax and garbage bags. I put my hand on the revivarium.

The palm of my hand tingled where I touched it. I was pretty sure I could hear a faint hum. I got the impression the revivarium might be running at some low level. Doing what, I had no idea.

I shivered and followed my friends back through the panel. No sooner had Freak finished sliding the panel back into place than Alf came striding into the ballroom. I pretended to polish the panel with the sleeve of my sweatshirt. Freak kicked me and I stopped.

"I don't wish to alarm you," said Alf, oblivious to what had just happened, "but Guernica informs me we may have an intruder. There's been a car parked on Breeland for the past twenty minutes. I want you to stay right here while I search the place."

"Don't bother," Freak told him. "It was a doghat. Maybe a cockapoo." Freak pointed to where I had dropped the doghat's doghat. "He went running out those doors a couple of minutes ago."

"The three of you scared him away?" Alf sounded unconvinced.

"Actually," I said, "it was your ghost who scared him. You *do* know your house is haunted?"

"It's not," said Alf.

"A little old lady? With an ax? And a detachable jaw?"

"Oh. Gram."

"She's your *grammy*?"

"Hologrammy. Yes. That's what I call her. She's a holo-gram. I modeled her after my father's mother. He was always scared to death of her."

"I can see why," I said.

"Oh, I exaggerated some things. She never used an ax. She preferred poisoned daggers. Hologrammy was my early attempt at a security system. She was supposed to scare intruders away. Even from the start, she behaved erratically. Then the part of Guernica that controlled her got damaged."

"Lost in a fire?" I said. I had put two and two together: The missing hassock had been in charge of Hologrammy.

"Why would you say that?" asked Alf suspiciously.

"I have an overactive imagination."

"Well, it was a good guess. It was a fire. And I haven't seen Hologrammy since. Otherwise, I would have warned you about her. But now something seems to have reactivated her. Maybe the three of you."

"Or maybe the doghat," said Freak.

"Right," said Alf. "The doghat. We should get up to the gallery and see what Guernica can tell us about our intruder."

Guernica replayed the gate-camera footage for us. The doghat had pole-vaulted over the front gate, collided with a low-hanging tree branch, landed on his head, and driven away. It would have been funny, if it hadn't been scary.

• • • • •

On Friday Alf presented us with waiters' uniforms. For the auction, he wanted us dressed in starchy white shirts, black vests, and black bow ties. We tried them on and Alf drilled us on how to walk around the ballroom with serving trays full of snacks. Shoulders back, no slouching. Always determine if the guests are right-handed or left-handed, then approach them from the opposite side so they can more comfortably reach across themselves to snag their snacks. Once they've sucked the cheese cube or the cocktail frank off the tooth-pick, present them with a smaller tray for discarded tooth-picks. Press a button on the underside of the tray to cause the tray to analyze the DNA in the saliva on the toothpick.

"Really?" said Freak.

"Really," confirmed Alf. "If the DNA matches that of Edward Disin, the tray will glow. The moment that happens, you signal me, and I will signal the federal agents."

"What if he's not hungry?" I asked. "What if he doesn't eat anything off a toothpick?"

"We will also be serving drinks. A used drinking glass turned upside down on the DNA tray will also register."

"Will these be alcoholic drinks?" Freak asked.

The question caught Alf off guard.

"Yes," he said after a pause. "But you don't have to serve them."

"Yeah," said Freak. "I would prefer that."

• • • • •

When I got home that evening, my aunt gave me the photographs I had asked her to get developed. There was an okay picture of me shaking hands with a guy dressed like Benjamin Franklin; and a pretty funny one of Freak looking guilty in front of the Liberty Bell, like he was the one who had put the crack in it; and three completely dark, blurry, useless pictures taken in the basement of Rodmore Chemical that could just as easily have been taken inside one of my socks.

Our dangerous trip to the heart of Hellsboro had gotten us nothing.

When I showed the pictures to Freak and Fiona, Freak

kicked the wall and Fiona pouted. The three of us agreed: If we had any hopes of stopping Edward Disin, it had to be by getting him arrested at the auction. We certainly had nothing to prove an unearthly portal existed in the basement of his chemical factory.

. . . . .

Saturday afternoon. The day of the auction. I couldn't sleep the night before. Freak and I were as hyper as Fiona had been ever since she'd quit her phone, and the three of us followed Alf around like cartwheeling monkeys, trying to make sure everything was perfect—polishing glasses, rearranging chairs, tugging tablecloths back and forth. Alf finally took us outside to help inflate the balloons.

He'd been correct about there being two colors: one for each.

Both balloons were on the patio, just outside the ballroom's French doors. Each was stuffed in its own canvas bag, leaning against its own wicker basket.

"Hot air balloons," said Fiona.

"Of course," said Alf. "What other kind of balloons would we be using?"

"These are, what?" I asked. "Decorations?"

"No," replied Alf. "They're scarecrows."

Alf went to the nearest bag and pulled open the drawstrings. He started pulling out yards and yards of brightly colored nylon fabric.

"The patio, and the lawn beyond it, is the only open place on the property where a helicopter might land," he said, indicating with hand gestures that we should help him unpack the fabric and spread it over the ground. "The trees make it impossible anywhere else on the grounds, and the steep pitch of the roof makes it impossible to land on the house itself. We're going to fill these two balloons with hot air and tether them side by side."

"You're expecting Disin to arrive by helicopter?" Freak asked as we teased the fabric into a large oval shape and spread it out over the grass. "Like Santa Claus at the mall?"

"I'm expecting him to arrive by automobile. I'm expecting him to try to *escape* by helicopter. He knows full well this is some kind of trap. But it's the nature of Compulsive Completist Disorder that he has to be here himself. He has to be planning to have a stealth chopper handy should he need to break and run."

"Couldn't the helicopter drop a rope ladder?"

"Not with all these overhanging trees. Not with the balloons filling in the empty space."

"Couldn't a helicopter just shoot down the balloons?" I asked.

"Bullets would pass right through. You'd have to strafe to bring one of these down quickly, and that much gunfire would be too dangerous to anyone on the ground, Edward Disin included. It would also attract too much attention at a time when Disin doesn't want anyone looking too closely at the town of Cheshire."

"Couldn't he escape by using one of the balloons?" asked Fiona.

"I hope he tries. Balloons can't be steered. He'd be a sitting duck if he tried to take one. Not to mention I've rigged these so I can release the baskets from a distance by remote control. There are explosive bolts at each connecting clip. Should Edward Disin try to ascend in one, he'll find himself falling back to earth very quickly."

"The balloons are a trap," I said astutely.

"They are a contingency plan, should the Feds have difficulty getting handcuffs on him."

We helped Alf inflate the first balloon, using ropes to secure its basket to stakes in the ground and then using a large electric fan to fill the nylon part—Alf called it the envelope—with air. When the envelope was half full, we heated the air in it with a propane-powered burner. The hot air caused the envelope to rise.

After about half an hour, the fully inflated balloon loomed over me like Morgue MacKenzie demanding all my lunch money.

We walked away from it and looked back so we could see it more clearly. It was a bright, orangey red.

"I've seen this balloon before," said Fiona.

We all had. Huge words in old-fashioned lettering appeared on its side. They said STATE FAIR OMAHA.

"It's a replica of the balloon seen at the end of the movie *The Wizard of Oz*," Alf acknowledged. "I bought it from the owners, who are big Judy Garland fans." He glanced at his watch. "Let's get the other one up."

The other balloon wasn't in the conventional shape of a balloon. This became obvious as soon as we spread the envelope out on the ground. The white fabric stretched out in a weird L shape.

"There are hot air balloons in the shape of Noah's Ark, the Taj Mahal, and George Washington's head," Alf said, starting up the fan. The stark white envelope began to stir. "There's a famous one of a pig with wings."

"What is this one in the shape of?" I asked.

"You'll see."

After a while the envelope rose into the air. It still had some folds and floppy parts that made it hard to see what it was.

"It's some kind of chair," said Freak.

"It's a big, puffy throne," said Fiona.

"Get some distance," suggested Alf.

As we ran out to the side, the hot air in the envelope filled out the remaining kinks and the balloon assumed its finished shape.

"It's a toilet," I announced.

It was a huge toilet bowl complete with a flush tank and a clearly visible flush lever. It must have been six stories high. The drainpipe was the hole in the bottom that the hot air rose up through. The basket dangled beneath the drainpipe.

"Its registered name is Porcelain Cloud," Alf said, coming up beside us. "But everybody calls it the Dear John, after the name of the company that originally commissioned it. Dear John, before it went out of business, was a supplier of portable privies to construction sites, county fairs, and balloonist conventions. I was able to get the balloon cheap when they were forced to liquidate their assets. And trust me, you don't want to be anywhere near a portable privy company when they're liquidating their assets."

The three of us stared upward, our mouths hanging open.

"Obviously designed by a man," Fiona finally said, and started to walk away.

"How do you know?" asked Freak.

Fiona tossed her head.

"The seat is up."

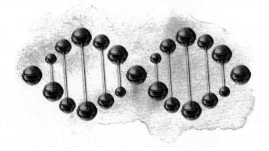

CHAPTER
21

Auction Lots and Lollipops

ifty-six people attended the zucchini crayon auction, including the two federal agents who were there to arrest Edward Disin. Freak and Fiona and I were kept hopping, serving everybody drinks and hors d'oeuvres. I kept looking over my shoulder, expecting to see a dangerous man with a small army come bursting through the door.

"That's not the way it's supposed to happen," Freak reminded me, nervously watching a tall man in a tuxedo we both thought looked like a possible villain. "He's supposed to be here in disguise."

"Any one of these people could be Disin," Fiona whis-

pered, using the shiny surface of her DNA tray as a rearview mirror to study a large woman standing behind her. "But most of them look so normal!"

"That's the scary part." I shivered. We had already met Edward Disin once. I was in no rush to meet him again, especially if I wasn't wearing a hazmat suit.

"Yeah," agreed Freak. "I've never trusted normal."

Alf circulated through the ballroom disguised with a beard and a wig and a reasonably convincing false nose. His own father wouldn't have recognized him. I assumed that was the point.

The federal agents didn't want to be there. I could tell. They shook our hands without enthusiasm when Alf introduced us. Ms. Beauceron was a tall blond woman in a stiff-looking gray suit, and she spent most of the time on her cell phone. Mr. North was a beefy-looking, square-jawed guy who kept his mirrored sunglasses on and had hair deliberately moussed to appear windblown. He was chewing a piece of gum, giving it one deliberate chew per minute. I thought maybe he was trying to quit.

Neither one of the agents smiled as they sat down near the back on either side of the aisle. Alf shrugged. "I have a friend in the Treasury Department. If she hadn't owed me a favor, I probably would not have been able to convince them to send anybody."

"What?" said Freak. "They didn't believe your story about a crazy billionaire risking his freedom to buy a crayon?"

"Sarcasm is not your best trait," Alf replied, and pointed at a guest who was looking around for a place to discard a toothpick. Fiona glided over and presented her DNA tray. The toothpick was not a winner.

"Check out the guy in the overalls," Freak whispered.

Alf told us the guy in the overalls was an artist named Avram Belize who wanted to win the zucchini crayon and then film a documentary of himself drawing a picture with it. He was bent over the glass case of the preview table, intently studying Jackson Pollock's coloring book.

"You think he might be Disin?" I asked Freak.

"I think he might be an escaped lunatic," said Freak. "Half the people here might be. They want to pay us thousands of dollars for a *crayon*."

I wasn't sure about thousands of dollars. Some people seemed like they had just come for fun. WaxLips was there. Lips turned out to be a middle-aged woman whose real name was Martha Ellinger. I overheard her saying she knew she didn't have a chance at winning *the* crayon, but she was absolutely thrilled to be in a room with so many other crayon collectors.

There was a tall black woman who stood ramrod straight and never smiled and didn't look like she had ever been interested in crayons, even when she was a kid. I overheard her give her name as Cicely Shillingham, but Alf whispered, "Alecto," in my ear when he saw me watching her.

The guests were divided pretty evenly between museum representatives and well-to-do toy collectors. The museum people, I noticed, ate more.

By far the most interesting person there was Sheik Geisel al-Rashid, a black-bearded man in full Arabian burnoose and headdress. He had arrived in an armored Hummer with diplomatic plates, which Alf insisted he park on Breeland Road along with the rest of the guests' cars. The sheik and his driver had walked up the hill to the house just like everybody else.

Sheik Geisel looked at us sternly as he entered and shook his head when I offered to take his hat. His driver wore a black uniform and kept his chauffeur's cap on and pulled down in front.

"Either of these guys could be a werewolf," Freak said to me out of the corner of his mouth.

We escorted the sheik to the ballroom. He gathered his

robes together and went to the display of auction items, lingering over a sketch by an artist named René Magritte showing a man who had crayons for teeth. He then continued on to the zucchini crayon, moving all around the display case to see it from every possible angle.

"I say, if he breaks the glass, we tackle him." Freak looked to me for agreement. I nodded. The sheik slipped something that might have been a glass cutter out of one of his sleeves.

"We need DNA proof!" Fiona hissed.

"Then we'll hit him so hard, we'll knock the snot out of him!" Freak was getting psyched. He tensed like he was listening for the starter's pistol.

The crayon was cradled in gray foam rubber in the center of a thin wooden box. The sheik flicked the object in his hand and a magnifying lens popped out of it. He asked Alf if he could see the crayon more closely. Alf hesitated, then slowly unlocked the display case and passed him the wooden box with the crayon inside.

I fully expected him to take the box and run. I got ready to give chase. Freak, I could tell, was about to spring. But the sheik merely looked the crayon up and down with his magnifier and then handed the box back. Freak stumbled forward as the tension broke.

I didn't waste any time before I approached the sheik with a tray full of pigs in a blanket. He looked at the tray, looked at me, and said, "We do not eat pork."

"They're not really pigs," I explained. "And they're not really blankets, before you tell me you don't eat wool. The caterer says they're all-beef franks."

He held up a hand.

"Nevertheless."

I moved away. A minute or two later I returned, having switched trays with Freak.

"Pizza roll?"

He looked at the tray and frowned.

"We are watching our cholesterol."

"The ones on this end are low-fat."

"Nevertheless."

I returned a minute or two later, having exchanged trays with Fiona.

"Champagne?"

He looked at me and sighed.

"We do not drink."

"You don't? Don't you get awfully thirsty out there in the desert?"

He studied me with a pained expression.

"We do not drink alcohol."

"Oh. Well. Can I get you a juice box?"

"Young man," said the sheik, "upon completing your education, is it your intention to pursue a career in the hospitality industry?"

I thought about it for a moment. "No," I said.

"Good."

The sheik held his hand out to his driver. The driver reached into the interior of his jacket, the way I had seen people on TV do when they were going for a gun, and pulled out a little yellow ball on a stick. The sheik stuck it in his mouth and began sucking on it. His driver held out his arm, indicating I should leave. I did.

Martha Ellinger—WaxLips—plucked a glass from my tray as I passed her, and I started to worry about what might happen to all the innocent people in the room if things got out of hand once we found Disin. Clusters of people were everywhere, chatting, laughing, totally oblivious to the possibility of a power-mad lunatic in their midst. I wanted to lean into their conversations and suggest they practice ducking.

Fiona and Freak were just as nervous as I was. It was getting late and we still hadn't found Disin.

"So far," said Fiona, "there are only three people I haven't been able to get DNA samples from. They've refused everything I've offered them. The woman from the Tate Gallery says she's on a diet. The sheik's driver won't even look at me when I come around with a tray. And the tall guy from the toy museum says he has something called irritable bowel syndrome and if he eats anything, it could seriously disrupt the auction."

"I don't even want to think about what that might mean," said Freak. "Why does Alf have us testing the women? Does he think Edward Disin is that good of an actor?"

"Who knows what he's capable of?" I said. "He made a pretty passable werewolf the last time we saw him."

Freak nodded and moved off to offer a woman from the Museum of Modern Art some cocktail shrimp.

"Sheik Geisel is sucking on a lollipop," I whispered to Fiona. "We have to watch and see when he's ready to throw away the stick."

I left Fiona watching the sheik and went outside to check on the balloons. Alf had instructed us to give them a blast of hot air every half hour. The State Fair Omaha was upright and straining at its tethers. The Dear John was listing slightly to one side. I climbed up into the basket and fired the burner the way Alf had shown me. After a couple of minutes, the toilet righted itself.

I looked around for circling helicopters and nearly jumped out of my skin when I saw a pair of eyes staring hungrily at me from a nearby tree. I blasted the burner again and the flame revealed an owl, who hooted angrily and darted away. I scurried back to the ballroom.

With only five minutes remaining until the start of the auction, we had yet to find Disin. What if he hadn't come? Or what if he was outside, waiting to pounce on whoever won the crayon? Or worse, what if he was there in the room, but he had figured out the DNA trays, and he was somehow using somebody else's spit?

"He can't be using somebody else's spit!" said Fiona, nearly spitting herself.

"It happens in movies all the time," I argued. "The bad guy needs certain fingerprints to unlock a door, so he cuts off somebody's hand to get them."

"What kind of movies do you watch?" muttered Fiona.

"How do you cut off somebody's saliva?" asked Freak.

"By showing them something unappetizing," said Alf, coming up behind us. "I assure you, he's not using anybody else's spit. If he's here, the DNA trays will find him. Now, get back to work! I'm about to start the auction—you have to find him soon! We're running out of time!"

While I had been checking the balloons, the guy from the toy museum had stepped out on the lawn and smoked a cigarette. Freak had retrieved the butt and placed it on his DNA tray. Negative.

Fiona had seen the dieting woman from the Tate put her auction program between her teeth as she used both hands to rummage through her purse. Fiona sneakily managed to snatch the saliva-laced program, replacing it with another so we could test the first. Again, negative.

The sheik was still working on his lollipop.

I saw the sheik's driver take a small bottle of spring water from his coat pocket. The bottle was only partially full. He tilted it back and finished it, then screwed the cap on and slipped the bottle back in his coat.

River Man made it his mission to steal the bottle.

"If you could all find a seat," said Alf, leaning forward on his auctioneer's lectern, "we're ready to begin."

The sheik's driver remained standing as everybody else settled in. I used Cicely Shillingham to block the driver's view of me as she made her way to her seat, and I wound up standing just a few feet behind him. Cicely—Alecto—sat in the back row like a tiger ready to spring.

I was really glad to see her there. Alecto had been

GORLAB's biggest competitor during the online auction, and if Fiona and Freak and I were going to get whatever the crayon sold for, it was important to us that Edward Disin didn't win it too cheaply.

I had thought that once Disin was arrested and there was no longer any threat of him taking over the world, it might be nice if my friends and I had a little spending cash. It might be nice to go a little crazy in Max Schimmelhorn's junk shop, where there was a ten-speed bike that I liked; and a really cool chess set carved, Max assured me, from the wood of a Boojum tree; and a piano that could replace the one my aunt Bernie had sold when our roof had to be fixed. But then the business between Freak and his father at the woodpile had happened, and I realized bikes and games and even pianos weren't all that important. I decided I wanted to give my portion of the money to Freak. He thought paying off some of his father's bills might somehow make his father a better person. If there were any chance of that, I would happily let him have my third. Or most of it, anyway. I planned to talk to Fiona about doing the same.

"I would like to welcome you this evening," declared Alf, "to an auction dedicated to all of us cerophiles. And by cerophiles, of course, I mean crayon lovers. And by crayon lovers, of course, I mean loonies."

Everybody laughed heartily, as if Alf had made a joke, although I wasn't so sure he had. I got up on River Man's tiptoes and snuck closer to the sheik's driver. The driver glanced my way and I bent down and pretended to tie my shoe. Alf finished his introduction and started the bidding.

"Auction lot number one," announced Alf. "An important box of Victory Garden crayons, containing fifteen of the original sixteen colors. There are two rutabaga crayons and, while there is no zucchini, the box does have a leek." Alf held up the box. Two crayons fell out of the bottom, which he deftly caught. "Do I hear one hundred?"

A crayon collector from Topeka scratched the side of his nose.

"Thank you, sir!" said Alf. "Do I hear two?"

Each bidder had his or her own way of making a bid. After a series of head nods, hand gestures, and harrumphs, plus a burp that turned out to be a real burp and not a bid, the Victory Garden box went to the Rochester Toy Museum for $700.

I took two baby steps and put River Man close enough to the driver to pick his pocket.

Alf had accumulated a number of items of interest to crayon collectors. When the bidding on a red crayon once used by the Surgeon General to draw blood reached $500, the sheik took the lollipop out of his mouth and raised it in the air. I was pleased to see the candy was almost gone.

"Six hundred from the sheik," said Alf. "Any advance on six? Any? Going once—"

The crowd was hushed. The sheik's driver leaned forward. I put my thumb and forefinger on the cap of the water bottle.

"Going twice—"

I eased the bottle out of the driver's pocket. River Man, in my head, clenched his fists and said, *YES!*

"Sold to Sheik Geisel al-Rashid for six hundred dollars!" said Alf, and banged his auction gavel. I scooted away from the driver and made my way over to my friends. Fiona held out her DNA tray and I placed the mouth of the bottle on the tray's surface.

The tray did not light up. The driver was not Edward Disin.

My palms started to sweat.

"We've tested fifty-three of the fifty-four auction guests," said Freak, sounding as worried as I felt. "The only one we haven't been able to test is the sheik. By process of elimination, he *has* to be Disin."

"What if he's not?" asked Fiona. "We have to be absolutely sure. The Feds won't arrest him if there's any doubt."

"You'd think Alf would know his own father," I said.

"I'm not so sure about that," said Freak. "There are days when I hardly know mine."

"Knowing and positively identifying are two different things," said Fiona.

"We have to get hold of that lollipop stick!" I declared.

"He's finished the candy," observed Freak, "but he's still sucking on the stick."

"Yeah," agreed Fiona. "My little brother does that."

We watched the sheik. He showed no signs of throwing away his lollipop stick.

"A coloring book attributed to Johannes Gutenberg just before he invented moveable type," said Alf, holding up a leather-bound book with some of the pages falling out. Dust billowed from the book's cover and Alf sneezed violently enough that his nose flew off and ricocheted off the forehead of the lady from the Museum of Modern Art.

"Pardon!" said Alf, slapping a handkerchief to his face and looking panic-stricken.

I froze, wondering if this would make Alf look like a fraud and bring the auction to a crashing halt. All of our work would be down the drain. How many people had actually seen it happen?

Freak fielded the rubber nose, snatching it up from the floor at the museum lady's feet.

"Is this performance art?" inquired the lady.

"It's latex, I think," muttered Freak, racing back to Alf with the nose. Alf turned his back briefly and restored it to his face. It became obvious no one other than the museum lady had really noticed. I began breathing again.

The Uffizi Gallery got the Gutenberg for a quarter of a million dollars. Jackson Pollock's coloring book went to a private collector for an equal amount.

With each lot, the excitement in the room grew. Everybody knew we were getting closer to the night's highlight. There was a louder and louder buzz among the bidders. Fiona, Freak, and I felt more and more panicky.

I glanced over at the two federal agents. They were looking at each other like they might be getting ready to leave.

Then, after forty-five minutes and eighteen auctions, only one auction item remained.

Alf had saved the zucchini crayon for last.

The Lord of the Crayons

Lot nineteen. An important zucchini crayon," said Alf, sounding a little nasal. "Who will start the bidding at one thousand dollars?"

"Why is everything he sells 'important'?" I wondered. "He keeps using that word."

"Maybe 'important' is auction-talk for 'stupid,'" said Freak. "Everything he's called important so far has looked pretty stupid to me."

"You guys"—Fiona sighed—"are so *important*."

I was right. She was beginning to like us.

"Five? Do I hear five? FiveFiveFiveFiveFive—six! Any

advance on six? Make your mark with a zucchini crayon!" Alf threw the comment at Avram Belize, who promptly bid six.

"Be the envy of all the other kids on your block, with your very own zucchini crayon!" brought a bid of seven from the guy from Topeka. "Hold it with your toes; stuff it up your nose—eat it with some cheese; kiss it if you please—if *you're* the high bidder!"

Alf, I could see, was getting cranked up. He was sounding more and more like the fast-talking auctioneers you sometimes saw on TV. What was worse, he was talking in hip-hop rhythm. "Scribble on your legs; fry it with some eggs—make you feel complete; wouldn't that be neat?"

"He's a crayon rapper," said Freak.

I realized Alf was taunting his father. His last rhyme had been a jab at his father's CCD, and it sounded like he was just getting started.

"Use it in the dark; feed it to a shark—you will be fulfilled, when you pay the bill!"

Topeka stood up. He weighed about four hundred pounds. It was possible he was Edward Disin wearing a fat suit. We had about ninety discarded toothpicks, though, that said he wasn't.

"Eight!" said Alf. "EightEightEightEightEight!" It sounded

like he was describing what Topeka had done to most of the hors d'oeuvres.

Avram Belize jumped up and glared at Topeka from across the room.

"Nine!" said Alf. "Any advance on nine?"

Belize and Topeka faced each other like gunslingers in a showdown. Topeka loosened his tie. Sweat broke out on his forehead.

"Twenty. Thousand. Dollars," said Cicely Shillingham slowly and deliberately from the back of the room.

Everybody turned and stared at her. She cocked one eyebrow and sat with her arms folded across her chest like she was ready to take on anybody there.

Belize scowled and threw himself back in his seat. "Out!" he growled. Topeka sighed and lowered himself back onto his chair. The chair creaked a little.

"I have a bid for twenty thousand dollars," said Alf. "Increments of two thousand, please. Do I hear twenty-two?"

Sheik Geisel al-Rashid quietly raised his lollipop stick.

"All right!" said Freak, nudging me with his elbow. "Here we go!"

"Come on, Alecto!" I cheered under my breath, making Cicely Shillingham the home team.

"I have twenty-two for an important zucchini crayon. Make your bid just right—take it home tonight! Do I have twenty-four?"

I held my breath. By the terms of our agreement with Alf, Fiona and Freak and I would share equally in whatever amount the crayon finally sold for. Twenty-four thousand dollars split three ways was eight grand each. I knew of one debt Freak's father had that eight grand would make a decent dent in. I wondered how generous I could bring myself to be with my share.

Then I remembered how Freak's father had treated him when we were trying to catch the cat. If it would help make Freak's life any better, I decided I could be pretty generous.

Cicely Shillingham pretended her hand was a pistol and shot it toward the ceiling.

"Twenty-four," said Alf.

The sheik raised his lollipop stick.

"Twenty-six."

Cicely fired another shot at the ceiling. She brought her index finger to her mouth and blew imaginary smoke away from her fingertip. We hadn't been introduced, but I decided I liked her.

"Write a little poem, when you get it home—BUT you can't begin it, until you win it! Do I hear twenty-eight?"

"Sure," said Cicely, folding her arms back across her chest like playtime was over for the year. "Why not?"

Alf looked at the sheik. The sheik looked at Alf. "No rhyme?" asked the sheik.

"Stick it in your ear; make it disappear," purred Alf.

The sheik once again raised his lollipop stick. By this time, the end of it was pretty well chewed.

"Thirty!" said Alf. "Any advance on thirty?" He looked at Cicely. The silence in the room was so deep, you could have heard a lollipop stick drop. Unfortunately, none did. I thought I saw Alf shake his head ever so slightly. Cicely stared at him and did nothing.

"Thirty thousand dollars for lot nineteen," said Alf. "An important zucchini crayon. Going once, going twice—sold to Sheik Geisel al-Rashid for thirty thousand dollars!"

Alf banged his auction gavel. Everybody applauded.

Freak and Fiona and I let out a loud *whoop!* then linked arms and danced around in a circle, stopping only when we realized we had linked arms and were dancing around in a circle.

"Thank you all for attending," said Alf, banging his gavel again. "Those wishing to settle their accounts may do so with me at the far table. Eight bidders were responsible for procuring all nineteen lots; this should not take long."

Alf headed for a folding card table set up in front of the French doors. As the auction guests started to get up from their seats, Sheik Geisel stood, plucked the lollipop stick from his mouth, and dropped it to the floor.

"Got it!" I said, and raced in with my tray.

I *almost* got it. A group of four people shuffled along the aisle where the sheik had been sitting and, after they had passed, the stick was gone.

The sheik motioned to his driver, and the driver walked briskly to the accounting table. He was not quite quick enough. The representative from the House of Wax, a crayon museum in Los Angeles, got there first. She proceeded to write a check for her auction lot.

I kept my eye on the four people. Fortunately, three of them stopped at the end of the aisle and got involved in a conversation. I ran over to them and shouted, "Congratulations!"

That was my entire plan. Shouting "Congratulations!" I had no idea what came next.

They stopped talking and looked at me.

"Hello," I said, a big smile frozen on my face. I looked desperately around the room. Freak gave me a "What the?" shrug. Fiona was oblivious, gazing down at her feet. Alf was looking desperately around the room, searching for a sign from us.

"One of you," I said, looking at the three expectant faces, "may have...won the door prize! Could you check the bottom of your feet?"

"Check the bottom of our...feet?" said a redheaded lady.

"We're looking for a piece of paper with the word *winner* on it."

"Aren't those things usually on the bottom of our *seat?*"

"Oh!" I said. "Seat! We thought he said feet. Could you check anyway?"

At the accounting table the sheik had produced three fat envelopes from within his burnoose. Alf opened the first envelope and slowly started counting one-hundred-dollar bills, all the while casting nervous glances around the room. The two federal agents positioned themselves on either side of him.

The redheaded lady obligingly sat and stuck her legs out. I looked at the bottom of her shoes. "No, I'm sorry," I said.

"Is that it?" asked one of her friends, bending her left leg back and craning her neck over her shoulder to see.

"No," I said. "That's toilet paper."

None of the three had the lollipop stick. I looked around for the fourth person who had been in the sheik's aisle. Avram Belize. He was standing at the end of the payment line. As I raced over to him, Alf was counting out the second envelope.

"Excuse me, sir," I said breathlessly, "but you've just won a free shoeshine!" I snapped my waiter's towel smartly and bent down. Belize stood solidly on both feet and refused to move.

"I'm wearing paint-spattered overalls," he growled. "Do you think I ever get my shoes shined?"

I stood up. "You've won a shoeshine OR the equivalent value in cash!"

"Really? How much?"

"I'll have to do an estimate."

I dived down again. This time, Belize picked up his feet for me. Stuck in the tread of his right boot was the stick. I grabbed it, stood, and raced over to where Alf could see me.

I held up my DNA tray, placed the lollipop stick against it, and pushed the button.

Nothing happened.

The tray did not glow. The DNA on the stick did not match that of Edward Disin. Alf looked stricken.

He finished counting out the contents of the final envelope. He smiled weakly and handed the box containing the zucchini crayon to the sheik. The sheik bowed formally to Alf and turned to leave. The male Treasury agent—Mr. North— whispered in Alf's ear. Alf shook his head and North frowned. The sheik headed for the door and nobody tried to stop him.

"I don't believe this," said Freak, coming up next to me. "How could Disin not be here?"

Fiona hopped over to us on one foot. She was holding one of her shoes in her hand.

"What's with you?" I asked.

"I stepped in gum," she said, waving her shoe under my nose. "Can you believe it?"

I couldn't believe it. Here, all of our plans had gone wrong, we weren't about to capture Edward Disin, the population of the planet Earth would soon be slaving away in his shipyards singing show tunes, and Fiona was worried about gum on her shoe. She started scraping it off with her tray.

Mr. North cleared his throat authoritatively and seemed to come to a decision. He bolted around the accounting table and trotted across the room, intercepting the sheik just before he and his driver made it to the door.

"Excuse me!" North bellowed, loud enough to get the attention of everyone in the room. "Sheik Geisel al-Rashid? Of the Unaligned Emirates?" The sheik nodded. "I am agent William North of the United States Treasury Department." North flashed his ID. "And I am arresting you in the name of the United States government. You have the right to remain silent..."

We listened, stunned, as North read the sheik his rights.

North's partner, Ms. Beauceron, seemed as much caught off guard as the rest of us, but she recovered quickly and raced over to assist him. Neither one of them had drawn a gun.

"What is the charge?" asked the sheik.

"There is probable cause to believe you are a key figure in a terrorist plot against the United States."

"I have come to this country only to purchase this crayon," said the sheik, waving the box Alf had just given him.

"A crayon," said North, "that could easily be used to draw plans, sketch maps, and send messages inimical to the welfare of the people of the United States. I will take that, thank you." North plucked the box from the sheik's hand. "Cuff them."

The sheik and his driver exchanged glances, and the sheik shook his head as the two were handcuffed.

"This is a very bad example of the worst kind of profiling," said the sheik.

"No," said North, tucking the crayon box into his jacket. "It's a very good example of the worst kind of profiling. Can you explain to me your reasons for wearing a false beard?"

North grabbed the sheik's beard beneath the left ear and pulled. The beard came off the sheik's face with a loud ripping sound.

"I am very self-conscious about the dimple in my chin," explained the sheik. "So I wear the beard to conceal it."

"Why not just grow your own beard?" demanded North.

"Then I would not match my passport photo."

"Your passport is no doubt bogus to begin with. The name Geisel, while similar to the name Faisal, is not a genuine Arabic name. It is, in fact, the real name of beloved children's book author Dr. Seuss."

"My mother was very fond of *The Cat in the Hat*," said the sheik. "You know nothing of the people of the Unaligned Emirates!"

"Watch these two," said North to Ms. Beauceron. "I'm going to the car to radio for backup." North turned to leave.

"Wait a minute," said Fiona. When no one paid her any attention, she shouted, "HEY! WAIT! DON'T LET THAT MAN OUT!" She sprinted toward the Treasury agents, waving her DNA tray in the air.

The chewing gum she'd been prying off her shoe clung to the tray, and the tray was brightly glowing.

There had been only one person in the room chewing gum. That had been Treasury Agent North.

All three of us had offered North and his partner things from our serving trays, but when both had declined, we hadn't pressed them. They were the agents Alf had invited there to arrest Edward Disin. It had never occurred to us that one of those agents might, in fact, *be* Edward Disin.

Fiona flashed her glowing tray at Alf as she ran past him. Freak and I charged after her, waving our arms in the air, shouting, "WAIT! STOP! THAT'S HIM! HELP!"

Alf shouted at Beauceron, "HE'S NOT WHO YOU THINK HE IS! IT'S *HIM*!"

Edward Disin, already at the double doors that led to the hallway, twisted the handles and tried to fling them open. They opened about an inch and stopped abruptly.

Disin threw his full body weight against the doors and they opened another inch. Then they refused to budge. His look of triumph was replaced by one that, to me, looked like panic.

We stopped short, realizing we were almost within grabbing range of him but weren't quite sure how dangerous it would be to grab him. He plowed his shoulder into the doors and still they refused to give. Through the two-inch gap between them I could just see what was holding them shut.

It was the back of a very familiar dark green sofa.

Up a Tree

E dward Disin threw himself against the door one more
time, but the door slammed shut, as if two strong furniture movers had shoved the sofa back up against it.

Somewhere overhead, I heard a *whumpa-whumpa* sound.

Disin took one step forward and grabbed the person closest to him, who happened to be Fiona. He got her in a head-
lock, then pulled something out of his pocket and held it to
the side of her head. He might have been holding a candy bar.
He might have been holding a zucchini crayon. He might
have been holding a gun. It was impossible to tell. Fiona
began thrashing wildly back and forth.

"Let go of her!" I shouted as Freak made an animal noise next to me.

"Back off!" Disin shouted. Those of us who were inching up on him stopped. Freak looked as though he might lunge at him at any moment. If Freak hit him high, I knew I could hit him low. I wondered if I could poke him in the knee with a lollipop stick. I looked around, hoping to find a better weapon.

"Let the girl go," said Alf, stepping forward and dramatically pulling off his beard and wig. His nose fell off on its own.

"Alfred! How unexpected!" said Disin in a voice that said he was fully expecting him. "That's almost as bad a disguise as the one you wore in Barcelona when I deprived you of Upchuck the Clown. I knew the whole zucchini-crayon thing had to be you."

"What's going on?" demanded Ms. Beauceron. She was holding a pistol indecisively down at her side.

"I assume this is not your usual partner?" Alf snapped at her.

"I never saw him before today!"

"Then *arrest* him!"

Beauceron raised her gun, but Disin shook his head. "I

have a better idea," he said. "Drop your gun and kick it over here, and this child won't get hurt!"

When Beauceron hesitated, Disin shifted the position of his hand against Fiona's head. Fiona attempted to bite his wrist, but bit his sleeve instead. He gave an urgent nod in Beauceron's direction. She dropped her gun, kicked it to him, and he crouched and picked it up.

It turned out Disin had been threatening Fiona with a pen.

"There's no need for this!" said Alf, taking another step toward his father.

"No closer!" Disin waved Beauceron's gun at his son, then swept it toward the rest of us. "Everybody down on your knees," he ordered. "NOW!"

I had to say something, even if it was totally obvious.

"It's just a crayon," I reminded him.

"No," corrected Disin, "it's not. By acquiring it, I enable myself to think straight. So it's much more than just a crayon. It's the elimination of a final distraction so I can concentrate completely on more important matters. I notice you're not kneeling."

Freak and I dropped to our knees. Next to Freak, Sheik Geisel was kneeling and bobbing his head, repeating under his breath, "I'm just an actor. I don't know who hired me. I'm just an actor."

"*I* hired you, you moron. Your check is in the mail," Disin informed him. "Alfred. You're still standing."

Alf stood defiantly in front of his father, his arms folded across his chest.

"I can't let you leave here," he said.

"*'You shall not pass!'* I get it! Very commendable. But how are you going to stop me? *I*, personally, would sacrifice a pawn." Disin joggled Fiona like he had just plucked her off a chessboard. She responded by kicking him in the shin. "But I know *you* wouldn't. What does that leave?"

"Reason."

"Reason? Right. Sorry, don't have time for it."

Disin dragged Fiona past Alf to the French doors and pushed one open. The helicopter noise got louder. Alf lunged for him but drew back when Disin lifted Fiona one-handedly in the air like a rag doll and swept the pistol up and down her length, as though asking where he should shoot her. Alf took an additional step back.

"I'm leaving now," Disin announced. "If I see anyone come through these doors in the next five minutes, I will use this." He pointed the pistol straight up and fired, ignoring the plaster that showered down on him and barely blinking when a small piece of crown molding bounced off his head.

"You can't take the girl, and you can't reopen the portal!" Alf bellowed, his hands clenched in frustration.

"I believe I can do both." Disin took one step out the door, then stepped back in with an afterthought. "There's a rumor going around that your sister may have survived somehow. If this is true, you need her germplasm to regrow her body, and I've got the last remaining sample on my mantel back in Indorsia. It's between her baby picture and her graduation photo, right under a framed copy of my order to have her executed. I would think that would be justification enough, for you, to reopen the portal."

He left then, taking Fiona with him and leaving me with the impression he was not a very good parent.

The moment the door latch snicked shut behind Disin, Freak was on his feet and running. I was right behind him. We got to the French doors and looked out through the glass. Light from the ballroom spilled onto the lawn and illuminated the underside of the State Fair Omaha.

We watched as Disin dragged Fiona kicking and screaming across the patio to a picnic table. He stood on the table, lifted Fiona over his head like she weighed nothing, and tossed her into the Omaha's basket. Then he caught hold of one edge of the basket and hauled himself aboard. Moments later, the balloon's gas jet sent a fiery blast upward, bathing the scene in a hellish light.

Alf stood stunned, watching, like he really didn't know what to do next.

"Of all the hostages he could have taken—" he said to himself, bewildered.

"He's got Fiona!" shouted Freak, yanking on Alf's sleeve. "If you're going to drop the basket, do it now, before they get airborne!"

Alf started slapping his pockets, doing the universal pantomime for I-can't-find-the-remote-that-will-release-my-balloon-basket. After about ten seconds of this, Freak got it.

"He picked your pocket!"

"I don't do well with heights!" Fiona screamed, loud enough that we could hear her through the glass. She tried clambering out of the basket, but Disin caught her and shoved her to the floor. He immediately started loosening the balloon's tethers.

"He's watching *these* doors," said Alf, suddenly sounding decisive, "but we can get behind him if we go out through the house and run around from the front! We can still catch him by surprise! Come on!"

It was the old Alf. I was happy to have him back. But as we turned toward the hallway doors, Beauceron waved a water pistol in Alf's face. She had pulled the pistol from the top of one of her boots, and it was identical to the one Cockapoo had threatened me with the previous day. It had to be full of deadly Hista Mime.

"I never *saw* him before today," Beauceron explained, expanding her answer to Alf's earlier question. "Before today, he was just a bulldog on a TV. Let's watch him escape!"

Freak and I ducked low and sprinted for the hallway doors. We were hoping Beauceron wouldn't see us as a threat. Maybe she wouldn't see us at all. I realized if the sofa was still blocking the doors, we were trapped.

"Hey!" Beauceron shouted.

Freak slapped the handle down and slammed into the door with his shoulder. To my relief, it flew open and he fell into the empty area beyond. By the time I got there, he was already running toward the house's main entrance. I raced down the corridor after him, passing the sofa, which had parallel parked between two tables. It was acting nonchalant.

Freak burst through the front door and circled around the side of the house. I knew I couldn't keep up with him, but I was pretty sure, fast as he was, he wouldn't get to the Omaha in time. I knew what plan B would be. I slackened my pace a bit.

By the time I rounded the house, Disin had launched his balloon. Freak was below it, but he failed to catch the dangling rope, and then it was out of reach. I saw the hovering helicopter rise to a higher altitude and head off in the direction of Hellsboro.

I scampered over to the Dear John and hauled myself aboard. Freak was right behind me. We started pulling frantically at the bowknots that would release the balloon.

"Has she still got Alf?" Freak shouted, yanking at his last knot.

I glanced across the lawn. Through the French doors, I could see Beauceron holding Alf at water-pistol-point. He was looking longingly in our direction and I knew he wanted desperately to join us. Everybody else was on their knees. It looked like a prayer meeting. I hoped at least some of them were actually praying.

"He can't get away! We're going to have to do this without him!" I yanked as hard as I could on my remaining knot. It came undone, and the Dear John began to rise.

"Tree!" screamed Freak as the balloon sluiced sideways and headed for the menacing branches of a massive oak.

I grabbed a sandbag from the floor and threw it overboard. The balloon bobbed upward, but the basket hit the tree and a branch came through the wicker, nearly impaling Freak. The balloon strained to rise, but the tree wouldn't let go.

"We have to break the branch!" I shouted, then climbed out of the basket into the tree limbs. I found a fairly solid perch and started kicking. I glanced up and saw the Omaha getting away from us. We couldn't afford to stay stuck long, but the branch I was attacking refused to break. Freak swung out of the basket and joined me. He stepped on a bird's nest and an angry crow started flying in our faces.

"I've seen that crow before!" I announced, pretty sure I recognized the angry flapping.

We kicked the branch together and it cracked. The pull of the balloon ripped it from the tree.

"That's done it!" I cheered.

"Yes!" Freak agreed triumphantly. "There she—"

"GOES!" we screamed in unison as the balloon took off without us.

No Such Thing as Steering

O ur flying toilet bowl rose rapidly above us. A rope whipped me in the face and I snatched at it desperately. I caught it, twisted my hands into it, and wrapped my legs around it just as Freak threw his arms around my waist. The rope, attached to the balloon's basket, yanked us out of the tree in a burst of exploding twigs and furiously flying crow feathers.

We skimmed the treetops and got whacked by the uppermost branches. The crow continued to swoop around us and attack. The wind was taking us in the same direction as the Omaha but at a much lower altitude.

A dangerously lower altitude.

"If we don't make it to the basket and fire the burner," I shouted, "we're going to crash!"

"No kidding," muttered Freak as he got his own grip on the rope and let go of me. "Get climbing!"

I was above him. Fortunately, it was another challenge requiring upper-body strength. I started pulling myself up hand-over-hand. The crow kept flying into my face, but I had gotten used to him. He was the least of our problems. The nylon rope kept slipping through our fingers.

The rope twisted as we tried to climb it. After a few moments we were spinning around and swinging back and forth, like a carnival ride you shouldn't be on immediately after eating.

"Tossing cookies!" Freak warned me before barfing above Breeland Road with enough spin to send it spraying like a rotary lawn sprinkler. It caught the crow in the eye and sent it squawking.

The balloon rose a bit after the loss of ballast. Freak had been sneaking a lot of the auction hors d'oeuvres. I wondered if it would help if I puked, too. I considered it, then decided I didn't have it in me.

The balloon was skimming the field just before our houses. I could see that Freak and I were going to be slammed against a roof if nothing changed. With one final effort, I hauled myself up the remaining section of rope and threw myself into the basket. I jumped up and pulled down on the burner-release lever with all my might.

With a roar, a huge flame shot up toward the balloon's envelope. The balloon immediately started to rise, but it didn't look as though it would rise fast enough to miss the houses. The basket just cleared a chimney, but I heard the rope lash against the bricks.

"Freak!" I screamed, and looked over the side.

My friend was clinging to the side of the basket. My hand shot out and clasped his, and I pulled him to safety.

"Got any breath mints?" he asked, then tumbled into the basket.

I kept my hand on the burner lever for the next minute or so. The bowl of the enormous toilet above me glowed intensely from the flame of the gas jet. It looked like a warning against overindulging in jalapeños. We rose to the same height as the Omaha, about three hundred feet.

When we had inflated the balloons that afternoon, Alf had explained the basics of hot-air flight to us. To go up, you either made the air inside the envelope warmer or you dropped ballast and made the basket lighter. To descend, you either allowed the air in the envelope to cool or, to descend more quickly, you opened the parachute valve at the top of the envelope and let the warm air out. That was all there was to it. There was no such thing as steering.

"We're gaining on them!" Freak sounded surprised.

"I think it's the flush tank," I said. "It's acting like a sail."

"Thank you, Science Girl," said Freak. We looked at each other, suddenly realizing how much we'd miss her if anything happened to her.

The wind was out of the west, propelling the balloons toward Rodmore. The night was clear, the moon was full, and we could see Fiona and Disin outlined in the basket of the Omaha. Fiona was unrestrained. But then, there was nowhere she could go. She was in the corner of the basket opposite Disin, gripping one of the ropes connecting the balloon to the basket and staring at her feet. I could tell she was concentrating on not looking over the basket's edge. As we watched, Disin tossed a sandbag out.

Freak and I winced as the sandbag hit Took Lane, the last street before Hellsboro, and burst with a sickening *splat!*

"If he decides he doesn't need a hostage any longer—" I said, leaving the thought unfinished as I suddenly got a lump in my throat.

Abruptly, the Omaha dropped. Fiona screamed. The balloon plummeted to within fifty feet of the ground, then Disin fired the gas jet full throttle and their descent slowed. After a moment, the balloon began to rise.

"Are you okay?" Freak shouted to Fiona. She shakily waved and nodded. We had gotten close enough to see small gestures. "What just happened?" Freak said, turning to me. "Why'd they drop?"

I tried to figure it out. I looked at the ground, where Took Lane was gliding by below us and the border of Hellsboro was rapidly approaching. I saw smoke curl from a Hellsboro fissure, and I knew.

"It'll happen to us, too!" I shrieked, jumping for the gas jet and pulling it down just in time. A tower of flame shot upward, heating the air above us.

We crossed the border between Sunnyside and Hellsboro. The balloon bobbed a bit, but it didn't drop as far as the Omaha had, because we had raised the temperature of the air inside it.

"The air above Hellsboro is warmer than the air above the surrounding countryside," I shouted, loud enough for Fiona to hear, because I hoped she'd appreciate how I was thinking the way she did. "A hot air balloon only stays up if the air inside it is much warmer than the air outside it. Hellsboro is a seriously bad place for ballooning."

We were now only thirty seconds behind the Omaha. Both balloons were level at two hundred feet. Fiona suddenly started screaming at us.

"Go up! Go up! The two of you! You have to climb!"

"Shut up!" barked Disin. "Or you'll join that sandbag!"

"She wants our balloon to go higher," Freak said. "Maybe she thinks we can come down on top of him!"

"No, that's not what she's saying—look at what she's doing!"

I pointed. Fiona, the girl who was terrified of heights, was climbing up the rigging. She was trying to tangle herself in one of the ropes. She was looking upward at the underside of the balloon. She had given up coherent speech in favor of whimpering. Still, I thought she was incredibly brave. Then Disin stood up on the edge of the basket opposite her and grabbed one of the ropes, and I knew what was about to happen.

"We have to climb!" I screamed. "Not the balloon! *Us!* Up the ropes! He's going to drop the baskets!"

Disin had picked Alf's pocket. He had the remote-control device that disconnected the baskets from the balloons. Alf had no idea which balloon Disin might try to escape in, so the remote, I decided, must drop both baskets simultaneously.

Our balloon's basket was about to fall two hundred feet to the smoldering surface of Hellsboro.

Freak and I scrambled to get ourselves into the rigging. We hauled ourselves up the ropes, trying to figure out how high we had to go before we were safe. I swung from rope to rope, trying to convince myself it was no worse than playing on monkey bars.

I looked over at the Omaha. Disin was about five feet above the edge of his basket. He was leaning into the center, reaching for something.

"What's he doing?" demanded Freak.

Disin snagged what he was reaching for. It was a blue plastic handle attached to a cord that disappeared into the Omaha's envelope.

"PARACHUTE VALVE!" Freak and I shouted together. It was the valve that opened a flap in the balloon to let hot air out. It was good to have if you needed to make a quick emergency landing.

I looked around for ours. It was midway between Freak and me. Neither one of us could reach it.

Disin dug into his coat pocket and pulled out the remote.

Unintentionally, he also pulled out a handkerchief. The handkerchief snagged one additional item. It looked, to me, about the size and shape of the box containing the zucchini crayon. It came out with the handkerchief and fell into the basket below. Disin, I could tell, hadn't noticed. If he had, he wouldn't have done what he did next.

He pressed the button on the remote and blew the baskets off the balloons.

"LOOK OUT!" Freak and I screamed at each other.

The bolts exploded. It was as though four M-80 firecrackers had gone off simultaneously at the four corners of each basket. Our basket, with its burner and propane tank, fell away, hit Hellsboro, and exploded. The Omaha's basket simultaneously fell, hit, and rolled without exploding. Both balloons rose rapidly and started to spin.

The motion made me dizzy, but I managed to focus on the Omaha as it swept past. Fiona and Disin still clung to its ropes. Fiona was shrieking. Disin opened the parachute valve, and the balloon began to descend. Rodmore Chemical was dead ahead.

"Is he going to land on the roof?" I shouted.

"Looks like!"

We, on the other hand, looked like we were going to sail

right over Rodmore and crash and burn on the far side of Hellsboro.

"Parachute valve!" I bellowed at Freak, above the sound of rushing wind. He nodded and lunged for it. His fingers just missed it and he lost his grip.

"Freak!" I screamed as I saw him drop.

He fell five feet and caught the last possible rope between him and Hellsboro. I reached down my hand for him but he was too far away.

"Valve!" he hollered up at me.

The parachute valve was beyond his reach. It was up to me.

I swung once or twice to build up momentum. *Monkey bars!* I reminded myself, and I let go.

I'd never felt more like a monkey in my life. I caught the valve and my full weight came down on it. I dropped three feet and felt something give, high up in the balloon. It was the lid of the flush tank opening. The Dear John began to drop.

I dangled from the valve and watched as Disin maneuvered the misshapen remains of the Omaha like a hang glider. The rapidly deflating balloon landed on the roof of Rodmore's main building and was carried along by the breeze.

Disin scrambled to his feet, still clutching one of the ropes. He caught an upright vent pipe, wrapped the rope around it, and stopped the balloon before it could go over the edge. This was good, since Fiona was still tangled in the balloon's ropes and would have gone over with it.

We hit the roof moments later. Freak hit first and rolled, taking the impact in his shoulders. I came down next to him, and yards and yards of porcelain-white fabric came down on top of us.

After lying there unmoving for a moment or two, I staggered to my feet and tried to find my way out from under the fabric. I thrashed around a bit and finally found an opening. Freak emerged a second or two after I did.

We were surrounded by doghats.

I Get Killed

ou'll enjoy being zombie workers," Edward Disin
informed us as we walked beside him along the balcony in the huge underground room with the icy wall. "Our
surveys indicate one hundred percent job satisfaction. At
least, we haven't had any complaints." He chuckled, and it
sounded like razor blades going around in a blender.

After the balloons had crashed, the doghats had grabbed
Freak, Fiona, and me and marched us into the depths of the
building. Disin had joined us a few minutes later and had
announced his intention of strapping unlimited-plan cell
phones to our heads and force-feeding us Piggie-O's—the

bacon-flavored breakfast cereal from Agra Nation®—until we were as receptive to his mind control as everybody else.

"But before we get to that," he said, rubbing his hands together, "I'm going to let you witness the opening of the portal. I need somebody staring in wide-eyed wonder, but all my subordinates have other assignments. I need an appreciative audience, even if it's only infants."

"We're not infants," growled Freak.

"By my standards you are. And I see Alf used my prejudice against me to put me off my guard. That won't happen again. You're infants, but you're very bright infants."

"And you're very important," I said. "And by important, of course, I mean stupid."

Disin no longer looked like Treasury Agent North, although he still wore North's rumpled suit and tie. He had pulled off his wig and peeled what looked like a thin layer of chewing gum off his face. He now looked pretty much like the man in the first photo we had seen of him. Like somebody you wouldn't get into a car with if he offered you a ride. Even if it was raining. Or hailing.

"Compared to me, Alexander the Great was merely mediocre," he said. He waved his cigar in the direction of the icy wall. "I didn't just conquer a world; I unified it. I unified it and got everybody in it to speak the same language. The immediate savings on dual-language road signs was tremendous."

"Everybody in Indorsia speaks English?" Fiona asked. We were walking a few paces behind Disin. As infants, we apparently didn't rate handcuffs or any other form of restraint. In front of Disin was the woman he called Jackal. She had a pistol in a holster on her hip. Walking behind us was the man we once knew as Doberman. He had a semiautomatic rifle slung over one shoulder. He had bruises on either side of his head, as though a sliding door had recently closed repeatedly on him. Disin no longer addressed him as Doberman. He called him Jervis. Somebody else's mind now looked out through Doberman's eyes.

"More correct to say there are some people here on Earth who speak Indorsian," replied Disin. He seemed pleased to take questions from the audience. "At some point long ago, a portal must have opened and a handful of Indorsians found their way back here. They brought with them an early version of the language you call English. And I have to say, you people have made an absolute hash of it. Whoever invented the word *infomercial* should be banished to Bogeyland. And don't get me started on *staycation*."

"Is Bogeyland a place in Indorsia?" Fiona asked.

"It's a place in a Laurel and Hardy movie. Quite unpleasant. Even without the singing."

We were walking with a madman. Alf was being held prisoner back at Underhill House. My friends and I were going to be enslaved through mind control. An invasion force from another world was about to take over our hometown, and from there, the world. Bogeyland couldn't have been any worse. My palms were sweating and I was on the edge of panic. I had been crazy enough to call the madman *stupid*. Fortunately, he didn't seem to have noticed.

We came up alongside the man we had once known as Coyote. He was standing at the balcony's railing, studying the huge metal spiderweb that stretched across one end of the cavernous room. He was holding a remote-control box with a small steering wheel on it.

Coyote turned the little steering wheel an eighth of an inch to the left. The metal spiderweb groaned. A numeric display on the remote went from 7.6 to 8.1.

"That's too tight!" snarled Disin, snatching the remote from Coyote and turning the wheel a half inch to the right. The display went from 8.1 to 6.2. The spiderweb sagged noticeably. "It's crash netting. You want it to act like a fishing net, not a trampoline. The transport will be coming through with enough momentum for it to bounce. That must be kept to a minimum." He handed the remote back to Coyote.

"Good help is so hard to find," Disin confided. "Even when you have the capability of upgrading their brains." He continued to lead us along the balcony. "Of the entire staff of the Disin Corporation, only nine people know what's really going on here. Most know nothing, and the remainder think it's some sort of project designed to stream TV commercials directly into people's brains. Nobody seems to find that last part objectionable."

"What did you promise the nine to get them to go along with this?" asked Freak.

"California."

Two or three people in hard hats were down on the main floor, making adjustments to the washing machine–sized boxes at the base of the ice wall. Otherwise, I couldn't see too many other people around. I was hoping that might somehow work in our favor.

On the opposite side of the cavern, high up on the wall, a clock was counting down minutes and seconds. It had gone from 45:18 to 41:22 in the time we had been on the balcony.

"What happens when the clock reaches zero?" Fiona asked quietly.

"The world changes," said Disin. "I force open a portal that has been closed since 1952 and it stays open long enough for a troop transport to drop through. Then it closes again for at least another few years, until a sufficient number of neutrinos pass through the chargers and it can be opened again. In the meantime, the troops who arrived on the transport will have been quartered in the homes of the good people of Cheshire; adjacent communities will have been taken over; and, by this time next year, I rule the world."

"Without opposition," said Freak.

"Certainly not from anybody who uses a cell phone and consumes any of the tasty products of the Agra Nation® food company. The mind-control module will enable me to conquer your world in much less time than it took me to conquer Indorsia. The good news for you, however, is that my troops and I won't be staying."

"You won't?"

"No. Why would I? Until I came here, I had no idea there was anything outside of Indorsia. I had claustrophobia and I didn't know it. The first time I saw your sky at night, I thought it had holes in it. I thought the world was ending. I spent an embarrassing amount of time hiding under an ice-cream truck. When I finally understood that the holes in the sky were stars, with planets like Earth circling them, I felt such a sense of release. The day after I conquered Indorsia, I looked out on it all and I said, *Is that all there is?* Now I know there's more, and I want it."

"That's probably just the Compulsive Completist Disorder talking," I said.

In an instant, Disin had grabbed me by the collar, slammed me against the wall, and slid me halfway up it. Somewhere, his avatar was probably howling. Freak and Fiona both went for his back, but Jackal and Jervis caught them before they could help me.

"If it is the CCD," said Disin, breathing cigar breath in my face, "there's nothing I can do about it. None of Indorsia's advanced medicine has been able to cure me. I would have been the owner of Earth years ago if I hadn't been periodically compelled to drop everything I was doing and run off in pursuit of some idiotic comic book or baseball card or odd-ball crayon." He looked down at my feet, which were dangling about a foot off the floor. "How tall are you?" he asked.

"F-four foot three and a half," I stuttered, grateful for the change in topic but leery of the direction it was taking.

"How old are you?"

"Thirteen in December."

"Perfect." He let me slide down the wall until I was back on my feet.

"You shouldn't do that to a kid," said Freak with an edge in his voice. I could tell he wanted to do something stupid. I was glad he had the sense not to.

Disin smoothed out the wrinkles he had made in my collar. To Jackal he said, "Have Setter come up here with a mnemocide bulb." Jackal turned and spoke into a walkie-talkie. Freak and Fiona and I exchanged uneasy glances. *Mnemocide* wasn't a word you easily forgot, even though it was the gas that destroyed all memory.

"No," said Disin, as though I had never interrupted him, "I will not be staying. It will take a little over twenty-eight years for the enslaved population of Earth to build a fleet of space habitats big enough to transport the people of Indorsia out to new homes in the stars. At the end of those twenty-eight years, the slaves will wake up, wonder briefly why they are so tired and emaciated, and pick up their lives where they left off. Some will still be young enough to have children. Of course, Earth will look like an apple with enormous bites gone out of it, completely stripped of resources, but you were doing that to yourselves, anyway. It would only have taken you about a hundred years more to accomplish what I will do in twenty-eight. You can't make an omelet without breaking coconuts."

"Yes, you can," said Fiona.

"Not if you're making a coconut omelet. And I love coconut omelets. Is that a cat?"

Disin scowled down at the cavern floor. We rushed to the railing in time to see a Mucus-colored streak dart in and out among the washing machines and disappear under the balcony.

"Nine lieutenants I've got," muttered Disin, "all codenamed after dogs, and they can't keep a single cat out of the place. Pathetic." He looked at us and spread his arms out, as if he were about to embrace us. "I am keeping the three of you alive, by the way—or at least two out of three—so that twenty-eight years from now you'll be able to tell everybody I wasn't a bad man. Just a driven one. Remember that, if you remember nothing else."

"You're *not* a bad man?" sputtered Freak. "How on earth can you think that?"

"Not being from Earth helps."

"Did you say two out of three?" said Fiona.

"Is Indorsia dying?" I asked. "Is there a plague? Is the whole place overpopulated?"

"None of those things. Why do you ask?"

"There has to be some reason everybody will be leaving."

"There is. I want them to. It's my whim. Most members of the healthy, well-managed population of Indorsia don't know they're leaving yet. They're contentedly tilling their fields and thatching their cottages and fletching their arrows and watching their 3-D TVs, happy with what little high-tech the Royals permit them to have, little suspecting that in less than thirty years, they'll be on the adventure of a lifetime. And yes, it probably is the CCD. So you can blame Miranda. I find myself wanting everything that's out there." He waved his arm over his head, flipping his hand in the universe's direction.

"What if they don't want to go?"

"They have no choice. I am their ruler. I say, 'Jump!' they'd better ask, 'To which star system?' "

"Probably not the first thing it will occur to them to ask," said Freak.

"What do you mean, *TWO OUT OF THREE*?" Fiona repeated, louder and more urgently. Disin ignored her.

"We opened the portal for six seconds two weeks ago as a test," he said, halting our stroll in front of the door marked MEN. The countdown clock now said 38:11. "We were only able to open it enough for radio waves to pass through. It was enough, though, for me to establish that my trusted regents still rule the place and for me to transmit orders to them. There was even enough bandwidth for them to send over a half dozen downloads of dead Indorsians who at one time had been helpful to me. Five of them now occupy the bodies of former associates of mine. The sixth is an assassin who will find it much easier to get close to his targets if he's occupying the brain of an adorable, tousle-haired twelve-year-old boy. I really am sorry about this," Disin said, giving a quick nod in my direction. "But then again, let's not forget you called me *stupid*!"

Somebody, probably Setter, had come up behind me and now pinned my arms to my sides. A hand reached around and clamped a plastic mask over my mouth and nose. A clear plastic bulb hung down from the mask. Rutabaga-colored gas swirled inside the bulb. It looked exactly like the gas Disin's werewolf had used to punish his employees.

Mnemocide, the gas that killed by wiping the mind clean.

Freak and Fiona screamed and sprang at my attacker, but Jackal swept Fiona off her feet and Jervis caught Freak around the waist. I kicked out with all my might, skimming Disin's pants leg but otherwise connecting with nothing.

The hand squeezed the bulb and the gas entered the mask. I caught a whiff of gym socks and asparagus and felt tiny needles in my nostrils as the gas swirled before my eyes like the atmosphere of a hostile planet.

I tried to hold my breath, but I had been caught off guard. After a moment, I had to inhale. My throat felt like I had been gargling broken glass, and things I knew and remembered were suddenly unknown and forgotten. The gas entered my lungs and a flash of white light erased everything I had ever been. I ceased to exist.

At a nod from Edward Disin, I had been killed. I was dead.

Bummer.

CHAPTER
26

Death Is No Picnic

I once read a book where it turned out the narrator was a
ghost. You didn't find this out until the end of the book.
The narrator got himself into a tight situation, failed to deal
with it, and got himself killed. He finished up the book by
describing how his friends, who were still alive, had gone on to
solve the story's problems without his help. His friends paused
every once in a while to say what a great guy he had been.

I really hated that book.

Shortly after I died, I found myself sitting on the edge of a
picnic blanket.

I was in the middle of a meadow on a warm summer's

day, with bumblebees and butterflies flitting here and there under a bright blue sky. Off in the distance, a grove of trees leaned over the banks of a meandering stream. Beyond the trees, mountains loomed.

On the picnic blanket, plates overflowed with my favorite foods. Fried chicken. Cheeseburgers. Fresh-baked chocolate-chip cookies, still warm from the oven.

But I wasn't looking at the food, and I wasn't admiring the scenery. I was staring at my parents. My father was sitting opposite me and my mother was on my right, close enough to hug. She and I were immediately in each other's arms, crying and laughing and making joyful noises. My father rushed around and joined us.

My mother was dressed the way she had been in the photo from the Rodmore company picnic. My father was wearing the fishing hat he had worn in the photo on Fiona's refrigerator. They both looked ecstatically happy. They looked exactly the way I felt.

"We've missed you so much!" my mother said.

"You realize," said my father, "we've been with you all these years, whether you were aware of it or not."

"I think I knew," I said. "I've always tried to do things as if you were around. I never wanted to disappoint you."

"We are so proud of you," my mother said, and hugged me again.

"But we don't have much time," said my father.

My mother let me go and wiped her eyes. "That's true; we don't," she said. Off in the distance, I could see two people in the grove. One of them appeared to be wearing armor.

"Don't we have all of eternity?" I asked.

"Uh, no," said my father, sounding uncomfortable. "*We* do. You don't."

"I'm dead, right? Just as dead as you are?"

"Well, yes. You are dead. But you're not as dead as we are. We are very dead. You're just...dead."

"What's the difference?"

"What your father is trying to say is...before you died, your mind—your essence, maybe even your soul—was downloaded."

"Downloaded?"

"A copy of your mind is now inside Guernica's circuits, being kept alive the same way Miranda's essence is. Guernica thought it best if we explained this to you. Guernica also recommended there be comfort food handy."

"So...the two of you were downloaded before you died?"

"No." My father shook his head sadly. "We were never

downloaded. We don't exist here in the same way you and Miranda do. There is no possibility of a second chance for us. We are just…visiting."

"Are you Guernica, pretending to be my parents?"

My father grimaced. "Possibly," he said.

"And possibly not," said my mother. "I prefer to think we *are* your parents. I certainly feel an overwhelming love for you. No machine could duplicate that. But sadly, there is no real way for you to know if we're your actual parents, or if we're being generated by Guernica, or if we're just your imagination working overtime to make something very strange feel more familiar."

"Unless, of course," said my father, helping himself to a piece of chicken, "your mother and I are able to share with you something only she and I would know, that you could verify independently at a later date."

"Such as?" said my mother, sounding hopeful.

"Oh, I don't know," said my father, chewing his chicken thoughtfully. "The combination to our safe."

"We didn't have a safe."

"It was just an example. Or maybe what our last words were."

"Nobody recorded them. There's no way for him to verify

them. And, as I recall, we both said the exact same thing. 'AAAAAAAAAAAAAAAAAH!'" my mother screamed. It wasn't alarming, because my father laughed, and then she laughed, and then he reached over and took her hand.

"Or something," said my father, "along the lines of 'There's a tin box hidden in the rafters of the garage with some of our old childhood toys that we were going to give to you as soon as you were old enough.'"

"That's good," said my mother. "Do we have anything like that?"

"We must," said my father, taking another bite of chicken and furrowing his brow in concentration. "How about what the name of my first dog was?"

"I don't know what the name of your first dog was," said my mother.

"It was Flash. No, wait. That was the turtle. The dog was Clyde. No, wait—it was Skip. I think."

"Is it written down anywhere?" my mother said with a sigh.

"No."

"I don't recall being downloaded," I said.

"Do you remember falling asleep on the sofa?" my mother asked. The two figures from the grove were approaching. I recognized the one who wasn't in armor as my English teacher, Mr. Hendricks. His suit still matched the sofa's upholstery. I knew he wasn't really Mr. Hendricks. He was the sofa. He was Guernica. I nodded in answer to my mother's question. "That was when it was done," she said.

I thought about this for a moment.

"So how come I can remember things that happened after I was downloaded? Shouldn't my memories end there?"

My mother and father looked at each other and smiled. "He's so bright," my mother said.

"Don't embarrass him," replied my father.

I must have been blushing. I know that dead people don't blush, so I thought this was a hopeful sign.

"Double Six transmitted periodic updates," my mother explained.

"Double Six was nowhere near me when Edward Disin had me killed," I protested.

"Double Six," said Mr. Hendricks, "was in one of the adjacent rooms at Rodmore Chemical when you died. Close enough to send one final update."

Mr. Hendricks and the figure in armor had come up behind my father. They knelt down on the picnic blanket on either side of him. The armored figure pulled off its helmet, and I was not surprised to see it was a woman. She shook her head back and forth and red hair billowed around her, like she was in some kind of medieval shampoo commercial. She was beautiful, despite having the same eagle beak of a nose that Alf had.

"You're Miranda," I said.

"I am a digital personification. But yes, I am Miranda," she said. "I'd say I'm pleased to meet you, but we've already met, and the countdown clock is now at fourteen minutes and we are running out of time. I have to make this brief. We are about to put you back into a flesh-and-blood body."

"Whose?" I said warily.

"Your own. The moment Guernica computed you were the most likely of the three children to get yourself killed, we cloned you."

"How was I the most likely?"

"Freak has faster reflexes and Fiona is more concerned with self-preservation. And neither of them has a history of being the frequent victim of friendly fire during dodgeball."

"Right."

"And of the three of you, you're the most imaginative and the most inclined to do what's right, meaning you might handle being cloned better than the others, as well as justify the trouble and expense of cloning you. I'd call it a no-brainer if, under the circumstances, that weren't somewhat tactless."

Mr. Hendricks, speaking with a voice I now recognized as that of Double Six, said, "The sofa took a DNA sample—you may recall getting stuck with a fishhook—and we worked from there. A revivarium can either force a new mind into an old body or grow a new body from scratch, which is what we did with you."

"I got stuck with the hook a little over a week ago," I protested. "You can't clone somebody in a little over a week!"

"You can if you use an accelerated growth program," Guernica replied. "The body you are about to occupy is, technically, the equivalent of you, physically two months older than you were when you died eleven minutes ago. This body has never had its legs broken, so you'll find it is somewhat taller."

"Taller?"

"By about an inch."

"You couldn't have given me an extra foot?"

"You wish to be a tripod?"

There was an awkward silence. I tried to decide how confident it made me, to find my life dependent upon a machine that could make such a mistake. Or had such a rudimentary sense of humor. I stuffed a chocolate-chip cookie in my mouth.

"Your old body," said Miranda, "has already been occupied by the mind of Greeves Stainer, an expert Indorsian assassin my father has employed in the past. In less than thirteen minutes, my father will force open the Indorsian portal and a troop transport will slide through, bringing two thousand of my father's storm troopers and additional downloads of disagreeable dead Indorsians my father intends to revive on Earth. At the same time, the mind-control module will start up, rendering everybody living within a ten-mile radius completely docile and accepting of storm troopers in their midst, and probably humming insipid tunes from *The Sound of Music*, to boot. This has to be stopped. You are going to help by creating a diversion."

"Me?"

"Oh, my poor dear boy," my mother said, brushing a lock of hair off my forehead. "In just a moment you're going to leave here and wake up in your new body. You'll be in a revivarium in a hidden room of Underhill House. The revivarium will split open. It will spill you out. There will be pain and screaming and second thoughts and a gloppy mess on the floor, but you survived natural childbirth once, so I know you can again."

"You are not going to have a belly button," said Guernica informatively. "I hope you are all right with that."

"I, uh, rarely use it," I mumbled, worried about other things.

"You can take up to a full minute to reestablish motor control, but no longer," said Miranda. "Then you have to be on your way back to Rodmore."

"How am I supposed to get there?"

"Throw yourself on the sofa."

"What—"

Before I could ask another question, my mother had jumped up and hugged me. My father joined her. I was lost in their embraces for a moment and then they vanished, like candle flames blown out.

Darkness surrounded me and pressure built up on all sides, like I was diving deeper and deeper into an ocean of pain, my lungs unable to fill with air. An enormous weight crushed me flat, folded me over, then flattened me again. My mouth and nose filled with liquid and I felt the terror of drowning, just as the world turned sideways and dropped me off a cliff.

Then I struck a hard, cold surface and thick, sticky fluid slithered down around me.

I opened my eyes, but I couldn't breathe. Screaming helped. Glop flew out of my mouth, and I was able to inhale.

I was in the room behind the secret panel at the far end of the Underhill House ballroom. Next to me was the revivarium, which had split lengthwise and opened like a clamshell. It dripped reddish goop, not unlike the Jell-O that Nails Norton had dumped on Fiona's head. As I sat up, I noticed the sofa sitting not too far away.

My legs felt like rubber when I tried to get up. I slipped in the goop. It took me four tries, but I finally got up and staggered across the room.

That's when I noticed I was naked.

I was all set to go skinny-dipping while the fate of the world hung in the balance.

Great.

I put my ear against the secret panel and heard a low murmur on the other side. I wondered if Ms. Beauceron was still holding everybody at gunpoint.

Suddenly, a maniacal cackle rang out from the other side of the panel, followed almost immediately by the sound of an ax striking wood. It sounded like Hologrammy was chasing someone. People started screaming. I cringed, wondering if my arrival had somehow set her off.

I snatched a black plastic garbage bag out of a box and used it to wipe as much of the red goop off me as I could. Then I tore a hole in the bottom of a second bag and pulled it over my head. I made holes on either side for my arms.

I realized I had a choice. Either I could find a way to open the panel and help Alf, or I could get back to my friends and try to help them.

I took a deep breath and threw myself facedown on the sofa.

I sank into the cushions as deeply as Fiona's fist had when she had punched it. The sofa shuddered.

And I felt myself being turned inside out.

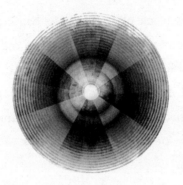

Open Late on Doomsday

essering is not a good way for a living thing to travel. It may be great for furniture and other inanimate objects, but for anything with a nervous system, it's very painful. For what seemed an eternity, it felt like every cell of my body was being ripped apart. I had thought rebirth hurt. It was nothing compared to tessering.

The pain lessened and the cushions beneath me got firmer, gently pushing me upward. I rolled off the sofa and fell on my back. After panting, blinking, and twitching for a few moments, I suddenly remembered there was a clock somewhere, and it was rapidly running out.

I scrambled to my feet. The sofa and I were in the same elevator that had taken us to the roof the first time we were in the Rodmore Chemical plant. The elevator opened into the room marked SERVICE, which had an exit onto the balcony where I had last seen my friends.

The balcony where I had been killed.

I was a kid, cleverly disguised as a bag of trash. I had no idea what I was going to do. I only knew I was going to do something. I had a score to settle. If nothing else, I had to save Freak and Fiona.

I stepped out of the elevator, reached back in, pushed the 3 button, and waved good-bye to the sofa. It needed time to recharge before it could tesser again, and this was the best I could do for it.

Running across the room, I suddenly detoured and skipped in a circle, stifling a laugh because I realized I no longer had a limp. I had to stop myself from dancing a jig. If the world still existed in the spring, I decided, I would try out for the school baseball team.

I opened the door just wide enough to stick my head out.

The icy wall was to my immediate right. It was now covered in fog. I could hear water dripping. The ice was starting to melt.

The countdown clock said 6:14.

Midway down the balcony to my left stood a cluster of people. Edward Disin was there, talking on Jackal's walkie-talkie. Coyote was still fiddling with his remote control, trying to get the adjustment on the spiderweb crash net just right. Jackal and Jervis stood on either side of Freak and Fiona, guarding them. Freak and Fiona were hugging each other like they had just lost their best friend.

Then it occurred to me that Freak and Fiona *had* just lost their best friend.

I wanted to show them I was all right, but I knew running down the balcony, ripping off my garbage bag, and shouting, "Hey, look, it's me!" might not be such a good idea. Cloning, I thought, would never be perfect until it included the cloned person's underwear.

I decided to try to find Double Six. It had helped us the last time we were in Rodmore, and I desperately needed help now.

Guernica had said Double Six was in one of the rooms adjacent to where I had died. The two most likely rooms were the ones marked MEN and HAZMAT SAFETY. HAZMAT SAFETY was closer.

I stepped out on the balcony and walked cautiously to the

left, keeping as close to the wall as I could. Everybody had their backs to me, and I was barefoot, so the sound of my footsteps, I hoped, wouldn't attract their attention. I glanced nervously at the countdown clock. It went from 5:58 to 5:57.

I was about halfway to my goal when Fiona turned, looked my way, and yelped. She immediately slapped her hand to her mouth, but not before Freak turned to see what had startled her. His eyes went wide, and I put a finger to my lips.

It was too late. Jackal noticed my friends' reactions and began to turn toward me. I looked around frantically for a hiding place, but I wasn't even near a door.

I sat down where I was, pulled my head inside the garbage bag, folded my arms across my chest, and leaned forward. I hoped, from Jackal's point of view, I would look like a bag of trash waiting to be picked up.

I held my breath. It was a good thing Alf didn't use transparent trash bags.

I heard footsteps approaching.

I tensed and prepared to burst from the bag like a wild animal jumping out of a Dumpster. I would snarl and claw and be all over my opponent. I almost shouted, "ARRRRRH!" but then I heard the footsteps stop, turn, and go back the way they had come, meaning whoever they belonged to had gotten close enough to be convinced I was an actual bag of garbage. I felt both relieved and insulted.

I peeked out, and only Freak was still looking my way. He had seen me gassed with mnemocide; he had to be wondering if I had somehow recovered my memory. The real explanation was so much more complicated.

I scurried along the wall until I got to the door marked HAZMAT SAFETY, and I quickly stepped inside.

Somebody was already in the room.

He was sitting at the conference table with his back to me. He didn't bother to turn around. Instead, he lifted the photo he was looking at, so I could see it over his shoulder. It was a picture of Alf. He pointed at it, and in a very familiar voice, said, "So, is he like you? Is he immune to arsenic? If he is, I can always shoot him between the eyes."

I picked up a chair and broke it over his head.

The most annoying teacher we have at school always uses the phrase "Go ahead, knock yourself out." I had just done it. The figure in the chair fell on the floor, and it was me.

I rushed over and knelt down beside him. We were identical. He could have been my twin. Red-haired, gray-eyed, handsome as anything. "I'm so sorry," I said. "I didn't mean to hit me. I mean you. Whoever it was I hit."

A loose flap of skin on his scalp trickled a bit of blood. I spit on my fingers and tried to stick the flap back in place. "A couple of stitches will fix that," I assured him.

He isn't me, I kept reminding myself. He was Greeves Stainer, an Indorsian assassin now inhabiting my former body. Edward Disin had apparently revived him so he could assassinate Alf.

Stainer was wearing a jumpsuit. I unzipped it and pulled him out of it. I ripped the garbage bag off myself and put on the suit. Then I picked up the photo of Alf, pushed my hair back so it looked the way Stainer had combed it, and stepped back out on the balcony.

This time I didn't cower along the wall. I strode purposefully over to Edward Disin. Freak's and Fiona's faces lit up when they saw me. I waved them away with my hand.

"Back off, small children," I said, trying to make my voice sound like Robert De Niro's in a gangster movie. "I'm an assassin. I don't have time for kids. I assassinate people. It's what I do. I'm on a mission. Assassination's my game. No time for autographs!"

"Stainer," said Disin. "You're just in time." The count-down clock said 2:09. "The portal is about to open."

"Yes, well," I said. "That's fine if you're interested in that kind of thing. Me, I have work to do." I waved Alf's photo at him. "I want to get to this guy before he has a chance to escape."

"Nothing to worry about there," said Disin. "One of my agents is holding him at gunpoint."

"Oh," I said. "Then . . . what do you need me for?"

"Your target is one of the Royals. You know the code better than anyone. It has to be done either by another Royal or by a compensated member of the guild. Beauceron is neither."

"Hey," I said. "I'm all about the guild. Just issue me a weapon, and I'll be on my way."

"This is hardly the time," growled Disin, trying to return his attention to the technicians on the cavern floor. He held the walkie-talkie to his lips and said, "Prepare to initiate mind-control module."

I caught Fiona scowling at me like I was an amoeba under a microscope. Freak was watching me appraisingly, no doubt trying to decide whether I was me or somebody else. I tried to give them a reassuring wink, but it came out more like a nervous twitch, and it only made them look more confused.

"I'm itching to do this," I said to Disin, tugging on his sleeve. It was not, perhaps, what an adult member of an assassin's guild would have done. "Just give me a gun and I'll be on my way."

Disin turned to Jackal. "Give him your gun."

"But—"

"Just do it! He's the best in the business and he's apparently full of adolescent hormones." Disin glared at me. "The sooner he's on his way, the better."

Jackal pulled her gun from its holster and handed it to me. I must have grabbed it the wrong way because the clip containing the bullets fell out and bounced off my foot. Fiona quickly bent down, picked it up, and handed it to me, saying under her breath, "It *is* you, isn't it?"

I nodded enthusiastically as I fumbled with the clip and repeatedly failed to get it back in the gun.

"This isn't the model I'm used to," I explained to Jackal, who was watching me, goggle-eyed. "You should see me with a bow and arrow."

I could tell she was about to pounce on me and take her gun back. I wasn't fooling her.

Freak stepped an inch closer to Disin, who had his back to us, but Jervis put a restraining hand on his shoulder. Fiona took advantage of the distraction and stepped behind Jervis. It looked like she was getting ready to tackle him.

The countdown clock said 1:46.

Suddenly, the room shook with the force of a tremendous explosion. Tiles and dust from the ceiling cascaded down to the floor. Disin turned around, looking wild-eyed. He spoke into the walkie-talkie, but he couldn't get a response.

"Find out what that was!" He pointed at Jackal. When she hesitated, he barked, "Now!"

Jackal sprinted to the far end of the balcony and disappeared into the stairwell. Jervis let go of Freak, unslung his rifle, and looked around nervously, as if he expected an attack from any direction. Fiona stepped away from him and squinted in the direction of Coyote, who was farther along the balcony adjusting his crash-net remote. I turned the ammo clip over and finally succeeded in snapping it back in the gun.

The countdown clock said twenty-six seconds.

Disin twisted something on his walkie-talkie, possibly changing the frequency, and snapped, "Report!" A voice crackled in response.

"Fifteen seconds to opening!" announced Disin. "Initiate countdown."

He walked briskly away from us toward the icy wall, then

stopped, leaned over the railing, and studied the wall like a traveler looking down railroad tracks for a train.

A mechanical voice started intoning the remaining seconds over a loudspeaker. It started with fifteen. The voice sounded like it was in a hurry. I aimed my gun at the countdown clock and pulled the trigger.

I did it to see if the gun's safety was on. The gun refused to fire.

I had no idea how to take the safety off, so anything I did with the gun would be a bluff. This was fine by me. I could never have pointed it at anyone—even Edward Disin—and fired it.

Out of the corner of my eye, I saw myself stagger out of HAZMAT SAFETY wearing a shredded garbage bag as a diaper and clutching my head. I staggered off in the wrong direction. It was so typical of me.

"TWELVE," said the mechanical voice.

I pointed my gun at Jervis. "Drop that rifle over the side," I said, in my best tough-guy voice. "Drop it or I drill ya."

Jervis stared at me in disbelief. When the mechanical voice informed me he had hesitated for longer than a second, I added, "I'm the best in the business and I'm full of adolescent hormones!"

I don't know if it was Greeves Stainer's reputation as an assassin or an adult's natural fear of adolescent hormones, but Jervis paled and tossed his rifle over the railing. Then he put his hands up.

Disin continued to wait for his train, bouncing on his feet like he could barely contain his excitement. At the other end of the balcony, Coyote was studying the cavern's big metal spiderweb, equally oblivious to what had just happened.

I looked back at Jervis. Jervis looked at me. I knew he was waiting for me to point my gun elsewhere. The moment I did, he'd be on me. I had no idea what to do next.

Freak did. He shouted at Disin, "Hey! You! You're not the only one who can pick pockets!" He ran up to Disin and snatched at his coattails. "Look what I've got!"

Disin shot him an annoyed glance. Freak waved the zucchini crayon in his face.

It wasn't the real zucchini crayon. It was the fake zucchini crayon Freak had taken from Alf's cigarette case. Disin slapped his pockets to verify he no longer had the crayon. He was unaware he had lost the real crayon during the balloon flight.

"SIX," said the mechanical voice. A warning siren began to wail.

Fiona started strolling toward Coyote, approaching him

slowly, as though he were a woodland creature she didn't want to alarm.

Disin brought the walkie-talkie back to his face and started to issue an order. He didn't finish it.

"I've got it—you don't! Come and get it, come and get it!" shouted Freak, waving the crayon in the air as he danced backward away from Disin. Freak started whistling like he was calling a dog. "Here, boy! Here, boy! Get the nice crayon!"

Disin glared at Freak, then returned to the walkie-talkie. But he couldn't bring himself to speak into it, and he turned back to Freak. He got red in the face and quivered like he might split down the middle. On one side, he obviously wanted to be in command when a project that had been years in the making and involved the fate of the planet Earth reached its most crucial stage. On the other, he needed to get his hands on a dark green crayon.

The Indorsian genius who had engineered Compulsive Completist Disorder had done a good job. Disin gave a longing look at the cavern's icy wall—"THREE," said the mechanical voice—and then he turned and bolted after Freak.

They ran past me and they ran past Fiona, who was standing only an arm's length from the totally preoccupied Coyote.

I looked at Jervis, shrugged, and chased after them with all the speed my new legs could give me.

Freak sprinted until he was opposite the door marked CAR-BOYS. Then he leaned out over the railing and tossed the crayon into the air. Disin got there just in time to catch the crayon as it fell, but it was a few inches beyond his reach. He lunged. The balcony's top railing, the same one that I had broken the first time we had visited, gave way under his weight.

Disin caught the crayon. Then he fell to the floor thirty feet below.

Freak and I looked over the railing. Disin was below us, grimacing, with both of his legs bent at unusual angles. The zucchini crayon was on the floor by his side.

"ZERO," said the mechanical voice, like it was keeping score.

Jervis, who must have been resurrected because of his intense loyalty rather than his acute intelligence, leaped from the balcony to assist his leader. He hit the floor and rolled. He staggered to his feet and limped over to Disin.

The portal opened.

The ice wall shattered and shards of ice hurtled through the room like stinging sleet. I turned my face away and felt myself buffeted by a fierce gust of wind. The railing I clung to felt electrified. The icy wind passed, and I looked back at the place where the ice wall had been. It was now a tunnel into nothingness.

The end of the room was the darkest, blackest night, without any stars, without any moon, and I imagined myself being sucked into it. I must have taken a step toward it, because I suddenly felt Freak's arms around my chest, holding me back.

A light appeared in the middle of all the nothing. It rapidly grew in size and then burst blindingly into the room. It was on the front of a huge metal cylinder that came barreling in with the roar of a dozen runaway freight trains. Everything around us shook. It was the troop transport from Indorsia, and it came at us like the hammer of an angry god.

The transport thundered in like it was on gigantic rollers. It filled the space from side to side, from top to bottom, and its curving hull eclipsed everything else. Through brightly lit portholes, I could see figures in armor moving around inside. The thing was teeming with Indorsian troops.

I aimed my gun at it. I felt like a mouse pointing a finger at a charging elephant.

The transport loomed like an avalanche over the spot where Jervis was trying to save Disin.

He attempted to drag Disin to the side, but Disin kept pulling him toward the crayon. The two of them became aware of a shadow bearing down on them. They both looked up, and then they were lost to view as the transport passed over them.

Fiona snatched the remote out of Coyote's hands, dodged his clumsy attempt to grab her, and raced over to us. Coyote was right behind her, but he stopped dead when I swung my arm around and made him my new target.

The transport collided with the crash net, which expanded like a fishing net catching a killer whale. Its metal cables groaned and screeched, as if it were screaming that this was too much for it. The transport slowed as the net stretched to what had to be its breaking point. I expected the net would be yanked from the walls and send broken fragments flying our way.

I prepared to duck just as the transport came to a halt. Fiona turned the wheel on the remote all the way to the right.

I immediately understood what Science Girl was trying to do. I also realized it was our only hope.

As she turned the wheel, the cables of the crash net tightened. The transport started to inch backward, trembling as its incoming energy got turned against it and it became a gigantic paper clip about to be shot across the room by an enormous rubber band.

Each of the portholes had a storm trooper looking out at us. Fiona raised her hand and gave them a little bye-bye wave. One trooper waved back. I imagined him being demoted in the near future.

The transport picked up speed as the slingshot Fiona had created flung it back toward Indorsia. The crash net gave out an earsplitting *SPROING!* like the world's biggest spring, and the cylinder was flying back out almost as fast as it had come in. It passed through the portal, its headlight became a tail-light, and then it vanished into nothingness.

With a sound like planets colliding, the portal snapped shut behind it.

Things With a Mind
of Their Own

A rocky wall appeared where the portal had been, and
frost immediately began to form on it.

Fiona and Freak and I looked over the edge of the balcony. We expected to see a bloody streak along the floor
where Disin and Jervis had been. I could see a streak, but it
wasn't bloody. It was thin and zucchini green. It told us the
fate of the fake crayon, but it didn't give us a clue as to what
had become of Jervis and Disin.

"Pardon me," said my voice, coming from behind me. I
turned and there I was, still clutching my head and holding

up my garbage-bag diaper. "I seem to have somehow injured myself. Is there an infirmary anywhere nearby?"

Freak and Fiona both jumped at the sight of my double.

"You have a twin?" Fiona squeaked, sounding the tiniest bit jealous.

"Not really," I hastened to explain. "That's my old body, with a new mind inside it. His name is Greeves Stainer."

"Is it?" said Greeves, sounding astounded. "What an odd name! Is there any place we can get ice cream? My head hurts!" He sounded like he was getting progressively younger with each sentence.

Fiona looked at his scalp wound.

"I hit him with a chair," I confessed.

"Why?" asked Freak.

"I didn't have the sofa."

Something warm and furry threaded itself between my ankles. I looked down. Mucus was on my feet. The cat hunched its shoulders and yawned, and Double Six fell on the floor in front of me.

"It's quite likely he has amnesia," said the domino. "A blow on the head so soon after a personality download can frequently cause it."

"He's forgotten he's an assassin?" I asked.

"For the time being. Aren't you going to pick me up?"

"You're covered in cat spit."

"And you have amniotic fluid in your hair. Your point?"

I bent down and picked up the domino.

Fiona turned away from Greeves, held me at arm's length, and peered into my face.

"It *is* you, isn't it?" she asked.

"Yeah, it's me. My mind is in a new body. I'm a little taller and I'll probably get chicken pox again, but it's me."

"We thought you were dead!" said Fiona, and I was surprised to see a tear run down her cheek.

"Me? Dead? Don't be hyperdiculous!"

Fiona crushed me to her and Freak joined the group hug. After a moment, Greeves hugged me, too. "I don't know who you are," he said, "but I like your face."

"None of you should move," said a voice. We turned our heads. Coyote was aiming the same type of water pistol at us that Cockapoo had threatened us with in Underhill House. Being part of a group hug made us a single target. It was an unexpected downside to group hugs.

Coyote's finger tensed on the trigger. Before he could pull it, a zucchini-colored blotch appeared on his forehead. He dropped the gun and put his hands out in front of him like he was pressing them against an invisible wall, then tilted his head back, opened his mouth, and tried to scream, but nothing came out. He had been dosed with Hista Mime.

"I do so hate biochemical weapons," said Alf.

Alf had arrived on the balcony just in time, wearing Cockapoo's doghat. Coyote must have thought the approaching figure was an ally and gotten caught off guard when Alf made Coyote his target.

Alf quickly leaned forward and injected Coyote with a syringe. Coyote collapsed but started breathing again. "The antidote," Alf explained. "Anti–Hista Mime. He'll be back to normal in about an hour or so, I'd guess."

"Alf!" the three of us cried. We moved to include him in the group hug.

"Let's not make ourselves an even bigger target!" he said, putting his hands up and refusing to be engulfed.

"How'd you get here so fast?" demanded Freak.

"The keys were in the sheik's Hummer. Fortunately, something triggered Hologrammy. She started chasing Beauceron with her ax, Beauceron tripped over my outstretched foot, and Opal Austin was able to subdue her."

"Opal Austin?" asked Freak.

"The private eye who found the zucchini crayon for me.

She was at the auction in disguise. Using the name Cicely Shillingham."

"Alecto!" I said.

"Actually," Alf admitted, "I've been Alecto from the start."

"So...Opal Austin was doing your bidding."

"You make it sound medieval. But yes, she was."

"I have a boo-boo!" Greeves announced.

"Who is he?" Alf asked me.

"Greeves Stainer."

"Ah. Notorious Indorsian assassin. Wonderful. Anyway, as soon as Opal disarmed Beauceron, my first thought was to follow the three of you. I drove the Hummer through three chain-link fences. Straight across Hellsboro. We have to get back to it before the tires melt."

"You didn't fall through the crust?" Freak asked suspiciously.

"The Hummer has sonar. It's the Luxury Landmine Edition. The cupholders are gyroscopic, so they don't spill your drinks."

A short bald man wearing a lab coat scurried across the floor of the cavern, a folder under his arm spilling a trail of papers behind him. He reached a door in the far wall and practically fell through it in his eagerness to leave.

"There must be a kennel full of doghats here," said Freak, squaring his shoulders and giving us a tough-guy look. "Shouldn't we round them up?"

"Or flee from them in terror?" Fiona suggested. Much more reasonably, I thought.

"No reason to do either," Alf assured us. "All of Disin's people, from Jackal and Cockapoo down to the lowliest lab tech, are corporate employees. Meaning they have no initiative or self-motivation. Without Disin to tell them what to do, they're not going to do anything. They are no longer a threat. Their main concern right now is who's going to sign off on their overtime pay."

"You're one hundred percent sure about that?" I asked.

"No. Perhaps we should get moving."

We led Greeves by the hand like a two-year-old and ascended the stairs in the stairwell. It didn't seem right to leave him behind. He was a twelve-year-old, half-naked kid with amnesia. We couldn't just let him wander.

At the top of the stairs, we found ourselves once again in the little room where safety began with you. Broken glass crunched beneath our feet and a breeze fanned us from where the door had been blown in.

"What happened here?" wondered Freak.

We found out the moment we stepped outside. The huge spherical gas tank that had concealed the mind-control module had exploded. Nothing remained of it except for some twisted support girders.

"Playground!" cried Greeves, and Fiona pulled him back before he could run off and play.

"What did this?" asked Freak.

"You did," said Double Six. "You're the one who dropped the double-headed coin into the works."

"It was a bomb?"

"So to speak."

"You could have told me."

"Most people get antsy when they find out they're carrying antimatter. I didn't want to alarm you."

"Antimatter?"

"The coin was only heads on the outside," Double Six clarified. "It was tails on the inside. It was programmed to detonate the moment the mind-control module became fully activated. Which occurred later than I anticipated. Slight miscalculation there. Sorry for any inconvenience."

"The domino talks?" asked Alf, not sounding pleased. "Guernica?"

"Hello, Alf," said Miranda, speaking through Double Six.

"Guernica and I have been advising the kids from time to time. It was my idea. I'll tell you about it later."

Alf looked at me. He pointed at the domino.

"May I have that?"

I handed it to him. He put it in his pocket.

The Hummer was parked in a gap it had torn through the fence.

"Shotgun!" said Greeves.

"You want to ride next to me?" Alf asked him.

"No, I want a shotgun!" Greeves's eyes went wide. "We can play cops and robbers!"

"Put him in the back," Alf directed us. "He needs rest."

We put Greeves in the space between the backseat and the hatchback, where there was space for him to lie down, and Fiona put a blanket over him. "'Night!" he said. He snuggled into the blanket.

"He looks adorable," I said.

"He looks like you," muttered Freak.

"That's what I said. I'm trying to figure out how I can send him to school in my place."

All four of the Hummer's tires were flat, forcing us to drive back to Underhill House on the rims. We stopped once to remove debris that had fallen from the antimatter blast from our path. The car's sonar—which looked like a device Alf had added, despite what he said about a "Luxury Land-mine Edition"—warned us not to try driving around it.

When we arrived at Underhill House a short time later, we got an unpleasant shock. We opened the hatchback and discovered Greeves's blanket was gone.

And so was Greeves.

* * * * *

"I wouldn't worry about him," said Alf two days later as he shared a coal-dust pizza with us. "If he survived Hellsboro he's bound to be picked up by the authorities the first time he's caught feeding himself from a Dumpster. The number of feral children in Pennsylvania is well below the national aver-age. Somebody must be keeping an eye out."

We were sitting around a table in the coachman's apart-ment in the carriage house on the grounds of the Underhill estate. Freak had moved in that afternoon. It was going to be his home for the next thirty days, while his father stayed in an alcohol rehabilitation clinic in the nearby town of Flanders. This had come as a surprise to everyone, especially Freak.

"Did you figure out the washing machine?" asked Alf. "You fill the tub with soapy water and scrub the clothes against the bumpy board. The dryer is currently broken, but all you have to do to fix it is retie the rope. Almost everything in here dates back to 1910. Some of it is rather funky."

During the week prior to the crayon auction, Alf had gotten in touch with Child Protective Services without telling anyone. On Saturday afternoon, around the time his son was helping inflate some hot air balloons, Frank Nesterii had been visited at home by a social worker. Mr. Nesterii was well into his second six-pack of the day and the interview had not gone well. He had been given the choice of entering rehab and cleaning up his act or losing his son to a foster home. Mr. Nesterii had thrown the social worker out of the house.

Later that evening, while sitting on his back steps and trying to sort things out despite the muddled thinking caused by an overpowering headache, Freak's father had a vision of where his life was headed. He described it to Freak the next day as he broke down and cried in his son's arms, vowing to enter rehab and make everything right. Frank Nesterii had been sitting there on his steps, looking up into the night sky, and had seen an enormous, fiery toilet bowl.

The vision had given him the final scare he needed to make his decision.

The computerized files of Child Protective Services had

listed Alf Disin as a neighbor who was also a distant relative and an acceptable guardian for Freak. I had no doubt that Guernica had tweaked the files.

Fiona and I helped Freak move into the carriage house, which was about a hundred yards down the hill from the mansion. The ground floor was filled with empty horse stalls and wagon bays, and the coachman's apartment where Freak would be living was on the second floor. Its floorboards creaked. There was no television. The only clock had to be wound with a key. I had never seen Freak so happy.

"The toilet flushes with an overhead pull chain," Alf added. "Did you notice that?"

"I thought it was a train whistle," said Freak. "To signal the butler in the main house if you ran out of toilet paper."

"That is most certainly incorrect, *François*," Alf replied lightly.

Freak usually winced on the rare occasions when someone used his real name—it was also his father's name—but he just shrugged and nodded. He didn't know it, but I had seen him hug Alf shortly after Alf had announced the carriage house was his if he wanted it. I couldn't really say at what point Freak finally decided to trust him. It had, over time, just happened.

"You know," said Fiona, thoughtfully munching on the tip

of a pizza slice, "if you need a body for Miranda, you could clone me. It would be like having a twin. I wouldn't mind that."

Alf stopped chewing his pizza and looked at her. He patted her gently on the shoulder. "That's very generous of you, Fiona. And there was a time when I might seriously have considered it. There was a time when I was seriously considering something even less ethical, and I'm ashamed of myself for that. I was of two minds, and I think it showed in the way I treated you all and how much I was willing to tell you. Miranda has made it clear the only body she will permit herself to be restored to is her own. And the only available cloning material for that is back in Indorsia, on her father's mantel."

"Then we should open a portal, go to Indorsia, and get it!" Fiona declared.

"Portals are not easily opened between the two places," said Alf with a smile. "It took my father decades to open the one under Rodmore Chemical. I doubt you'll be seeing a controlled opening of a portal anytime soon, and your chances of being present at the site of an *uncontrolled* one are astronomically unlikely."

"Is Edward Disin dead?" I asked.

"Possibly," said Alf. "There are rumors that the Disin Corporation is currently without its CEO. Which is why whatever

349

doghats may still be out there don't pose a threat. I told you this in Rodmore a few days ago, and I'm even more convinced of it now. No one pursued us. Beauceron, Cockapoo, Jackal, and all the rest no longer have their alpha dog; they won't make a move without him. I've got Opal Austin tracking down the pack, so I can keep an eye on them. Don't lose any sleep over it. My father was done in by his own troop transport. 'Those who live by the sword—' "

"The floor looked pretty clean to me," said Freak.

"His body may have been swept back to Indorsia with the transport."

"Could he have downloaded a copy of himself?" asked Fiona.

"If he did, it's back in Indorsia, and it hasn't been updated since 1952. The technology for downloading is only available in Indorsia."

"The sofa didn't have too much trouble doing it," I said.

"The sofa is unique," said Alf. "I increased the computing power of the entire furniture set when I got here so I could have a well-disguised computer in an age when Earth's computers were little better than adding machines. I did not realize Guernica would evolve. The sofa is the only thing outside of Indorsia that can download living minds. It is also the only thing, here or in Indorsia, that can tesser. I have no idea where it gets it from."

"Anybody seen it lately?" asked Freak.

"I am sure it will turn up. It knows how to take care of itself."

We had told Alf the story of our adventures, including everything his sister and Guernica had helped us do behind his back.

"All these years, I've pretended Guernica has a mind of its own," he admitted. "Imagine my surprise to find out it does."

"Sort of like the surprise your father got when he found out the three of us had minds of our own. He called us infants." I was still insulted.

"And that mistake led to his downfall," said Alf.

He left us then, after reviewing with Freak an intercom system between the coachman's quarters and the main house through which Freak could reach Alf any time of the night or day. He promised to check back with Freak at regular intervals.

"I don't need to be tucked in," Freak announced.

"I'm sure you don't," replied Alf. "Just make sure you lock the doors and brush your teeth."

"Imagine," said Fiona, after he had left, "if we'd never sat down on that sofa."

"I believe *I* sat on it first," said Freak.

"I *slept* on it," I reminded them.

"*More importantly*" Fiona replied, through gritted teeth, "imagine if we hadn't searched between the cushions. Don't forget that *I* was the one who suggested that."

"Yeah," said Freak. "We wouldn't have had all those adventures that resulted in you becoming a less annoying person. Oh, wait—"

"There would be Indorsian troops occupying our town," Fiona interrupted him, counting things off on her fingers. "Most of the world would be enslaved; most of the planet would be strip-mined; Edward Disin would be a global dictator—"

"I would be an inch shorter," I threw in, because she was missing the important stuff.

"And Freak's dad wouldn't be getting the help that he needs."

"You said 'hi' to me in the hall today," I reminded her. "Even though you were with your friends."

"She did?" asked Freak.

"I'd say 'hi' to you, too," Fiona informed him. She looked down at her feet. "You two guys aren't all that bad."

It crossed my mind that I wasn't the only one who had

grown. I didn't say it out loud, though. It sounded way too goopy.

"And," said Freak, adding one of his fingers to the six or seven Fiona was holding up, "my father would still be in debt."

I had given Freak most of my share of the money from the sale of the zucchini crayon. He told me later that Fiona had done the same. She had sworn him to secrecy when she did it, but he figured telling me didn't count. The money had pretty much paid off all of the Nesterii family's bills. Freak was convinced having a clean slate would help his dad recover. I hoped he was right.

"So," continued Freak, "thank you—*both*—for that."

• • • • •

When I got home a little later, my aunt Bernie was darning socks while watching TV. I hugged her tightly, then hurried off to my room.

The previous day, Sunday, when I finally woke up, I had skipped breakfast. I had gone straight out to the garage, set up a stepladder, and poked around in the rafters. Way in the back, tucked in between a stack of burlap bags and a bunch of paint cans, I had found a tin box.

A tin box full of toys.

I looked through the contents of that box, now, for what had to be the twentieth time.

There was a deflated basketball in it, and a slingshot, and a small cardboard box containing a complete set of dominoes—hard plastic, rather than the wood Double Six seemed to be made of—and a plastic bag full of partially used crayons. Bubble wrap protected a single dark green piece of dollhouse furniture, like a force field around a spaceship. A hand puppet in the shape of a Siberian husky hung its head when I picked it up. There was a fancy chess set, still in its original packaging, where the pieces were modeled after characters in *The Lord of the Rings*. At the bottom of the tin box was a thirty-year-old *Superman* comic book.

They were toys that had once belonged to my parents. I got teary every time I looked at them. Each time I returned to the box, I felt a different emotion or had a new thought. This time, for some reason, I thought about how Indorsian stories told around campfires were usually about campfires, and I wondered what kind of story might get told around my box full of toys.

I picked up the comic book. It wasn't worth the million dollars Edward Disin had paid for *Action Comics* number one. To me, it was worth a hundred times that.

I studied the artwork on the cover, then put the book aside. While I had always liked Superman, I was in no hurry to read about his adventures. My friends and I had had some pretty incredible adventures of our own, and I wasn't entirely sure they were over.

As far as I was concerned, Superman had nothing on River Man.

Acknowledgments

"Our bomb-sniffing dog keeps barking at your manuscript" is not, I am relieved to say, anything I heard from my editor, Andrea Spooner, even during the book's earliest incarnations, when it gave off a distinct pong of gelignite. What I did hear from her were many words of encouragement and advice that vastly improved the final product.

Editorial Assistant Deirdre Jones changed her name midway through the rewrite, but insists it was not out of embarrassment over being connected with the project. I thank her for her many helpful suggestions and, obviously, tact. And I thank copy editor Martha Cipolla for her knowledge of fantasy realms—particularly the color of a certain wizard's balloon—and her unflagging flagging of words that repeated too closely in the text.

My agent, Kate Epstein, has been extraordinary throughout, and really knows her Wallace Shawn movies. Judy Mitchell and Barbara Keiler both read an early version of *Sofa* and furnished me with suggestions that benefitted the book while convincing me not to quit my day job. Oldest friends Harrison Hunt and Paul Feldman were both twelve years old when I was twelve years old, and influenced the book's characters in ways only my subconscious may be fully aware of.

And finally, special thanks for the support I receive daily from my daughter, Elyse, and my wife, Kathy. As Tarzan was fond of saying to Jane, "Because you're mine, I walk the lion."

Tarzan not being known for his wit.

Discussion Guide

1. Do you think River, Freak, and Fiona would be friends even if they didn't live close to one another? How does their friendship change from the beginning of the story to the end?

2. Who do you think is the leader of the group and why? Can all three kids be leaders in their own way?

3. Which one of the three kids are you most like? Which one would you want to be your best friend?

4. Why doesn't Alf tell the kids the whole story when he explains that Edward Disin is a billionaire who wants to find the zucchini-colored crayon? Should he have trusted the kids with the information that Disin is actually from another universe? Why or why not?

5. If you could own only one of the amazing pieces of technology in this story (like the DNA-analyzing tray, the double-six domino, the Hologrammy, etc.), which would it be and why?

6. One of the plot points of this story is that Edward Disin invented cell phones in order to control the minds of everyone in the town of Cheshire. Does everyone in your town have a cell phone? Do you think the author was trying to make a point about how cell phones control us in real life when he wrote this part of the story?

7. At the end of the story, River sees his parents, who died several years before the story takes place. Do you think he really saw them and talked with them, or was it just Guernica creating a scene from memories inside River's mind? Why do you think so?

8. What do you think will happen to River, Freak, and Fiona now? Do you think Edward Disin is really gone?

9. This story is full of jokes and puns and an imaginative adventure, but it also contains an important message about curiosity. Do you think the author believes being curious is a good thing? If you found a zucchini-colored crayon in the cushions of a couch by the side of the road, what would you do next?

River Monroe's Field Guide to Things Most Frequently Found in Sofas

Okay, the absolute top thing found *in* sofas is foam rubber, but of course what I mean by the title of this essay is the things most frequently found *between* a sofa's cushions. Here, we're talking about sofas like the one in your living room, and not some weird sofa out by the side of the road. A sofa out by the side of the road is probably a good place to find bedbugs, or worse, sofa bugs. Under ordinary circumstances, I would steer clear of it.

I'm sure some of you, after you finished reading *What We Found in the Sofa and How It Saved the World,* immediately searched your furniture for strange items that might start you off on an exciting adventure defending Earth against alien invaders. Either that, or you were looking for something to eat. That got me thinking about the things I *should* have found when I reached into the sofa by my bus stop but didn't.

Over the course of a week, I did a lunchroom survey of most of the kids in my school to find out what things, if any, they had ever found in their sofas. Even school bully Morgue MacKenzie came over and volunteered an answer: "Nunchucks," he said. I figured it was his way of telling me he owned nunchucks, but then Freak suggested it might be Morgue's way of telling me he owned a sofa. (Morgue's house is even more run-down than Freak's, and it's nowhere near Hellsboro, which at least would explain the neglect. Fiona says not to judge because we don't really know Morgue's "backstory." But then, Fiona reads a lot.)

Here are the results of the survey, arranged from the least commonly found things to the most commonly found things:

9. NUNCHUCKS AND HAMSTERS (tie)

One person said "nunchucks," one person said "hamsters," and they weren't the same person, which is probably good news for the hamsters. Rudy Sorkin said he found his pet hamsters in the sofa after he "looked everywhere else." They were probably there, he said, "because of the Cheerios."

8. ARMY MEN

Army men got two votes: one from Orv Cello, who said he's always finding the little plastic figures from his World War II play set down in his sofa's trenches; and one from Sybil Krepulski, who said her older brother, when he's home on leave from the army, likes to barricade himself beneath the sofa cushions and doesn't like people entering the room unannounced. Maybe it's a stretch, but I'm putting the two together.

7. MONEY

Money, of course, is the main thing you're looking for when you search for stuff in a sofa. Money is the jackpot. It's like you're panning for gold and a nugget shows up. Five kids said they found money, including one who said he had found two dollars and eighty-seven cents after his uncles spent the afternoon on the sofa playing the action-packed video game *Zombies Can't Find Your Brain*.

6. USED TISSUES

Yuck. This is particularly gross when somebody in the house has been sick and they've been using the sofa as their sickbed. Once they recover, the best thing you can do is float the sofa onto the nearest lake, set fire to it, and give it a Viking funeral. Most parents won't approve of this solution, so wait until they're out of the house and the babysitter is asleep. (If the sitter is asleep on the sofa, think twice.)

5. PENS, PENCILS, AND CRAYONS

Other kids have actually found crayons in their sofas, but none of them was zucchini green. (The crayons, I mean. Not the kids. Anna Bannerjee found a very old pink crayon that was labeled "flesh," but it didn't match her flesh or the flesh of half the kids in our school. Fiona researched it and found out the flesh-colored crayon was discontinued in 1962, when the crayon company, as Fiona put it, "came to its senses." "The crayon company was way ahead of the makers of adhesive bandages," she added, and went off to write an indignant article about it for the school newspaper.)

4. FOOD

The decision you have to make when you find food in a sofa is whether or not you should eat it. Basically, you have to ask yourself two questions: *How old is this food?* and *How hungry am I?* If the answer to the first question is "Less than a year," and the answer to the second is "Very," you are probably going to eat whatever it is. But I personally wouldn't eat chips or popcorn that I found in a sofa. Cheerios are all right if you're a hamster, but eating spaghetti is out. A slice of pizza is borderline. It depends on what's on it. If it's, like, extra cheese, it can be very tempting. But if it's dust bunnies or clumps of hair from your grandmother's wig, it's not. And never, ever chew chewing gum you've found between sofa cushions. Even if it's only a little bit fuzzy. It's like eating a squirrel.

3. CELL PHONES

You are much more likely to find a cell phone in your sofa today than your grandparents would have when they were young. This is because kids today are more observant.

Here's a fun thing you can do with a cell phone and a sofa. Program the phone with a ringtone that sounds like somebody farting. Then hide the phone under a sofa cushion. Wait for somebody to sit down, then call the phone. It works just like a ninety-nine-cent whoopee cushion, but you can do it with a three-hundred-dollar smartphone. The advantage to the smartphone is that you can slowly increase the volume. This is progress. It would definitely make buying a smartphone worth it.

2. VIDEO GAME CONTROLLERS

Video game controllers live in sofas. It's their natural habitat. They're like barracudas in coral reefs or raccoons in Dumpsters. The National Geographic channel has shows about video game controllers living in sofas, filmed by guys with cameras hiding in hassocks. The camera guys endure all kinds of hardships, like family sing-alongs and fathers with smelly feet, waiting for that perfect shot.

And finally, the thing most commonly found between the cushions of a sofa—

I. TV REMOTES

Why are TV remotes the thing most frequently found between a sofa's cushions? Because, after everybody has gone to bed, sofas like to watch TV. They love to watch late-night talk shows because talk shows have sofas on them. The guests sit on the sofas. The next day, that's all the sofas can talk about—what celebrity sat on what sofa the night before. And was the sofa wearing a slipcover that clashed with the celebrity?

I'll bet you didn't know that.

It's true.

Stay up late some night and see.

Fiona's answer to this survey was "magic." This was after our English teacher, Mr. Hendricks, had all his students write short stories about kids who find weird things in their family's sofas and how those weird things cause the kids to have exciting adventures. When everybody read their stories aloud, we heard about how some kids found keys that unlocked mysterious doors, and other kids found lost toys that came to life, and still another kid found a letter that revealed the location of a family treasure. Fiona believes all stories are magic, so her answer to the survey isn't as hyperdiculous as it might sound at first.

It's certainly a better answer than "nunchucks."

A Chat with Authors Karen Harrington (*Sure Signs of Crazy*) and Henry Clark (*What We Found in the Sofa and How It Saved the World*)

Henry Clark: Are you going to eat those fries?

Karen Harrington: Not until they bring out the spicy ketchup, my new favorite condiment. So, in the meantime, keep away. No, wait, I'll share. But now just try to segue out of a potential french fry fight into a conversation about middle-grade literature.

HC: Hmm. Try this. Your novel *Sure Signs of Crazy* has been published as a middle-grade book, but I think it skews older, and any adult who's read *To Kill a Mockingbird* should love it, since your main character writes letters to Atticus Finch. Were you aiming for the middle school reader when you wrote it?

KH: Impressive segue.

HC: Thank you.

KH: No, I didn't envision the story for middle-grade readers, but I really wanted to capture the life of a twelve-year-old, so maybe it was subconscious. The story began because I'd received a letter from a reader of my first novel, *Janeology*, which asked me: Whatever happened to Jane's daughter, Sarah? This question really piqued my curiosity. I began writing with a huge "what if" in mind: What if you had a giant family secret and always lived in fear that everyone—from the lady who bags your groceries to the boy you have a crush on—would find out? You, too, might end up talking to a plant like Sarah does. Plants don't tell your secrets!

Now what about you and your terrific adventure novel, *WWFITSAHISTW*? Whew, is that a title abbreviation or a town in Wales? What was your "what if" when you began writing *What We Found in the Sofa and How It Saved the World*? Was there a question that kept you up at night and made you want to write this story, or did you find a zucchini-colored crayon in your sofa and ponder its origins?

HC: Not too many people know that the actor Richard Burton was born in a town called Wwfitsahistw. It's just north of Llanfairpwllgwyngyllgogerychwyrndrobwllllantysiliogogogoch, which is in the Guinness book as the Town Name Least Frequently Tweeted. What was the question? Oh, origins of the book. One morning I walked by an old sofa dumped by the side of the road, and I wondered, as any writer out looking for discarded deposit bottles would, whether there might be enough change between the cushions to get myself a cup of coffee. There wasn't, but I did find the germ of an idea, which is why I always carry hand sanitizer. I started writing the book when I got home.

KH: I'm amazed you were able to pronounce that Welsh name with your mouth full. And by the way, that last french fry is mine.

HC: Definitely. Now, so far you've written three novels that take place in Texas. Your upcoming one, *Courage for Beginners*, is practically a love letter to the Lone Star State, and I was wondering how you manage to write such intimate and human stories in such a big and sprawling place. Any thoughts on how environment affects the creative process? If not, what's your favorite color?

KH: Thanks for saying that about my writing, and zucchini green is my new favorite color. What I love about Texas is the can-do spirit—the attitude that hard work yields success and that it's okay to dream big. I think this is a universal quality that people everywhere are drawn to. So I like to bring that aspect out in my characters.

HC: Harper Lee is an obvious influence. What other books and authors do you feel you owe a debt to and why? In the formula "Readers who enjoyed X, Y, and Z might also enjoy *Sure Signs of Crazy*," what titles would you hope first come to mind?

KH: Yes, Harper Lee and her fantastic book are some of my longtime favorites, and my book wouldn't be possible without the creation of a character like Atticus Finch. As a reader, I love coming-of-age stories that show a young person in a tough situation and how he or she works it out with hope and courage—whether they be in the children's arena or in adult fiction. So if you're like me, you would love Gary Schmidt's *Okay for Now*, Kaye Gibbons's *Ellen Foster*, and Jayne Pupek's *Tomato Girl*. These are books I reread constantly. And recently, I've become a huge fangirl for *Twerp*, by Mark Goldblatt.

And for *Sofa*, the connection to *A Wrinkle in Time* must mean it's one of your favorites, right? I'm curious, Henry, what books on your shelves are your perennial favorites?

HC: *Wrinkle* came out when I was ten, so I read it before it had that big, distracting gold medal thing on the cover. And yes, it's been a major influence, along with some of the lesser-known books I was reading around the same time, like E. Nesbit's *Five Children and It*, Evelyn Lampman's *The Shy Stegosaurus of Cricket Creek*, and Robert McCloskey's *Homer Price*. If I was smart, I'd now be reading somewhat more contemporary authors, but even though I've downloaded E. L. Konigsburg's *From the Mixed-Up Files of Mrs. Basil E. Frankweiler* to my Kindle, I have yet to read it because its 1967 publication date makes it seem a little too recent....

KH: I'm always curious about how writers find the names for their characters. You have very original character names in your novel—the trio of main characters are Fiona, River, and Freak. And then there's this cat named Mucus. How did you arrive at these names?

HC: I didn't know River's name until midway through the writing process, when I realized his mother was named Willow. Then I pictured her bending over him. So he had to be River. Or Big Wet Rock, which didn't work quite as well. Freak, whose real name is François, got his nickname on the first day of middle school when he sank two difficult basketball shots in gym and later, in English, he surprisingly knew the meaning of Onomatopoeia—the small town in Greece where the actress Irene Papas was born. (This detail was actually in the original manuscript, but I have an editor.) I've always liked the sound of Fiona, and Mucus, being an acceptable alternate spelling of Mew Kiss, seems a perfect name for a cat. I once had a cat named Herr Ball, which I also think is a pretty good name, especially since the cat was from Düsseldorf.

KH: Ha! So do you have an ideal reader in mind when you are drafting, or are you really in touch with your inner seventh grader? Any character names left on the editing-room floor? Is there a Mr. Burpenfart, perhaps?

HC: Girls mature faster than boys, so while you may be in touch with your inner seventh grader, I'm in touch with my inner sixth grader—the grade during which I wrote a series of stories featuring two goofy boys modeled on the comedy team of Abbott and Costello. The kids' names were Merlin Kicamore and Wilfred Whiffletree, and they were the first human beings ever to combine vanilla ice cream with asparagus, inadvertently creating an anti-gravity substance that put a flying ice-cream truck at their disposal. My idea of plotting has never advanced beyond this. When I write, I write for that sixth grader. And I steal his jokes.

Would it be self-serving of us to mention your website at karenharringtonbooks.com and mine at indorsia.com?

KH: Yes.

HC: Oh look, the spicy ketchup has arrived.

KH: But you ate all the fries!

Enter a world where magic bubbles just below the surface....

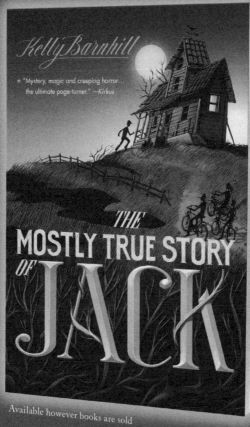

KELLY BARNHILL

★ "Mystery, magic and creeping horror... the ultimate page-turner." —Kirkus

THE
MOSTLY TRUE STORY
OF JACK

Available however books are sold

Now in paperback, Kelly Barnhill's debut tale of magic, sacrifice, and friendship.

 LITTLE, BROWN AND COMPANY
BOOKS FOR YOUNG READERS

lb-kids.com

BOB451

A delicious adventure from award-winning author

WENDY MASS

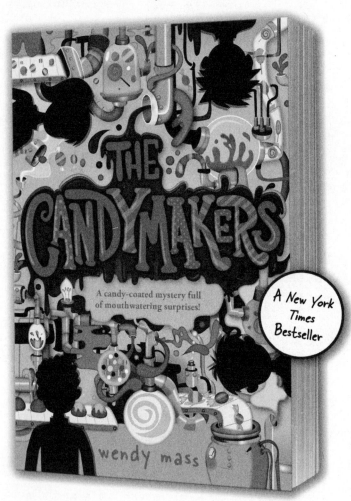

A New York Times Bestseller

A sweet and delectable story about four children,
a candy contest, and a mystery that will change their lives forever

  LITTLE, BROWN AND COMPANY
BOOKS FOR YOUNG READERS

lb-kids.com

Available however books are sold

BOB456

SCHOOL OF FEAR

Sharpen your pencils and put on a brave face.
The School of Fear is waiting for YOU!
Will you banish your fears and graduate on time?

IT'S NEVER TOO LATE TO APPLY!

EnrollinSchoolofFear.com

LITTLE, BROWN AND COMPANY
BOOKS FOR YOUNG READERS

Available however books are sold

BOB449

Henry Clark is a couch potato, which is how he got the idea for *What We Found in the Sofa and How It Saved the World*. He has contributed articles to *MAD* magazine and published fiction in *Isaac Asimov's Science Fiction Magazine*, in addition to being the head phrenologist—if that is not being redundant—at Old Bethpage Village Restoration, a living-history museum in New York. He lives on Long Island, and he invites you to visit his website at indorsia.com.